ALSO BY BRIAN DRAKE

<u>Sam Raven</u>

Terminal Memory

Wicked City

Lady Death

The War Business

The Kill Fever

No Name on my Grave

Bullet Alley

Vengeance Strike

OCTOBER BLOOD

JACK SLAYTON
BOOK 1

BRIAN DRAKE

ROUGH
EDGES
PRESS

October Blood
Paperback Edition

Rough Edges Press
An Imprint of Wolfpack Publishing
1707 E. Diana Street
Tampa, FL 33610

roughedgespress.com

Paperback ISBN 978-1-68549-458-2
Ebook ISBN 978-1-68549-457-5
LCCN: 2026936235

OCTOBER BLOOD

1

Three CIA Ground Branch operators, weapons drawn, advanced along a dimly lit hallway. Hanging bulbs flung their shadows onto the walls and across the floor. Smoke clouded the ceiling—the building was on fire after three harsh minutes of fighting. They stopped at the top of a flight of concrete steps. The cracked steps lead down into a narrow space with a door at the bottom. The basement waited beyond the door. They had to get in there before the jihadists destroyed their files. And the clock was ticking.

Jack Slayton, codenamed "Slayer," stood in the lead. Heavy boots on the floor above thudded through the ceiling. Taking the first step, his automatic rifle tucked into his shoulder, Slayton focused on the basement door. He wore tan military fatigues, like his two teammates, with body armor and assorted weapons. The uniforms and weapons were unmarked; none of the gear suggested they were US assets. It was hot outside and stagnant inside. Slayton sweated and felt wetness all over his body.

Gunfire crackled outside the walls and on the floors above. The fighting wasn't letting up.

The narrow stairwell seemed to close around Slayton, but he ignored the sensation. The muted beam from the small light mounted on his helmet highlighted the smoke and dust drifting before him. He took each step carefully, placing one foot flat before moving the other. With the beam focused on the door, darkness cloaked the steps and his boots. He had to go by feel. *Don't slip,* he thought. *This is the wrong place to slip.*

The basement was Slayton's responsibility while Bravo Team cleared the rest of the building. HQ said the terrorists kept the "good stuff" in the basement. Computers, documents, files listing the group's leadership, all for the taking if they could get the material in time. The terrorist group called itself October Blood, and the CIA wanted as much data as possible. Slayton figured he was heading for a jackpot.

Slayton reached the door and turned to the two operators behind him, Ellis and McCoy. McCoy aimed his rifle down the hallway they'd come from, where a trio of jihadi bodies lay. The three had been guarding the basement but fell quickly when the CIA sharpshooters opened fire. Ellis watched the stair passage over Slayton's shoulder. Both men gave Slayton a thumbs up. No further threats.

He shined his light on the door. Rusty knob, hinges on the other side. The door opened inward. The wood looked solid. Slayton gestured for Ellis to join him. Ellis applied a M112 C-4 charge to the door with expert efficiency, his practiced hands leaving no detail neglected as he tore the wrapper and mounted the block of clay-like substance above the knob.

"Base to Alpha."

Slayton paused. The voice sounded loud in his earpiece.

The speaker overpowered the ringing in his ears, the result of the battle so far.

He replied, “Alpha. Go.”

“Be advised you have a tank rolling your way.”

Slayton scoffed. “That’s one way to kill us all. Copy. Bravo, acknowledge.”

“Bravo copies,” yelled back another voice. “We’re on the upper floors, heavy resistance.”

“Copy.”

Ellis signaled the C-4 charge was ready. The three operatives hustled back up the steps to take cover around the corner. Ellis pressed a remote detonator button and the C-4 exploded with a flash of fire. The narrow space intensified the blast; it shook the walls and rattled their bones. Smoke and chunks of debris filled the passage, but the doorway was now open—the door blasted off its hinges and flung inside. Slayton whipped around the corner and down the steps, stepping over the shattered pieces, then ran through the gap into the basement. He never let his men go ahead of him. Going into danger first was a leader’s responsibility, and he took his role seriously. He probed the darkness with the muzzle of his rifle, the light on his helmet acting as a spotlight.

Thick concrete pillars supported the ceiling, and he ran to one on his left. Seven jihadists had been working at two rows of folding tables. Items of importance cluttered the tabletops, and the items now went ignored as the fighters grabbed for pistols or rifles. Several coughed from the dust of the explosion.

Slayton zeroed his sights on the nearest gunner. He fired twice. Target down, a thud on the floor, a tumble of arms and legs. Ellis and McCoy opened fire. The loud pops of the 5.56mm ammunition filled the room. The sharper smacks of return fire from the enemy's Kalashnikovs added to the chaos.

Slayton moved forward, pivoting right. He fired twice. Another shooter dropped, the gunman's stray burst of auto fire pock-marking the ceiling. Shards of chipped concrete rained on the fallen fighter. Slayton swung left. A jihadi rose from the far end of the table and fired a pistol. The high-velocity round zipped over Slayton's head to smack into the pillar behind him. Slayton fired back, feeling the comforting kick of the rifle against his shoulder. The man cried out and fell back.

Slayton raced to the table and crouched. The shooting stopped as fast as it had begun.

"Ellis!" Slayton shouted.

"Clear!"

"McCoy?"

"All set!"

A blast shook the building. The force flung Slayton, Ellis, and McCoy to the floor. The building danced on its foundation.

McCoy snapped, "The tank is here!"

Slayton stood. He slung the HK rifle and removed a canvas sack from his back. "Fill 'em up and let's go!"

Another heavy blast rocked the building. Dust shook off the basement walls. The floor vibrated through Slayton's boots. He shoved items from the table into his sack. A laptop. Another laptop. Lots of papers and file folders. He jammed them all in without regard. Let the analysts figure out what the material meant.

A third cannon shell struck. Slayton yelled as he fell, landing hard. When the shaking stopped, he climbed to his feet. Another sound, a guttural shout, garbled Arabic, made Slayton turn. The last jihadi he shot, the front of his shirt a river of blood, rushed at him with a knife raised high. The beam from Slayton's headlamp glinted off the long blade. And Slayton's hands were full of canvas sack.

But the sack had weight. Slayton swung the sack into the knife man's face. The blow wasn't hard, but it forced the jihadi off his lunge. Slayton dropped the sack as the jihadi spun to face him. He slashed up and down, Slayton rushing close to block the swing, grabbing the man's knife arm with his left hand, bashing his right elbow into the killer's chin. Slayton pivoted, his back to the jihadi for a moment, and tried to get the knife out of the man's fist. The jihadi held tight and slammed a knee into the back of Slayton's left leg. Slayton lost his balance but fell against the jihadi and forced him into the wall. The jihadi exhaled a rush of hot air on impact; Slayton caught a whiff of the stench as it passed under his nose. The jihadi broke his knife arm free of Slayton's hold and plunged the blade downward. Slayton screamed as the razor point ripped through his uniform top and cut into his left shoulder. He slammed his head back into the killer's face, heard teeth crunch; thrust his right elbow into his belly. The man bent in half with the blow, then dropped to the floor. Slayton snatched a Glock-17 from his thigh holster. He fired into the killer's chest, the pistol spitting flame out the front and ejecting spent shells from the side. This time, the shots did the required damage. The jihadi wheezed a final breath and died.

Slayton stifled a cry. He stowed the Glock and leaned against the wall a moment.

Ellis reached him. "How bad?"

"Left arm...messed up," Slayton said through clenched teeth, fighting pain and dizziness.

Ellis examined the wound but couldn't see much with Slayton's uniform covering the slice. He shoved his full canvas bag at Slayton, who grabbed it with his good arm. Ellis hurried to finish filling Slayton's bag.

Another salvo from the tank hit the building, and the wall Slayton leaned against cracked. The splits in the concrete sounded louder than any gun shot.

"No more time!" Slayton yelled. *And we might already be too late...*

He slung Ellis's bag, grabbed his fallen rifle, and held the HK416 in his right hand. His left remained useless. They raced for the doorway and back up the stairs. Slayton heard somebody from Bravo calling them over the radio, but he didn't answer. McCoy supplied the reply, informing their teammates they were on their way.

Slayton's vision tunneled; the dizziness continued; shock taking effect. He'd need help to reach Bravo and get to the extraction point. His men had never let him down before. They wouldn't fail him this time either.

2

Slayton felt a pinch as the doctor drew the stitch line through the gash in his shoulder.

"You got lucky," the doctor said. "Barely an inch."

"Thought it was a mile."

He'd need a sling for a few weeks, he already knew; this wasn't his first injury in the line of duty.

"With all the wounds I have to sew up for you guys," the doctor said, "I'm starting to feel like a seamstress."

"It can be a whole new career for you, Doc. Open a boutique."

The doctor managed a chuckle. Slayton sat shirtless on the exam table and felt the chill of the room. The A/C worked overtime. The medical unit was part of a larger CIA operating base "somewhere in the desert." Outside, it was hot, dry, and miserable. But a jet waited to take him and his men back to the United States.

The doctor's gloved fingers were cold against his skin as well. Cold hands, warm heart? He didn't know her well enough to be certain. Dr. Olivia, as they called her, might spend her off hours dissecting live cats; he had no idea. He didn't go out of his way to sit in her office for long periods.

"At least I wasn't shot this time," Slayton continued. A second pinch as she drew another line through.

"How do you keep track?" Dr. Olivia asked.

"I just ballpark it now."

Noticeable scars decorated his upper body. Slayton had been taking punishment in one form or another his entire adult life. Boxer in college, where he lost more than he won, but learned a lot. He learned how to predict his opponent's movement, and how to counter before they executed. He learned how to lose. And he learned how to hit back. Then the navy, a ship posting, then the SEALs. Decorations for valor and promotion to chief petty officer and later commander. Postings throughout the world; missions he could never talk about. Now he worked for the CIA's special activities center and the covert efforts of Ground Branch. He'd broken his nose once, but nobody could tell by looking. Two scars dotted his face, one on his chin, the other near his hairline.

Dr. Olivia said, "Ever think of a less dangerous career, like washing windows on a high rise?"

"I'd die of boredom."

"Well, I tried," the doctor said. "You're going to need rest. Couple weeks."

"Already got plans for nothing but R&R."

"Good."

A snap and Dr. Olivia cut the last stitch line. She applied a bandage and gave instructions for changing the dressing. She also fitted him with a proper sling once he had his shirt back on.

Slayton knew the sling was temporary, but with it he was a bird with a broken wing. Birds needed to be free to fly; he needed to be free to fight. He didn't fight because he wanted to. He fought because he could, because others lacked the ability to defend themselves. He'd etched a portion of the SEAL creed into his brain: *I will never quit. I persevere and thrive on adversity. My Nation expects me to be physically harder and mentally stronger than my enemies. If knocked down, I will get back up, every time. I will draw on every remaining ounce of strength to protect my teammates and to accomplish our mission. I am never out of the fight.*

It was more than a bunch of words to Slayton. While others said they joined special ops to do "cool shit," Slayton had bigger goals in mind.

And he got to do cool shit too.

He settled his frustration with a deep breath. And the knowledge he'd have company during his imposed vacation. It would be a well-deserved break with a wonderful woman...

* * *

Before he exited the exam room, Dr. Olivia explained he'd feel lingering pain once the numbing agent wore off. It wouldn't be anything two extra-strength Tylenol capsules couldn't cure. He'd hoped the prescription might be a shot of whiskey, but no. She told him to avoid alcohol and vigorous activity for at least a week.

He stepped outside the medical unit and into the hot afternoon. It was a temporary structure on the operating base, located next to the main building. The analyst and mission control people worked in the main building, a cadre of intelligence experts on a three-month rotation.

Operatives occupied separate barracks. The barracks and other general-use buildings weren't fancy. Two rows of identical Quonset huts opposite each other, with posted signs identifying their purpose. They might have been at a secret base in the Middle East, but the environment resembled Arizona. Long stretch of desert all around, mountains in the distance, blue sky above. Slayton grew up in Tucson and he tried not to confuse the two.

After stepping out, Slayton wanted to take off his shirt again. The heat hit him like a sobering smack.

He started for the Quonset serving as the Alpha Team barracks; Bravo slept next door. He entered. A/C blew cold again via machines mounted in the windows, and bunks lined either side of the wooden floor. His men were packing their bags, cleaning the floor and bathroom. And they were in a hurry. Slayton didn't understand the urgency. He found Ellis and McCoy near his bunk and went to them.

"How's the boo boo?" McCoy said.

"Awful. No beer for a week."

Ellis looked alarmed as he closed up a pack, and Slayton realized the pack was his own. He frowned. Ellis explained.

"Some of the guys in Bravo convinced the pilot to leave an hour early."

"They *what?*"

"We packed your gear," McCoy said. Ellis handed Slayton his overstuffed pack, which he took with his good arm. He looked around. The rest of Alpha was hurrying to load up too, and most appeared finished.

"I'm gonna have a chat with Bravo when we're airborne," Slayton said. It was a fourteen-hour flight back to the States. He didn't want to spend it in a bad mood, but here he was ready to chew out grown men who only wanted to head for home. He didn't blame them, but they had a schedule for a reason...

3

FOURTEEN-HOUR FLIGHTS *SUCKED*.

Slayton made it suck more by launching into a lecture as soon as the jet leveled off.

"Goddammit, you clowns," he started. While his men lined the seats along the fuselage, he stood at the front of the plane. He felt an itch under his bandage, like sandpaper grinding against his flesh. *How nice.* "We have a schedule for a reason. There was *no* reason to leave early, and there was *especially* no reason to make life difficult for your *boss*, who is *me*, and I *hate* flying anyway, so I am not pleased, gentlemen."

Silence. Only the hum of the engine filled the space. Blank stares from his men. Only Ellis and McCoy, seated in the back, kept eye contact with him.

Until someone finally spoke.

"Where did we put the beer?"

One of the Bravo smart asses. A blond-haired shooter named Wittstrom. *Every time*, Slayton thought. *Try to be serious for two seconds...*

Laughter erupted. Even Ellis and McCoy succumbed.

Two of the Alpha guys grabbed cans of beer from a cooler in the back and began passing them out. Tabs popped, beer flowed down necks, and chatter replaced quiet. Slayton shook his head and wished he could partake. Then he decided the hell with it, yelled to Ellis, and Ellis tossed him a can. He snatched it out of the air. If his wound was going to itch, and he had to sit on a plane for fourteen hours, he wanted a beer. One wasn't going to hurt. And the way his guys drank, one was all he was going to get.

The post-mission revelry settled down, and the men resumed their seats. Some took out books or tablets; Ellis took out a deck of cards and announced a poker game. Slayton joined. As usual, they gambled with their combat pay, keeping track on notebook paper. Slayton lost more than he won and decided it simply wasn't his day.

Midway over the ocean, the card game broke up, the men settled down, and presently Slayton enjoyed the sound of his crew snoring louder than the throb of the engines. A nice touch of levity after almost getting killed "somewhere in the desert." He could never sleep on airplanes, either coming or going from a mission. He paced the floor, sat and fidgeted; he didn't like flying but it came with the job. Long flights were the worst.

Slayton and his men happily exited the jet when they landed near DC. The jet touched down on a private, out-of-the-way airstrip encircled by a security fence, cameras, and authorized lethal force warnings. They'd gone from hot days and dust on the other side of the world to chilly night-time and humidity at home. Slayton didn't notice the extremes any longer. He said goodbye to each of his team members and watched them leave in a variety of cars and trucks. They'd see each other again soon, but for now it was time to put the battle behind them. As the last vehicle departed, Slayton stood alone. He imagined he looked silly standing by himself with his left arm in a sling. Where was Reema?

Within ten minutes, a blue Honda pulled up alongside the tarmac. Slayton smiled and climbed into the car and leaned over to kiss the woman behind the wheel. It was a long, lingering kiss. Her lips were warm and wet and tasted like strawberry Chapstick. He wanted to spend more time in contact with those lips, but not in the middle of nowhere at a classified airstrip where eventually a patrol would find them and tell them to scoot. When he pulled back, he smiled. She didn't. He frowned.

"You okay?"

"I heard a jihadi almost turned you into a shish kebob," she said. But he noticed she didn't answer his question.

"It's only a flesh wound."

"And the sling?"

"For sympathy."

"Fat chance." She laughed. "Next time, get out of the way."

His door remained open, the overhead lamp shining on her face.

Reema Ashraf wasn't someone you easily took your eyes from. A light complexion concealed her Arab-European heritage, but her accent gave her away. She was as tall as Slayton, toned and athletic. With her long dark hair and matching eyes, she never went unnoticed. She knew a variety of hand-to-hand combat techniques. Her skills with a rifle and pistol were equally up to par. But for every skill she'd learned and kept up to date, she wasn't a field officer. Her expertise was studying data and coming to conclusions which eluded others.

She was a former Iraqi intelligence officer who defected

to the US and joined the CIA. Her knowledge of the Middle East and counterterrorism made her an effective asset.

Slayton examined her face, and she watched him. When she finally smiled, her eyes didn't light up. *Find out later*, he decided. Slayton shut the door and buckled his seat belt. Reema made a U-turn and drove off the airstrip property to the main road.

When they reached the highway, she asked, "You tired?"

"If I doze off on the way, don't wake me," he said.

"Bed's all ready," Reema said, "and I bought stuff for breakfast tomorrow so we'll get an early start."

"I'm not sure how good I'll be with one arm," he said.

"You're never very good with two arms, babe."

"Come on," he said. She grinned but didn't laugh. *She should be laughing*. "I've had a rough day. I can't drink beer for a week."

"I can smell it on your breath, sweetie."

"It was only one."

"Sure."

They had three weeks, with no work cell phones, in Ocean City, at a cottage on the beach. If Dr. Olivia had known, she'd have told Slayton he had the right idea.

"What did the doctor tell you?" Reema said.

"You're supposed to wait on me at all hours and never refuse a request."

"Want me to wear a bikini and veil every day, too?"

"Only the veil."

"You ass." She jammed a fingernail into his left leg.

"Ouch! Stop or I'll need more stitches!"

He laughed. Reema only smiled with her lips pressed together. Her faraway gaze wasn't only fixed on the road. *She's either going to dump my ass or there's a problem she doesn't want to tell me about.* Then he explained Dr. Olivia's real instructions.

"Much better," Reema said after. "And if you're good, we'll see about the veil anyway."

"Oh, I plan on being very, very bad, honey."

She squeezed his leg but didn't say more.

Neither Slayton nor Reema were rich. Nobody achieved significant wealth on a CIA salary if they were honest. But they had stashed away enough pennies to rent the beach cottage. Wounded or not, it had been the plan when Slayton returned from the sandbox. And after his chat with Dr. Olivia about his history of bad breaks, he wanted to talk to Reema about their future plans. As in, maybe the time had come to hang up his guns and find a cushy private security job where nobody was shooting at him.

But he had to find out what was on her mind first.

Reema turned on the radio, keeping the volume low, and Slayton dozed off.

* * *

Good. He won't talk anymore.

It wasn't as if Reema *didn't* want to talk to Jack, but what she wanted more was for him not to ask why she was late picking him up. If she told him what was on her mind right away, she'd ruin their vacation.

An unexpected gathering at CIA HQ delayed her arrival. Several pieces of intel from Jack's raid were too urgent to let sit. The desert base analysts transmitted the data once they finished translating the pages. After discussing the implications, the director of the Central Intelligence Agency gave Reema a choice. A bad one. But there was no other answer but yes, and now she had to find a way to tell Jack. The decision hung over her like a cloud. She didn't want to ruin the vacation, but it would be their last together for some time. She would leave the conversation to the last possible moment, and hoped Jack didn't take it the wrong way.

She didn't want to leave him.

But the mission required her to go.

She'd been working on the October Blood case for several months. The new jihadist group sprung up overnight and surprised even the most watchful analysts. They had personnel, weapons, equipment, and an unknown leadership structure. But how had they materialized without the CIA knowing? Finding their training camps had proved a challenge. It was as if they had none. Weeks of digging through data and questioning informants provided endless hours of frustration. Then they found what the analysts named the "western headquarters" deep within Syria. Jack Slayton's Ground Branch team went fishing. And caught a whale.

4

Slayton dared not look behind him. He didn't want to know if Reema was gaining.

The surfboard was alive under his feet, a beast to control, man and object working to thrash the waves fighting against them. Slayton used his weight to keep the tip in the direction of the shore. The roar of the waves drowned out all thoughts except one. He had to reach the beach before Reema or he'd never hear the end of her gloating.

After two weeks of sun and sand and taking it easy, Slayton decided the hell with it. No more *watching* Reema surf, as alluring as it was. He knew he was taking a chance, but the wound looked good and appeared to be healing without problems. If he was going to feel the aches and pains associated with his injury, he deserved to try and have some fun too.

Salty water pelted his lips and face. He stood with his knees bent, his arms out for balance. The limited movement of his right arm made him compensate at the core.

The board glided over the frothy water. The rush of forward momentum gave him a sense of falling through space.

The shoreline grew as they approached. *Almost there.* Slayton squatted for less drag and finally stole a glance behind him.

There she was!

She'd tied back her dark hair, and her skin tone contrasted nicely with her red bikini. And Reema's smile shone as she closed the distance between them. Knees bent, feet apart, her arms up on either side. She was a picture of competitive desire, one tiger racing another for the kill.

She came alongside Slayton, putting them almost neck and neck, and then Slayton lost his balance and crashed sideways into her. They tumbled into the cold water. Slayton sucked a breath tinged with salt spray and put his arms behind his head. He didn't want to collide with either board. He felt one brush his right elbow. He bent and twisted to avoid the pair as they *thunked* above. He and Reema surfaced, breaking through the surface like gophers, spitting water, the ocean slamming against them. They swam at a quick pace to the stray boards. Slayton kicked with his legs and used his good arm; he held his left alongside his body. He struggled, but reached his board, hopped back on straddle-style, and paddled his way to shore. Reema was on her board and ahead of him. *Terrific. I lose on a technicality...*

They rested on the sand with waves lapping ashore only a few feet away. Slayton spoke once he caught his breath.

"Your fault."

"Mine?"

"If you hadn't been so close, I wouldn't have tumbled."

"Nuts! You can't keep your balance with that broken wing."

She jumped to her feet, spraying sand at him. Grabbing her board, she started for their cottage. Slayton shook off the sand and followed her.

They placed the surfboards upright against the outer wall and went inside. Reema stopped in the kitchen to make coffee. As she spooned grounds into the maker, Slayton unzipped the front of his wetsuit and told her he was going to the shower.

"What happened to ladies first?" She flicked the switch to start the coffee maker after adding water.

"Ladies first when you don't knock me off my board." He followed the hallway to the bathroom, laughing as she yelled a reply he didn't bother to acknowledge.

Slayton shut the bathroom door and turned on the shower. He twisted the knob to hot. Climbing out of the wetsuit wasn't glamorous. He had to pull it off his body like peeling a banana, but once free, he left it on the floor and stepped under the hot spray.

He didn't hear the bathroom door open, but the shower curtain snapped back with a hard push. Slayton blinked as Reema stretched one long leg, and then the rest of her naked body, into the shower.

"Hi," she said.

"You weren't first, so you're going to crowd me?"

She took the soap from the holder and pulled him to her.

"You might use all the hot water."

They did.

* * *

Her side of the bed was empty when Slayton awoke the next morning.

He took his time rising, letting the throb in his left arm settle. He sat up and moved his arm around, then reached for the sling on the nightstand. He put his arm through after settling it around his neck. He didn't hear Reema elsewhere in the cottage, and figured she was on the deck with her coffee watching the ocean.

But he didn't smell any coffee. She'd have left some for him.

"Reema?" he called. He walked through the cottage and then checked outside. She was sitting on the sand midway down the beach.

Slayton tied his bathrobe tight and joined her. He didn't call her name until he was close enough for her to hear him over the ocean. The wind blew cold, and seagulls hovered nearby, flying in circles, looking for crumbs on the sand. She looked up and smiled, but the smile was weak.

"Are you okay?"

"Woke up early," she said. The wind blew her hair into her face. She brushed it back, then hurriedly tied it in a ponytail. "I couldn't get back to sleep."

"Bad dream?"

"We need to talk about something, Jack."

"Whoa. Nothing good ever comes from a statement like that."

"Remember I was late picking you up from the airfield?"

"Yeah," he said.

"I was late because the DCI called a meeting about some of the information you collected in Syria. You brought back more than we expected. We found the name of the man who leads October Blood."

"Reema, I don't understand what this has to do with *us*."

"The leader of October Blood is my brother."

"Your *what?*"

"Well, he's a half brother, but still."

"I'm sure nobody suspects you of any involvement."

"They don't."

"So..."

"Faisil still thinks I'm in Iraq doing my old job."

"Oh." *Now I get it.* "I see."

"The DCI wanted to know if I was willing to go undercover, get close to my brother—"

"And see what else you can learn?"

"Yes."

"When do they want you to leave?"

"Soon as we get back."

"Okay. We can work together on it. I'll be your handler. Point of contact. Something goes wrong, I'm already there."

"No, Jack."

"What do you mean *no?*"

"It has to look natural. I gotta go in clean. Faisil is too smart to fool."

"If he's so smart, you showing up after a raid on their headquarters won't seem suspicious at all."

"We grew up together," she said. "He won't suspect me."

"Reema—"

"I have to."

"Why? Tell me *why.*"

"This makes no sense! He was never radical. *Never.* This isn't *only* about work."

Slayton stared at the ocean. The waves landed on the beach in a never-ending cycle. A predictable pattern.

At least something in life is orderly.

He didn't hear the waves over the pounding of his pulse. Reema wasn't a field operative. She spent her time behind a desk, studying data, making recommendations, coordinating missions. There were others who could do the job, but none had her connection to the target.

Which meant there really *wasn't* anybody else.

"I need to find out why he's doing this, and convince him to give it up," she said. "If this goes on, he's only going to get killed. He's the only family I have left, Jack."

"How long, do you think?" he asked.

"As long as it takes."

"Reema—"

"We can't rush."

"I know! I know we can't rush. *Goddammit* do I know."

She turned to him, but for a moment he didn't meet her gaze. He watched the water and wished life followed the same rigid pattern.

He finally turned to her. Her eyes pleaded...*something.* He wished he could read her mind. Was it fear in her eyes? More than fear? He'd dig a little deeper in the time they had left. He'd discover the answer. If he asked, she might even *tell* him.

Slayton traced a line through the sand.

One thing for sure. He had no power to *force* her not to go. The decision was hers alone. All he could do was try and keep her from harm. Give her pointers. Provide the survival skills required. Anything to *be there* without being there. How else could he protect somebody he loved?

"We only have one more week," he said.

"Yeah."

"Then I suppose we better not waste the days. I'll get breakfast going. We have a lot to talk about if you're going to make it through this." He stood and extended his right hand. Reema grasped hold, and he helped her to her feet.

5

THREE YEARS LATER

THE OLDER MAN WHO SAT IN THE BACK OF THE SILVER ROLLS-Royce didn't look like a warlord. But in his private moments, Max Hudson thought the nickname a perfect fit. His business was war.

He read the sports news on his tablet computer and took in every last detail, stat, and figure. He wore a conservative gray suit, white shirt, blue tie. He could be mistaken for an experienced lawyer or engineer. At seventy-two, Hudson was fortunate to have retained a full head of thick hair, and he didn't mind where the gray showed. It added to his stature as a guru to the younger people who worked under him. He knew they one day hoped to be as influential as he.

The Rolls sped along the tarmac, a shark in a sea of minnows. Hudson looked through the tinted window to see other drivers inspecting his gleaming vehicle. He returned to his sports pages.

Hudson was the chairman of Hudson Enterprises Ltd., a benign name hiding the company's true expertise. Hudson operated defense firms and think tanks for both left and right. The jewel of the corporate crown was a private military corporation called the Eagle Alliance. He was heading to the Eagle offices for a meeting. His visit wasn't for fun; it had nothing to do with gloating over earnings or successful missions. He was going there to help manage a crisis.

Hudson had never served in the military, but he had no problem sending volunteers with such experience into action—when the price was right.

The Eagle Alliance was one of many specialized private military corporations around the world. They had an eager line of potential employees to select from, men and women fresh out of the military, with the proper training and requisite skills. They weren't soldiers for hire—they became "security consultants" or "contractors." The US and other western powers outsourced intelligence gathering and covert operations to PMCs to take advantage of their built-in deniability. Their lack of red tape and efficiency provided another attractive trait. The US alone paid several *billion* dollars a year to such organizations.

It wasn't long before privately owned PMCs caught the attention of investors looking for a share of those billions. Men like Max Hudson.

War was good for business.

As long as there was a war to fight.

* * *

Hudson's driver turned off the freeway. He followed a two-lane road through two blocks of anonymous business parks. Hudson, done with his sports reading, watched the scenery go by.

Sometimes the government actually achieved defensive goals, destroyed enemies, and sent other threats running for cover. Hudson's empire made no money with peace and victory. When the prospect of defeated enemies loomed, it was possible to create new threats, cultivate them like flowers in a garden, and unleash them on the world. Oh, look, now we have to stop this new danger; how about another ten billion dollars to make it go away, Senator?

The Eagle Alliance created October Blood. Hudson wanted a continuing threat to keep the government from reducing anti-terror budgets. The cuts would have ruined Hudson's bottom line.

But what had seemed like a good idea at the time now spelled potential doom. Hence his meeting at the Eagle Alliance headquarters.

The Rolls passed through the business parks and approached a line of trees at the end of the roadway. The trees formed a crescent around the Eagle offices, shielding the company from prying eyes. Fences around the perimeter displayed "No Trespassing" signs. Any passersby would think the signs warned them away from a government facility. Such signs were common in the area. But what went on at the offices of the Eagle Alliance was far more interesting than any other dull government job.

The Rolls stopped beside a guard shack at the main gate. The guard stepped out to check the driver's credentials. He wanted to see Hudson's too. The older man was happy to lower his window and display his ID. He let the guard see his face for visual confirmation. A careful guard meant a well-trained one. Hudson was not going to make the man's job difficult by pulling rank and being obnoxious.

The guard returned to the shack, and the automatic gate opened. The driver pressed the gas and drove through. When Hudson gave the guard a final passing glance, the man was on the telephone advising of his arrival. He'd be speaking to a man named Spencer Wolf.

* * *

Wolf waited in the lobby with his hands clasped behind his back. With his grim expression, he resembled a man on the way to face a firing squad.

He had bad news to deliver.

Problems with ongoing missions were nothing new to him as director of operations. But the current problem, if not contained, would land him in prison. Or worse. Wolf feared the *or worse* part the most.

He didn't resemble a wolf or any other aggressive predator. Spencer Wolf was slight, thin despite the near bowling ball belly under his shirt. His receding hairline and doughy face did him no favors. He was an expert at intelligence gathering and covert action, but nobody would mistake him for the type of spy Hollywood liked to portray. He was the Everyman. But he'd prevented many terrorist incidents which otherwise would have claimed thousands of lives. What kept him awake currently was the terrorist group he had helped *create*. The creation had rejected its creator and was now roaming on its own.

The automatic lobby doors whispered open and Max Hudson entered. Wolf stepped forward with his hand out.

"Hello, Max," Wolf said. They shook hands. Hudson's hand was soft, fleshy, and cold.

"Are you ready to tell me what's going on, Spencer? The wait has been tremendous."

"I have everything ready."

They stopped at the security desk for Hudson's guest badge, and Wolf led the way to the elevators.

6

"I smell coffee," Hudson said.

"Made fresh a few minutes ago," Wolf said. He poured a mug for the older man but none for himself.

They stood in a conference room with a long table lined with chairs. A large screen television hung on the forward wall. Wolf went to the head of the table, while Hudson took a seat on one side.

"Don't pull any punches, Spencer."

"I won't." Wolf remained standing. "We've lost touch with Faisil Ashraf, our man in Syria. He's missed his last three check-ins, and we cannot reach him using the secure phone."

"Is the phone functional?"

"It rings. Nobody answers. If the phone had a problem, he could reach us through the backup channels. He has not."

"What was his contact schedule?"

"Once a week."

"He's been dutiful all other times?"

"Once a week, on the dot, Wednesdays at noon. For three *years*, Max."

"And now nothing."

"Correct."

"Have you sent a team to investigate?" Hudson asked.

"I wanted to talk to you first before committing resources."

Hudson sipped his coffee. "Up till now, our only problem with October Blood was the CIA raid."

"A lot changes in three years."

The CIA's raid had been costly, but not unexpected. Wolf and Hudson knew the agency would act once they learned of the group, and only foot soldiers died. Learning how much information the agency collected proved impossible. Even with Wolf's inside connection, they had failed to discover how compromised the project became. Faisil and his people instead furrowed further underground, found better ways to hide their activity, and fell off the radar. The CIA maintained an interest but hadn't picked up any threads since.

"What do you think happened?" Hudson said.

"They may have been hit, or Faisil Ashraf is the victim of a forced change in leadership."

Hudson's face paled. "We'd know about a hit. The other option means—"

"We no longer control October Blood."

"Disturbing."

Wolf flinched. He'd expected more than a muted reaction.

He'd get one soon enough.

Hudson said, "What else?"

"More you won't like, and it finally solves the mystery of what the CIA found three years ago."

Wolf pressed a button on the electronic panel at the end of the table. The large screen filled with a woman's face. It was a snap of an Iraqi passport. The woman had dark hair and dark eyes. The name displayed identified her as Reema Ashraf.

"And she is?" Hudson asked.

"Reema Ashraf. Long history with Iraqi intelligence. Believed to have been working freelance after the US pulled out."

"She's related to Faisil?"

"Half sister," Wolf said. "And her backstory is a ruse."

"How do you know?"

"From our insider. She defected and joined the CIA. She's been undercover in October Blood for three years."

"Since the agency's raid. Jesus, Spencer, since we *started.*"

Now he gets it. "Yes. The CIA learned more than we realized, and they sent Reema because of the connection with Faisil. He may have told her *everything*, Max."

"And we are only learning this now because—"

"My source wasn't on a need-to-know footing regarding this case till forty-eight hours ago," Wolf said. "This is what happened. Reema went in as planned but vanished after six months. They considered her killed in action. Now she's reappeared. She's in hiding and wants an escort home."

Hudson remained quiet a moment, and Wolf did not press him for a statement. The older man stared at the screen and made slow circles on the table with his coffee mug.

Finally, he said, "We've lost touch with Faisil because he's dead. The woman escaped whatever took place and is running home to explain what happened. We must find this woman and kill her." Hudson sipped his coffee.

"Won't be easy. Reema isn't flying home. She knows the CIA is suspicious about the length of her disappearance. She has asked for a specific person to come get her. The only clue to her location is in a code she provided, and only this person understands what the code means."

"Who is the mystery man?"

"I didn't say it was a man," Wolf said.

Hudson scoffed. "Who else? Show me."

Wolf typed another command, and Jack Slayton's dossier photo appeared on the screen.

"This is Jack Slayton," Wolf said. "He and Reema were lovers once, and the code is for him."

"Where is Slayton now?"

"On a mission in Rome."

"Find him. They both need to die."

"Shall I send a team to Syria to find out what happened at the base?"

Hudson shook his head. "They have vacated by now. Somebody learned of Faisil's alliance with us and disapproved. October Blood is now exactly what we wanted; unfortunately, it may also be the end of us. No. Focus on the woman and Jack Slayton. If she's the only one who knows our secret, keeping her from talking will keep our secret safe."

Wolf paused. They were stepping deeper into an abyss sure to swallow them if they made any missteps. But decisions made long ago gave him no choice. He might have been in over his head, but there was nothing to do except charge forward.

"Is there a problem, Spencer?"

"No," Wolf said. "I know exactly who to call."

"Who do you have in mind?"

"Our old friend Rylen Cannon."

7

Amaan el-Hadi, terrorist mastermind, lived with two bodyguards. At least one stayed with him at all times. The other remained at the apartment. He was there for security in case any US or Israeli spies tried to enter and plant a bomb or listening devices. El-Hadi lived in hiding, under an assumed name, because he was a wanted man.

For fifteen years, el-Hadi worked as the chief strategist for the Al Haman terrorist group. Al Haman was one of the many off-shoots of the PLO, but didn't confine their terrorist acts to Israel. They attacked the US and other NATO nations too. El-Hadi planned the bombings, kidnappings, random shootings, the hijackings, the sabotages. He was never in the fight himself. The Al Haman leadership deemed him too valuable to let loose in the field. But to US intelligence, he was as responsible for the hundreds of deaths as the men sent to commit the atrocities. It took too many of those fifteen years to identify el-Hadi and then put a target on his back. When it finally happened, Al Haman sent him into hiding. He'd been living in Rome under his fake name for almost five years.

El-Hadi traveled with his bodyguard to the corner grocery store. It was close enough to walk, and they took advantage of the brisk night and its lack of activity to run the errand. El-Hadi liked to walk; he liked fresh air. Nighttime was especially nice, because it was quiet—especially in their neighborhood. They lived in a lower-income area. No tourists, not much traffic; people kept to themselves. The pair left the apartment at a quarter after nine and returned twenty minutes later. El-Hadi carried the bag as his bodyguard led him through the lobby and up the stairs. Their apartment was on the fourth floor.

The stairwell was well-lighted and clean, with white walls. It was a path el-Hadi and his gunmen traveled every day. They didn't trust the elevator, which was often not working, anyway. El-Hadi wasn't in as good a shape as he once was; he huffed and puffed up each flight. His younger, fitter bodyguard had no such issues. A black leather jacket concealed the guard's trim build. The jacket was two sizes larger than necessary to hide the man's Glock-18 machine pistol. El-Hadi, paunchy and white-haired, played the role of an elderly father living with his two sons. El-Hadi thought he was safe in Rome. He wasn't. He'd been under CIA surveillance for six weeks. An assassin waited to deliver the justice long denied his victims.

They passed closed doors with each flight. On the second landing, the door to apartment 201 seemed as non-threatening as usual. It was currently unoccupied. No light showed below the bottom gap. If el-Hadi or the bodyguard dropped to hands and knees to examine the gap, they'd see the business end of a snake camera. The micro-lens caught their entrance and ascent of the stairs.

El-Hadi shifted the bag of groceries as they started up

the third flight. The bodyguard kept glancing around out of habit. They were the only ones in the stairwell. Television noises came from behind other closed doors; the sound filled the space. Nothing out of the ordinary. And then the door to apartment 201 opened and a man stepped out holding a suppressed handgun. The bodyguard turned but had no time to react. A subsonic 9mm hollow point cored through the bottom of his nose.

* * *

JACK "SLAYER" Slayton sat beside the door inside 201. No lights. The apartment needed to remain dark and "unoccupied." He'd lived in the dark for five days while watching el-Hadi's movements. The old man took a walk every day, one of his men always in tow, and never went out to eat. His excursions consisted of circling the block a few times, and shopping. And el-Hadi always carried the bags so his bodyguards had their arms and hands free to fight.

From the first day of his watch, Slayton noted the apathy of his targets. They weren't afraid of anything. The guards kept watch, but not carefully. Too long in hiding, with no sign of opposition surveillance, had dulled their sense of danger. They thought they were home free. Slayton knew from the Stalker Team reports of the previous six weeks he wasn't seeing anything new. He simply confirmed with his own eyes what the advance team saw. It worked in his favor, but he wasn't going to cut any corners.

Slayton was glad he'd pulled the assignment. El-Hadi had escaped justice for too long. And the President and CIA decided he wasn't worth taking for questioning. They wanted his death to send a message to his terrorist buddies.

No matter how well you hide, we'll find you. Slayton had no problem being a mailman in this case.

He watched their arrival via the snake camera. He'd connected it to his Android phone via a USB adapter, and the display showed their progress. They passed the door to 201. They turned their backs to go up the third flight. Slayton set the phone down, *slowly* rose from his chair, and reached under his jacket. He removed from a shoulder rig his CZ P-10C, the polymer-framed, striker-fired pistol a familiar and trusted piece of equipment. It wasn't much larger than a Glock-19, and as easy to shoot as the bigger Glock-17 he'd carried in Ground Branch for so long, but he preferred the CZ's crisp trigger to the Austrian option. The extended suppressor made the gun a little heavier than normal. But the suppressor was key to the mission.

El-Hadi had two guards. He traveled with one. The other remained in the apartment. Both guards carried heavy hardware—Glock-18 machine pistols. Slayton needed to hit them both and get out before the second bodyguard joined the fight. He didn't want any loud gunshots giving him away. He didn't want enemy gunfire punching through walls or doors to strike innocent people. The apartment wasn't the best place for a hit, for sure. Slayton would have preferred another area. But el-Hadi didn't travel far enough to provide an alternative. And what better way to freak out Al Haman than to shoot their mastermind at his own home?

He had to be careful. Make no mistakes. Leave nothing to chance.

Slayton turned the knob and pulled open the door. The hinges didn't squeak thanks to an earlier application of WD40. The door moved without noise. The stairwell light spilled into the dark room.

The bodyguard turned as Slayton, framed in the doorway, raised the P-10C. He fired once. The slug punched a hole under the guard's nose and exploded out the back of his head. Blood and bone splattered el-Hadi's back. The bodyguard dropped and tumbled down the steps to the landing. He came to rest only a few feet from Slayton.

But the bodyguard made a loud racket on the way down. *Thud...thud...THUD*. The neighbors would notice. But Slayton didn't think about their reactions. He shifted his aim to el-Hadi. The old man turned much faster than his advanced years and heavy breathing seemed to allow. He screamed and put out a free hand with a "No!" for good measure. Slayton remained unmoved. El-Hadi had deserved this fate for a long time; his punishment well overdue. Slayton fired twice. The CZ nine-millimeter spit and the action cycled. The spent casings bounced off the right wall and tinkled onto the landing. El-Hadi's body tipped forward. He made more thuds as he tumbled, coming to a stop atop his dead bodyguard. The bag of groceries spilled with a crash. A red apple rolled to a stop at Slayton's feet.

A door opened above. A man shouted—he yelled with a questioning tone, his voice rising in urgency.

Slayton moved fast. He clutched the P-10C in his right hand, grabbed the apple, and hurried down the steps to the first floor. The yelling above continued, then feet stomped on the steps. Getting louder. Slayton pushed the exit door open, the cold night air drying the sweat on his face. A car rolled to a stop at the curb. He jammed the apple in his mouth, opened the car door, and the woman behind the wheel yelled, "Behind you!"

Slayton whipped around and brought his pistol to eye level. The second bodyguard, grasping his Glock-18, shoved through the door. He had murder in his eyes and rage on his face. He died with a twisted expression as Slayton fired round after round into his upper body. The gunner landed on the sidewalk and rolled over once. Slayton shot him in the head to make sure he stayed put. Then he swung into the car and pulled the door shut.

The woman behind the wheel accelerated.

Slayton stuck his gun under his right leg, bit off a piece of the apple, and chewed.

"Target dead?"

Slayton glanced at the woman behind the wheel. A short brunette with her hair tied back. She was a member of the Stalker Team sent to watch el-Hadi. One of the many anonymous CIA warriors prowling the globe for scum like el-Hadi. She steered the car through the light traffic as if none of the slower obstacles existed. He didn't know her real name, but she'd introduced herself as *Angela.*

He swallowed the bite. The apple was sweet and made his mouth water for more. "If he's with his seventy-two virgins," Slayton said, "he's explaining how old age makes him unable to get it up."

"Good," she said.

She drove on.

Slayton took another bite of the apple.

* * *

Slayton told Angela to let him off a block from the embassy.

"I'll walk the rest of the way."

"Okay." She slowed the car and pulled over.

"Thanks for the ride."

"No problem. Good job on the hit. We'll do it again sometime."

"Good night." He left the car, stepped onto the sidewalk, and started walking. Angela stuck her hand out the window to wave as she drove away.

Slayton approached the embassy gate at Via Vittorio Veneto 121. He showed his credentials to the on-duty Marines and they let him through. Slayton crossed the grounds at a steady pace. The complex of concrete and glass didn't look too bad in the middle of the night. During the day, it resembled a prison, complete with barbed-wire fencing and armed patrols. It was an example of bland efficiency. Nothing fancy, only what it required to exist.

Slayton used his magnetic key card to unlock a side door and went through. The overnight staffer at a desk asked for his ID and logged the time of his arrival. Slayton pressed the elevator call button and rode the car to the basement. He used the magnetic card again to access the restricted level. It was where the CIA kept offices.

The elevator opened on a carpeted hallway with white walls. Slayton turned left. A door reading "No Access" barred further movement; he used the key card again. The locks snapped and he opened the door. Most of the desks in the room were empty, but three overnight staff officers sat in front of computers in the far corner. They stopped their chatter long enough to give him a look, then returned to business. Slayton was about to pick out a workstation at which to type his report when the overnight supervisor came out of his office and approached.

The supervisor was young and dressed casually, a benefit of working when the higher-ups weren't around.

"Your boss is here."

Slayton frowned. "What?"

"He flew in a few hours ago. He's in the SCIF, end of the hall."

Slayton followed the supervisor's gesture and passed other doors along the hall. He stopped at the end, knocked twice, and opened the door.

The embassy's Sensitive Compartmented Information Facility was wired against acoustic and electronic eavesdropping. The room contained a desk, secure workstation, telephone and corner television. Slayton paused in the doorway. His boss, Dylan Sharp, sat at the computer playing solitaire. He moved the cards into position with the mouse. Slayton cleared his throat.

Dylan turned. "Hi."

He'd loosened his tie, and his dress shirt looked wrinkled. A thick head of hair topped his narrow face. While seated, he didn't appear taller than Slayton, but he was—by a good inch and a half. He had the skinny frame and long legs to show for it. While he stayed lean, he never went for big muscles, or the bulk Slayton's clothing concealed. Close-set eyes, high forehead, deep lines across his face. He was too young for so many, but the stress of the job put them there. They weren't scars with a history like Slayton's, but they were uniquely his.

"What are you doing here?" Slayton said.

"Emergency with a capital E. Come in and sit."

Dylan faced the computer and closed the game. As Slayton pulled a spare chair over and sat next to his boss, Dylan clicked a folder and the item within. A sound wave file filled the monitor.

"Mission accomplished?" Dylan asked.

"Yup." Slayton explained what happened.

"Good. Now, another issue has come up. Once I play this audio, you'll understand."

Slayton grunted and folded his arms. Dylan pressed the space bar and the sound file played through the computer speakers.

A woman's voice.

Reema's voice!

8

Slayton shook from a chill. He leaned forward.

"This is Darkstar, number 76050. Reema Ashraf. Who am I talking to?"

"My name is Dylan Sharp."

"I don't know you, Sharp. Where's Cruz?"

"Peter Cruz is no longer with the agency."

"What about Jack Slayton? Let me talk to him."

"Mr. Slayton is not available."

"Then I guess I'm talking to you. I need to come in and report."

"Miss Ashraf, you've been gone a long time and presumed dead."

"Presumed...what?"

"I'm running a voice scan to determine if you are who you claim."

"Then shut up and listen, Sharp."

Slayton reached for the space bar, struck it, and stopped the recording. He said, "It's her."

"We know. Voice analysis confirmed."

Dylan pressed the space bar again.

"My brother is dead and I'm on the run. October Blood was created by my brother and a US private military corporation called the Eagle Alliance. We need to—"

"Hold on. You're telling me—"

"Yes," Reema said. "It sounds crazy but I can show you proof. I'm sending you pictures and coordinates of their base in Syria. If you hurry—"

"Where are you?"

"No. I'll only deal with Jack. He has to come get me. Tell him d'abord. *He'll understand and know where to find me."*

Dylan stopped the recording and turned to Slayton. "Voice analysis also suggested she's highly stressed."

"No shit?"

Dylan raised an eyebrow, then turned back to the computer. He closed the sound file and opened another program. Slayton's mind raced to comprehend the recording. It took a moment to realize a picture now occupied the computer display.

The photo showed a building in the desert. A half-circle of mountains filled the space to the south of the building, and Dylan zoomed in. It wasn't a simple square, but a larger center structure with a 90-degree branch making the building resemble the letter L.

"October Blood's base," Dylan said. "Reema sent this picture after our conversation."

"And?"

"We have satellites watching. There *is* activity. Plenty of armed men, and what looks like a mass grave a hundred yards away that they're filling up with sand."

Slayton stood up and paced. He was breathing hard, like he'd run a sprint. He put an arm out, leaned against the wall, and took a deep breath. He looked down at the carpet.

"This is our first glimpse of October Blood since Reema

went undercover," Dylan said. "How they've kept off the radar is a mystery to me."

"I *knew* she wasn't dead."

"You said so many times," Dylan replied.

Slayton snapped his eyes to his boss. "You ordered me to stop looking."

"I had to."

Slayton knew it wasn't Dylan's choice. The two men were the same age and had shared a dorm at The Farm in their rookie years with the agency. They'd forged a strong bond during the training period, and it hadn't broken in the ensuing years. Dylan later gravitated toward management while Slayton stayed in the field. Slayton had wanted nothing more than confirmation, a body, to give a sense of closure to Reema's loss. But the suits on the seventh floor weren't happy with him using CIA resources to chase a ghost.

He'd done all he could to prepare her for a mission he didn't think she was ready for. Guilt over not doing enough almost ended his career. His work became sloppy. Other missions failed because of his mistakes. Luckily, Dylan talked sense into him when he needed it most. Which included ordering him to back off and let go. It also included Dylan securing Slayton's transfer out of Ground Branch and into his special access program—a unit called Z Section.

Special access programs covered a variety of responsibilities, but all SAPs had one thing in common—their work was above top secret. Z Section handled what the other covert sections couldn't.

"I'll go get her," Slayton said, "and we can finally get some answers."

"Tell me about this code word."

"It's a French word," Slayton said. "It means *first*."

"First for what?"

"My guess is the first time we went away together. We had to hide our relationship in the beginning. We didn't want the brass sticking their noses in our business. Then we found out nobody cared. That first trip was when we finally relaxed."

"Then *get* her, Jack. As fast as you can. We need her here in one piece. What she's suggesting is—"

"I can't contemplate it right now."

"Go back to your hotel and get some sleep. Well, if you can. I'll get your flight booked, just tell me where you're going."

Slayton moved away from the wall. "I'll take a copy of that recording, if you don't mind."

"Already done." Dylan pulled a thumb drive from his shirt pocket and handed it to Slayton.

"Book me a flight to Biarritz, France," Slayton said. He pocketed the thumb drive. He started for the door. "Something bad happened at that base, Dyl. Nobody digs a mass grave for nothing."

"We'll know more when we talk to Reema. Get some rest."

Slayton opened the door and went out.

* * *

SLAYTON RETURNED to his hotel and began packing his suitcase. He hurried, stuffing clothes inside. Then he had to repack and organize his clothes and shaving kit to be able to zip the case closed. He told himself to slow down. Take a breath.

D'abord.

The memories came back as a flood. He let them flow. The day they met when she noticed his car. *"Hey, little red Corvette!"* The nights out; dinner, dancing, checking their trail to make sure they didn't meet anybody from work in public. The day of relief when they realized they no longer had to hide.

There was no way for Slayton to miss the meaning. When a person you loved has been on your mind for three years you remember everything. All the moments. All the happy times. You try to keep the happy times alive when there are none. You hope, if you wish hard enough, what ended badly might have a different outcome. Slayton didn't want to get his hopes up, but his wish could be on its way to reality.

D'abord.

The first step, the beginning of the process, of their growing relationship. She wanted to remind him of their first holiday together. Who could forget the small village of Espellete in southern France? It sat near the border of Spain and was part of France's Basque country. You could travel south into Spain or hop a boat and hang out in the Bay of Biscay. It had been a wonderful three days, all the time allotted. The best part was their relationship no longer remained a secret.

Finally, Slayton zipped the suitcase closed, stretched out on the bed, and tried to sleep. But Dylan was right. Rest didn't come. He was too keyed up. He didn't need to replay the recording on the thumb drive because it played in an endless loop in his mind.

He needed action.

Answers.

He wanted Reema back in his arms.

Soon.

Hang tight a little longer...

* * *

REEMA ASHRAF WAS tired of waiting.

How tough could her code be?

Unless Jack gave up years ago and wasn't coming...

No.

Reema knew Jack wouldn't abandon her. The real question was, would Sharp keep the mission quiet? She wasn't sure who to trust at the CIA any longer. Not after what she'd learned while living with Faisil the last three years.

Reema wore a hat with small veil and sunglasses to hide her face. She sat on the patio of what had become her favorite café in Espellete. The village was full of tourists, busy sightseers, exactly the kind of cover she required. Plus, the village had been the most obvious signal for Jack. She hoped he was on his way. She'd provided no way to communicate, and she didn't want to risk exposure by reaching out to Sharp again. She had to trust and wait.

Reema finished her wine, paid, and left the café. She mixed with the tourist crowd for the short walk to her hotel. She'd picked the Euzkadi Hotel because it was the first hotel she and Slayton stayed at. She'd even booked the same room. All she had to do was wait. She wanted to go home and put the last three years behind her. She wanted a long rest. She wanted Jack. She wondered if he still wanted her.

She made a pit stop halfway. She visited Antton Chocolatier and asked for a few pieces of their spiced candy. The Espellete Red Pepper grew in the region, and the town's red motif came from the population's celebration of the pepper. The color red was everywhere, and a feature on building trim. The hot flavor gave the chocolate an extra kick, and it had become a comfort food during her stay.

Back in her hotel room, she opened the window to let the streets sounds inside. She sat against the wall two feet away and listened to the noise while eating the chocolate.

Jack.

They'd lost three years.

Three years.

She wanted a chance to get the time back.

...you've been gone a long time and presumed dead...

Presumed. The official designation of her employer.

Had Jack presumed too?

Her thoughts drifted back over the last three years and the violent events leading to where she sat now.

9

THE MISSION

Reema entered Syria under an Iraqi passport with her real name. They weren't going fancy with her cover. She was on her way to her brother, and there was no need to deny the reason for the trip. If October Blood had any operatives at the airport, her name showing up for review might alert Faisil. Which would make her job easier if he came to collect her.

She spent the first night in Damascus and then met an agency contact in the morning. The contact furnished a Toyota Land Cruiser, map, weapons, fuel, and water. The Kalashnikov provided had no stock and dents and scuffs marked the metal. But the contact assured her the weapon functioned. He supplied spare magazines and ammunition. Reema added extra water. Ammo was great but water was vital.

Three hundred and twenty kilometers. The equivalent of two hundred miles. East. Into the desert. The Toyota fired to life on the first twist of the key and she began her drive out of the city.

The air conditioner worked at full power but the heat competed to cancel out the air flow. She aimed two vents at her face to keep perspiration at bay.

She set the coordinates on the in-dash GPS and double-checked the paper map too. The map would be her primary resource. GPS was great, but she didn't want to rely on it one hundred percent when she reached the middle of nowhere.

Watching the desert stretch to infinity in all directions brought comfort to Reema. She wasn't *home*, per se, but it was close enough. She wished the Middle East wasn't embroiled in so much turmoil. The world should appreciate its beauty and the people's hospitality. With conflicts affecting so many, the beauty vanished. It was a shame. But for now, as she drove, Reema found time to appreciate what she saw. Someday the violence would end and allow people all over the world to see what the Middle East truly had to offer.

She traveled east through Damascus into the open country. The ride seemed peaceful so far, but the terrain held danger for sure...

* * *

SHE HAD NO WARNING.

The Land Cruiser passed between a rocky rise carved down the middle to accommodate the road. Reema watched the top and road ahead. She was passing through a bottleneck. The sort of place to expect an ambush. Only one way in and out, hemmed in by rock on either side.

Ahead of her, at the other end of the rise, a truck full of

armed men screeched to a stop. The truck blocked the roadway. Reema slammed the brakes. The tires screeched despite ABS. The armed men jumped out of the truck. She pulled the gear lever into reverse and stomped the accelerator. She grabbed the AK from the passenger seat and held it out the window in her left hand. She hosed the ambushers with a swarm of 7.62x39mm death bringers. The full-auto weapon clicked empty with no discernible effect. She checked the rearview mirror and screamed. Another truck moved to block the other way out.

Return fire pecked at the body of the Land Cruiser and then the rearward momentum came to a screeching halt. Bullets shredded the rear tires and the back end sunk with a *thunk.* Rubber flew off the tires; the steel rims gouged the asphalt with a spit of sparks and a shriek. The Toyota ground to a stop. The group from the front truck ran toward her. She ejected the empty mag from the AK and had a full mag half inserted into the receiver when somebody wrenched open the driver's door. She screamed. Hands grabbed her and pulled her violently from the off-roader. The AK flew from her grasp and she landed hard on her back on the hot blacktop. Her breath rushed out and pain filled her body. Only legs and booted feet surrounded her. She tried to rise. The first blow from a rifle stock struck her in the chest. Reema screamed again as a buttstock impacted with the side of her head. Then she stopped screaming as her world faded to darkness.

* * *

She came to. Her head spun with dizziness. She vomited violently, covering the front of her clothes. What didn't land on her shirt and jeans made *splat* noises on the floor.

She couldn't take stock till the retching ceased, and as she spit the residual from her mouth, she looked around.

She was dangling over a stone floor. They'd hung her by the wrists via shackles. The iron braces bit hard into her skin. The chains connected to the shackles were anchored into the jagged ceiling. Did they have her in an underground lair of some sort? Curiosity overcame panic—for now.

Her head hurt. Patches of blood mixed with the vomit on her clothes. Reema took mental inventory of her condition. Throbbing soreness traveled throughout her body. She hadn't been exposed or assaulted. Yet. She didn't detect any broken bones, but it didn't mean much. The beating with the rifle stocks could have broken a rib. Or two.

She didn't think October Blood had grabbed her. She was the victim of roving bandits.

Reema looked down. She dangled a foot or two off the floor. Another pair of rusty shackles held her ankles together. Her arms, straight above her head, felt like they were about to separate from their sockets. Creeping numbness was her friend and would disguise the pain as more time passed. Especially when the pain grew worse.

Voices echoed from somewhere distant. Men talking fast. An open arch marked the doorway to the chamber in which she hung. The wall and walkway beyond showed more rock. Rough, jagged, unforgiving, but with dim, flickering light. They had to have her underground, but where?

Reema closed her eyes and let her body hang. There was nothing else to do but wait for her captors to check on her. Her mission was over before it began, and a sense of dread fell over her.

She faced not ever seeing Jack again.

Reema fought back the urge to sob. No. This wasn't the

time to get weepy. She had to reach down deep for reserves of strength and power through. Nothing mattered now except survival.

And getting home to Jack.

A man with a rifle entered. He stood about five-five with a youthful complexion. She made eye contact and remained silent. The man noticed her state of alertness and yelled somebody's name. He departed. The name he yelled was Muneer. Reema committed the name to memory. It didn't ring any bells. No jihadist so named had crossed her reading at headquarters or anywhere else.

Reema breathed deep—and winced. Her ribs did hurt. But she didn't feel the ache in her arms or shoulders any longer. They'd gone numb. She wished she'd have no way to feel anything else they'd soon subject her to. Best case was a bullet in the head. It wouldn't hurt. *Oh, Jack, I'm so sorry...*

Muneer entered with the young gunman. Muneer stepped close while the younger man remained at the opening. Muneer carried no weapons. He was big, and not all muscle. A thick and bristly beard, gray at the chin, covered his face. He examined her with little interest, as if she were an insect he found in his bedroll.

"Who are you?" he said. He spoke with an accent Reema identified without error. *Damascene.* He was from Damascus. Another piece of info to file away.

Stick to the story...

But don't make it too easy.

"You know my name if you saw my passport."

Her voice had no strength. She sounded hoarse in her ears.

"Tell me."

"I am Reema Ashraf. Mean anything? My brother is a

powerful man. Turn me over to him and he will reward you."

Muneer pressed his lips together. His beard and mustache joined as one. He shrugged.

"I know of no such man named Ashraf."

"October Blood."

A shake of the head. "There are many groups with fancy names. Means nothing to me. Why are you traveling alone?"

"I'm going to my brother."

"For what?"

"We fight the jihad."

Muneer shook his head. "I don't think so."

"Then you tell me."

"You are a spy," he said.

"For who? I'm an Iraqi citizen."

"You could be spying for anybody, including our rivals."

"Look for my brother. He has a camp near here. Don't do anything you'll regret."

The bearded man laughed. "You can't scare me. I'm a powerful man too. Your brother is nothing. He may not even exist except in your imagination."

"You are very close to finding out the hard way. Don't you like money? Weapons? Supplies? My brother will hand you a fortune in exchange for me."

"We have what we need. Your vehicle alone is worth more than anything your so-called brother can provide." He added, "Once we repair the damage."

"Then kill me. Get this over with."

"You haven't told us why you're here," Muneer said. "We have ways of persuading you to talk. You will tell us everything we want to know."

Muneer turned and started for the opening. His sandals scraped on the rock floor.

"You're making a mistake," Reema said.

He stopped and looked back.

"No. *You* made the mistake of driving through our territory. We will continue this conversation later."

Muneer departed. The young gunman remained. He stared at her.

"My brother will pay you a lot of money to get me out of here," she told him.

Muneer shouted a command from the passage. The young gunman hurried away.

Reema sighed. Alone again. The pain was a little worse now...

* * *

THE ARMED FIGHTERS moved with ease over the rough desert terrain. As if they were one with the environment. They were. The men blended among the moonlight shadows, using rocks for cover. They were mere meters from the cave entrance when Faisil Ashraf let out a low whistle. The signal to halt.

His second in command, Kameel al-Rashid, took a knee beside him. No sentries stood at the mouth of the cave.

"No guards because there's no way to survive going in," Kameel said.

Where Faisil was handsome and dashing, with sharp good looks, Kameel wasn't as polished. Genetics hadn't been as kind to him as his commander. He wore a thick beard and mustache. The beard concealed a knife scar along his jaw. Both looked bulky with muscle under their thick clothing.

"It's not your sister they're holding, Kameel."

Word had not taken long to reach Faisil once Reema identified herself. Faisil salt-and-peppered informants into the bandit gangs in the area for such a case as this. His seeding served a broader purpose. The gangs refused to affiliate with the jihadist cells. They might very well be hired by Western intelligence to fight people like Faisil. For a price. He wanted to know if it ever happened.

But Faisil had never expected to learn of his half sister's capture through one of those informants.

"And you forget, my friend," Faisil continued, "we have help inside."

"He's a kid. A *child*."

"He's old enough. And *smart* enough to get word to me. His follow-up about their torture plan was most urgent."

"Then Allah be with us."

"He is," Faisil stated. Another whistle, a shrill one-two signaling the fighters to go forward. Faisil took the lead and flicked down the safety lever on his AKM rifle. His men kept up behind him.

He knew of Muneer, knew him as one of the most stubborn hard cases in Syria. His refusal to listen to sound advice would now cost him his life.

Faisil passed through the mouth of the cave. He followed a downward slope to two tunnels—one right, the other left. He'd find Reema on the right-hand side, in a chamber. The bandits congregated in rooms at the end of the left tunnel. Faisil and Kameel cut right with two fighters behind them. The rest went left. They punctuated their battle cry with the chatter of automatic weapons spitting hot lead.

* * *

The gunfire jerked Reema awake.

Deafening noise. Echoing screams. A living nightmare.

But in her sleepy daze, she questioned her connection with reality. She was imagining the fight. The rescue. It was her mind's way of deflecting the true nature of her situation.

Her heart jumped, senses at full alert, as the young gunman she'd seen twice before entered the chamber. He held his auto rifle tight in both hands.

"Your brother is here."

No.

No, it wasn't true. Reema's imagination was playing a cruel trick. But the young gunman hadn't finished talking.

"I'm with your brother. I sent him a message."

The gunfire continued to rage. And the screams.

The young man slung his rifle and produced a ring of keys from under his long robe. Reema decided she couldn't be imagining him inserting the key into the shackles at her ankles. The steel clamps fell away with a clang. The young man grabbed a metal stool from a corner. She hadn't been able to see the stool earlier. He stepped up to unlock the shackles from her wrist.

"I'll fall," Reema said, with more strength than she thought she possessed.

"Allah will guide you down."

He was close to her; the scratchy *keffiyeh* around his head smelled. Reema screamed as the shackles loosened. Her arms were rubber, useless. Her back and shoulders remained numb. She had no way to break her fall or protect her head on landing. But the young man's arms wrapped around her as the shackles opened, and he helped her to the ground. He set her down on her side, where she lay unable to move. She had to remember to breathe. Her heart pounded in her chest. *Fight or flight.* The natural reflex demanded a response, yet she had no power to move.

He dropped to his knees beside her and brushed her hair from her eyes. "Please have no fear," he said. More gunfire echoed. Less screaming now.

Reema didn't have the words to tell him she wasn't frightened. She lay powerless and damn near *terrified.*

* * *

FAISIL, Kameel, and their two backup fighters kept to the left wall of the tunnel. They advanced at a quick pace.

The tunnel opened wide. U-shaped cutouts along the wall provided hiding spots. Faisil and his men moved from one to another. A check of each chamber they found along the opposite side revealed no prisoners despite each showing the capability of holding captives. Chains hung from the walls or the center of the ceiling. Had they moved Reema? Or had they not reached her yet? Faisil tried not to panic.

She must be here!

Faisil took a step and stopped short. He heard a short, sharp scream. A woman's scream. His sister wasn't far away.

He moved from another cutout and stayed low as he followed the wall. Candles above his head, mounted on stands in the rock, provided dim light. The gunfire elsewhere remained intense, but not loud enough to block out his hearing. Footsteps, running, echoed ahead. Men breathed hard. Somebody with a deep voice gave a command.

"Take cover!" Faisil shouted. He dropped flat. It was too late to reverse. He fired as men came at them from around the corner, return fire careening off the walls to ricochet back and forth.

Faisil tensed as the bouncing bullets whined off the rock. But he had Allah's protective hand over him. None of the wild rounds struck him. He jumped to his feet and ran to the next cut out, his AKM spitting flame as he ran. He fired from the hip and only cared about keeping the enemy at bay till he found cover. The weapon clicked empty. He moved out of the walkway to reload.

The tunnel ahead curved, and he fired at the figures clustered there. Less than twenty meters separated them. The low light flashed over dirty faces. Several of the enemy fell as Faisil's bullets found them. The rest hunkered low.

"Muneer!" Faisil shouted as the two parties ceased fire a moment.

"Who are you?" the bandit leader called back. "Why are you doing this?"

"I am Faisil Ashraf! *You know my name!*"

A burst of gunfire screamed along the passage. Faisil fired back.

"You have somebody who belongs to my family! Give me my sister and we will leave!"

"You have slaughtered my men! You will both die here!"

Another burst crackled. Ricochets landed near Faisil, sparking off the rock floor. They continued their deadly bounce before losing energy and skidding, the slugs flat, across the floor.

The gunfire in other parts of the cave complex faded. Faisil only had to wait. Any of his men who survived would follow the way Muneer had come, and box the bandits into a death trap.

Faisil glanced back as Kameel led the other two fighters

to his position. The four settled into the cutout. Kameel scooted close to his leader.

"Grenades?"

"We'll hurt Reema. I think she's between us and them."

Muneer's men began to shout in alarm. More rapid gunfire popped, louder now. The noise pierced Faisil's ears. He told Kameel and the other two to get back. Then the gunfire stopped, and another voice yelled Faisil's name.

One of his.

Faisil rose. Kameel clamped a hand on his arm.

"Careful, Faisil."

"It's okay," Faisil said. He stepped into the walkway with his rifle ready. He reached the chamber where Reema and his young contact waited, both on the floor. His contact clutched his weapon but quickly set it aside so the muzzle didn't point at Faisil.

"Don't shoot!" the young man said.

"I see you," Faisil told him. He called for Kameel and the other two to come forward. They tended to Reema. Faisil made eye contact with her and raised one finger. Then he found his men in the passage. They were removing weapons and items from the dead. Two of his men stood over Muneer's body. Faisil joined them.

"Step aside."

Blood leaked from Muneer's body, but he turned his eyes to Faisil. A moan escaped his lips.

"You made your last mistake." Faisil held his AKM at his hip and shot the bandit leader in the head.

The fight was over. Faisil yelled for his men to regroup outside. He handed his rifle to Kameel, took Reema across his arms, and carried her out. Her unblinking eyes stared at him in disbelief. He smiled at her.

* * *

HIS DAMN SMILE.

The cocky know-it-all smile he'd used to charm so many. Women especially, but also their parents whenever he needed to get out of trouble. Reema never thought she'd see it again and kept the image in her mind as she lay in the bed of a truck. The vehicle bounced as it chugged over rough ground.

Feeling returned to her body slowly, and with feeling came pain, more than before. She'd need a long rest.

Her thoughts remained clear, though. All she had were the clothes she wore. She had nothing from the Toyota off-roader. The communication gear for contacting HQ was gone. She had no way to report.

It wasn't supposed to be like this, Jack...

None of his lessons had covered *this* particular kind of emergency.

The truck rumbled on. She stared at the night sky, and the warm air helped bring her back to life.

She'd find a way.

She *had* to find a way.

* * *

REEMA HAD no sense of time during her first few weeks at the October Blood camp.

Faisil said they were in the middle of making the camp a true headquarters. He wanted a building in the center where he could oversee training. There'd be plenty of open space for his fighters to practice. The camp doctor treated her injuries with expert care. He pronounced her banged up really bad but also told her she'd survive. She remained confined to a bed in a small tent while she recovered and spent the days listening to the construction sounds throughout the camp.

Faisil visited daily with her food, and they talked. She managed to thank the young gunman who'd freed her. His name was Illias. He accepted her thanks with graciousness.

Time crept by. Soon Reema was back on her feet and drawn into Faisil's inner circle. Kameel al-Rashid, the second in command, remained distant. He didn't trust her but caused no problems. She made sure not to ask any questions or behave in ways which caused any suspicion.

Months passed. Work crews finished the camp building. The fighters trained and Faisil and Kameel ran the camp with disciplined skill. Now and then, teams ventured out to practice missions. Reema sat for the debriefing sessions where the teams described what went well and where they needed improvement. Faisil updated the training program based on the feedback.

She settled into the camp routine while noting the possibilities of getting word to HQ. Any use of the camp radio equipment came with too big a risk. She needed to get to a city where the task would be easier.

But after a few more months and then the first year, Reema wondered if she'd ever have the opportunity. She couldn't force the issue. Her brother assigned to her another woman, named Hafsa, who stayed with her at all times. Did Faisil really trust her? Or was Hafsa there on the request of Kameel? She assumed Hafsa reported on her activity. Reema made sure to go about her tasks and chores without error.

Her opportunity to call home only arrived after another two years. And the last time she saw her brother alive.

* * *

REEMA BROKE the last piece of chocolate into two but then returned them to the paper bag. Memories of Faisil took away her appetite.

She'd made it out, but at a heavy cost.

Reema stared at the carpet, then left the chair to stretch out on the bed, too depressed to cry. Flashbacks to the camp didn't last long, but a weight lingered after.

Now another challenge faced her.

She had to rebuild her life. And she wasn't sure she could.

10

On the flight back to the US, Dylan Sharp did his best to finish the paperwork and reports on his trip. He didn't like being the only person aboard the CIA jet—it felt like a waste of resources. But he was the only one, so he tried to enjoy the solitude. The plush leather seats were perfect for his long legs. On commercial flights, he struggled to get comfortable, because he never had enough legroom. He admonished himself he could do better if he wasn't such a penny-pinching piker, but he refused to upgrade his seat only to avoid aching legs.

He wound up at his office at CIA headquarters to finish the final details.

He completed his tasks after an hour, saved his work on a secure laptop, and sat back with a sigh. There was no easy way to fly back and forth across the ocean and not feel exhausted one way or another.

The phone on his desk rang. He picked up the handset.

"Yes?"

"You snuck back without telling me," a woman said.

"I wanted to be in and out, but you caught me."

Emily Chapman laughed over the line. "I had help. Somebody downstairs told me."

"Figures."

"Finish your work," she said, "and I'll drive you home."

"I'm done."

"Then come to my office in five minutes."

He sensed the smile in her voice. It was infectious. Dylan smiled too and the weight of work lifted from his shoulders. For the night, anyway. He wasn't much in the mood to play with Emily though. A quiet night on the couch before bed seemed like the right idea.

Dylan would freely admit he and Emily didn't have a lot in common, but that didn't hurt his attraction to her. She was *thick*—and he liked 'em thick.

* * *

DYLAN FOUND Emily down the hall five minutes later. She worked in the Z Section control room, what they called the bullpen. Analysts sat at open desks. Mission controllers occupied cubicles with a trio of computer monitors spitting real-time information. Managers watched from glass-fronted offices on the side. Dylan preferred his private office. He conducted his work down the hall with periodic visits to the control center.

He found Emily in one of the offices behind the glass. She handled afternoon shift overwatch.

"How was the trip?" she said. She filled out her slacks and blouse nicely—round in all the right places. She'd told him when they started going out that she no longer wanted to force herself to stay skinny like she had in the Marines. In other words, when she wanted a cheeseburger, she was going to get one.

She grabbed a blazer from the coatrack beside the door and pulled it on over her blouse. She wore black slacks instead of her preferred skirts. During a ride on their bicycles the weekend previous, she'd taken a spill. Her right shin showed a large bruise.

"I told Jack," he said, "but we don't have all the answers yet."

She drove him home knowing she'd need to bring him back in the morning. He figured she'd stay the night. Emily had plenty of clothes and other items stashed at his place for such sleepovers. They'd been together the last two years; Dylan wasn't sure where they were going, but he enjoyed the journey so far. During the drive, he filled in details of his meeting with Slayton.

Once they reached his house, she waited while he took a shower to wash off the travel and wake up a little. He tied on a robe after drying off and found Emily in the living room. She mixed a gin and tonic, his favorite, and passed him the glass. She didn't make one for herself. They sat on the couch and she snuggled close.

"You look tense," she said.

"Can you blame me?"

"We'll figure it out. Always do." She leaned her head on his shoulder.

"Yeah." He sipped his drink, then put an arm around her. The warmth and softness of her body felt good. For now, they could forget work. But tomorrow was another day.

* * *

SLAYTON PLANNED to take the long way to Reema. If the enemy had a target on her back, tracing her connection to him wouldn't be difficult. If the enemy was onto him, he had to make sure. Leading the enemy to Reema wasn't an option. It meant taking his time. Being patient. Fighting the urge to hurry.

"We can't rush, Jack."

"I know! I know we can't rush. Goddammit *do I know."*

Their last conversation on the beach was a memory he didn't want to face. He'd blocked it out because it was painful. But he let everything play through his mind. Now wasn't the time to fight the emotions. He needed to embrace them. Letting them pass would lead to healing. Healing meant he could renew his connection with Reema and work to forget the past. Treat it like a bad dream.

He chose Biarritz as a place to start. It was within driving distance to Espellete, where Reema waited. He checked into a hotel using the cover identity cooked up by HQ. He left his luggage in the room along with a few basic burglar alarms. Old-school traps. A strand of hair across the gaps of drawers. Baby Powder on suitcase locks. If any appeared disturbed when he returned, he'd know his arrival had not gone unnoticed.

If his trail was clear, he'd head for Reema in twenty-four hours.

If not...

Biarritz enjoyed an active surf scene. Slayton took the time to wander to the nearest beach, La Grande Plage, and its busy boardwalk. He scanned the ocean with a pair of compact binoculars. Several surfers attacked the waves, riding them like pros. It was another memory to confront. The memories of surfing with Reema kept him from getting on a board since she left. Soon, he'd ride the waves again. Because Reema was back. Nothing settled his mind like surfing.

Slayton turned his attention to the crowd around him. No obvious surveillance, but he knew it didn't mean somebody *wasn't* watching.

He strolled the boardwalk and stopped for a drink at a small bar. Slayton looked around. Patrons sat jammed together at small tables. Two bartenders worked the center counter. Two waitresses took care of the tables on either side. Typical ocean junk made up the wall décor. Included were rough pencil sketches not worth the cost of their frames. But somebody had liked them enough, and acquired them cheap enough, to stick in the bar. Patrons could treat them as a guessing game. How drunk did one have to be to spend real money on a three-year-old child's refrigerator drawings? And then it dawned on Slayton. The drawings belonged to the owner's kid.

He found a seat left of the entrance and sat with his back to the wall. The position allowed him to see the pair who entered ten minutes later. He was a few sips into a Makers on the rocks when they arrived. The two men played tourist very well—white Americans out of their depth in the Basque territory. But they were good at casting around quick glances. One blew the charade. He did a double take when he spotted Slayton watching them. It wasn't the only tell. The two men wore laced shoes, same as Slayton. The rest of the clientele preferred sandals or flip-flops or slip-on footwear. But covert operatives always wore laced shoes because they didn't fall off when it was time to run.

Slayton wanted to raise his glass in salute but resisted the temptation. He sipped his Makers and let the two men approach the bar.

Slayton finished his drink, paid, and left a decent tip. He walked out and ducked into the narrow alley beside the bar.

He tried not to breathe the foul stench from the dumpster a few feet away, but no such luck. His new friends did not disappoint. They exited two minutes after him and split up to cover both directions since they had not seen him go. Slayton waited in the alley a few minutes more in case Mutt and Jeff had other friends. Nobody showed. He walked to the opposite end away from the boardwalk. He was already burned. Now he needed to get one of them to talk and see if he could learn something about who was after Reema.

Slayton returned to his hotel. Nobody appeared to have tampered with the lock on the door. Hacking electronic locks was so easy he knew a visual examination wasn't productive. The real truth waited inside.

11

He entered the room and investigated the old-school alarms. Suitcase: tampered with. The baby powder showed traces of fingerprints. The searcher hadn't cared. They'd also opened the x-ray proof compartment of the suitcase. His pistol remained inside. *Thanks for not stealing my gun, boys.*

He checked the dresser. Neatly packed clothes: disturbed, askew, hastily removed and thrown back. Nightstand drawer: opened a crack. The opposition had given the place a thorough once-over. It meant they didn't know where to find Reema, but they knew all about *him*. And short of cracking open his head, they'd fail to get the answers they wanted by searching his personal items.

Slayton sat on the edge of the bed and used his secure cell to call Dylan back in the US.

Dylan answered with a groggy hello.

"Did I wake you?"

"I plead the fifth. Everything all right?"

"They're onto me. Whoever *they* may be. Two followed

me on the street and another searched my room. How did they know I was here, Dyl?"

"I don't know."

"What's scary is I picked this place at *random*."

"Do you have a plan?" Dylan asked.

"Make one talk. The hard way, if I must."

"What about Reema?"

"I'm miles and miles from Reema. I'm not going anywhere near her until I know my ass is clear."

"Be careful."

"In the meantime—"

"I'll start looking on our end, yeah," Dylan said.

Slayton ended the call. He decided to get dinner at the hotel restaurant, then hit the street again. He'd look for his new friends a second time. If they showed up, he'd find an out-of-the-way place for a quiet conversation.

He'd be sure to bring a pen.

* * *

SLAYTON HAD no luck on his second try. *Must have gone to bed early*, he thought.

But on the evening of his second day, they didn't let him down.

He paid for dinner at the hotel and wandered back to La Grande Plage. He spent time on the boardwalk window shopping, taking in the view of the ocean and people watching. Mutt and Jeff appeared right away. The pair kept up their tourist act but by now had to know he was as onto them as they were to him. Where was their backup? Who'd broken into his room while they'd covered him at the bar? The last thing he needed was an ambush from Number Three while dealing with Mutt and Jeff. Since the third man had not seen fit to show himself, Slayton decided to take his chances with what he had.

Even if he succeeded in getting the first pair out of the way, Slayton had no intention of relaxing his vigilance. There could be an army watching him. If they wanted to find Reema, they'd need more than two guys.

Shops and restaurants along the boardwalk began to close as the sun set. The tourists thinned out to return to hotels. Within an hour, the boardwalk would be empty, with the tourists transitioning to the city's night spots. Slayton shivered as the temperature dropped. The ocean raged. He wore no jacket or windbreaker. He wanted his arms free of entanglements. He'd also left his gun at the hotel room. No need for artillery when you only wanted a quiet chat. Right?

Right.

But he'd brought a pen, a simple push-button ball point writing instrument. A simple tool for a simple job. A weapon in the right hands.

Slayton left the boardwalk and followed General de Gaulle Road. It ran perpendicular to the ocean. He didn't look back. Mutt and Jeff were behind him, or they weren't, and his combat senses told him they were.

He cut right to a concrete observation platform overlooking the beach and ocean. A U-shaped stone wall around the edge stood to keep people from falling onto the sand below. With the darkening sky, the view ahead was a dark abyss with an ocean wave soundtrack. A line of trees shielded the platform from the road. Slayton stopped at the far end of the stone wall. He took the Bic pen from his shirt pocket and clicked the button. He put the pen back. The pen was mightier than the sword, as somebody smart once opined. Slayton was happy to prove the point.

Presently he turned his back to the ocean. Mutt and Jeff approached.

"Hey," Slayton called.

Both men stopped but didn't reply. They watched him.

"I don't have time to fool around. Let's get it on."

Slayton walked toward the pair. Mutt took two steps away from Jeff. Jeff flexed his fingers.

Mutt opened. He came at Slayton, swinging his right fist; Slayton ducked, and Mutt's fist swept through the air. Slayton countered with a side kick. One blow to the belly as Mutt rose, a second to his face. Mutt flailed as he stumbled back, tripped on a crack in the concrete, and toppled hard onto his back.

Jeff swung at Slayton's head. Slayton dodged; Jeff kicked him in the side as Slayton shifted left. Slayton shot his right fist forward. Jeff collided with the bunched knuckles as he stepped in for another attack. Jeff's nose went *crunch* and he shouted "Arghh!" and Slayton swept his legs out from under him. Jeff landed on his bottom and tried to get up. Slayton grabbed the pen from his shirt and rammed it into Jeff's left arm. The ball point broke through the skin before the tip jammed against bone. Jeff stopped trying to get up. He screamed instead—loudly. Slayton held onto the pen like a video game joystick. He jerked it back and forth. Jeff hollered. The crashing ocean drowned out his cries. Slayton then grabbed the front of his shirt and pulled Jeff's face closer to his.

"Who sent you?"

Jeff stared back with pain etched across his face.

"Who are you working for?"

Jeff squirmed and bit off another yell. Flashing a hand under his shirt, he hauled out a gun. The suppressor attached to the muzzle caught on the waistband of his jeans. Slayton twisted the gun in Jeff's grip, heard fingers crack, and took the gun.

Slayton fired twice. Jeff stopped screaming. His body jerked before becoming still. His eyes remained open.

And then Mutt woke up.

Mutt rose, gaped at his partner, and clawed for his own gun.

Slayton pointed the pistol at Mutt's left eye. "Don't!"

"You son of a—"

"Tell me who sent you!"

"Killed my—" Mutt jerked out his gun. Slayton shot him. Mutt flopped flat again and didn't move.

"Shit!" Slayton hissed. He pivoted to throw the suppressor-fitted autoloader into the ocean. Then he started running. He hurried across the street and kept running for two blocks, then slowed to fast walk to his hotel.

He had to get on the road before the third man realized Mutt and Jeff no longer belonged to the present plane of existence.

12

Slayton used his key card to unlock the door to his room. He stopped in the doorway. A chill drifted up his neck. The smell inside wasn't right.

"Stay where you are, Mr. Slayton."

The third man.

The speaker stood opposite the bed, shrouded in shadow. The partial light from the hallway didn't give Slayton a good look at his face or body.

"Come forward and close the door."

"I'm turning on a light. I like to see who I'm talking to," Slayton said.

"Shut the door first."

Slayton let the door swing shut under its own weight. He flicked the wall switch and added light to the room. The bulb blazed above him. Most of the light was on Slayton, but it threw enough into the room for him to get a look at the man speaking.

The man wore dark clothes and a leather jacket.

Two more men stood nearby. They held pistols.

I knew they'd need more than two guys...

The man in the leather jacket showed empty hands.

"Very good, Mr. Slayton. We have questions for you, and we suspect you have the answers."

"Anybody want a drink? I got a bottle of gin on the dresser."

The speaker said, "We aren't talking here. But I admire your attempt. We know you have a weapon stashed."

The man spoke in a low tone. He wasn't a fellow to raise his voice.

Another American.

Slayton had a reply in mind, and halfway out of his mouth, when shuffling on his left made him turn. A fourth figure lunged from hiding in the bathroom and slammed Slayton into the wall. Slayton cried out in surprise, but not for long. A needle plunged into his left arm—a sharp stab he had no defense against, and the reaction took effect within seconds. His limbs turned slack, and he collapsed at the feet of his attacker. A curtain of darkness enveloped his eyes. It had nothing to do with the light in the entryway and everything to do with what was in the syringe. He knew firsthand. He'd injected many bad guys with the same stuff over the years.

* * *

SLAYTON AWOKE SLOWLY. Senses returned one by one. He did not know where he was, the light was low, and they'd tied him to a narrow bed. A hospital gurney on wheels. Tight leather straps bound his wrists and ankles to the metal frame rails on either side. *Okay. Bad news, I'm trapped. Good news, I'm breathing.*

He needed to determine much more if he wanted to survive.

We have questions...you have the answers.

They needed him alive. For now. And he knew what questions they wanted to ask. *Reema.* They'd used a powerful drug to knock him out. If they used another potent cocktail to question him, he'd have to fight harder than he ever had in his life. He *had* to resist giving up Reema's location.

The biggest lesson he taught Reema was nothing mattered except survival.

And as long as they needed him alive, he had a chance to get away.

All he had to do was wait. They'd be with him soon enough.

* * *

A DOOR OPENED BEHIND HIM. They wanted to keep him confused, play with his senses. Preventing him from seeing who entered, or identifying sounds, aligned with the strategy. Slayton began to wonder if the CIA had grabbed him. The process was similar. Whoever had him knew the playbook.

A woman stepped into his line of vision. She stood to his right, and a man joined her. The man in the leather jacket. Finally, he had a decent view of the man's face. The man was having a long day judging by the facial stubble. He had a small nose and the eyes of a dispassionate exterminator. *I'm here to chew bubblegum and kill bugs and I'm all out of bubble gum.* He looked fit and trim under his dark clothes.

The woman was another story.

Slayton wondered what her real face looked like behind the shell of makeup and lipstick. Her small mouth made a flat line and her eyes—green eyes—held nothing but curiosity for the bound subject. Blond hair tied back in a ponytail, and a similar taste in clothes to Leather Jacket, but skin tight, with no coat. Leather pants instead. Her slender neck looked longer than average. Slayton Christened her Long Neck.

"Nice to see you awake, Mr. Slayton," said Leather Jacket. He kept his voice low as he had at the hotel.

"Where am I?"

"You're safe. As long as you cooperate."

"Tell me what this is about, and you won't need to use force."

The man smiled. The woman stifled a laugh. She covered her mouth with a hand but laughed behind her eyes too.

Red nail polish, slender fingers, no ring...

Slayton wanted to remember as much as possible about the pair. He intended to see them again when he wasn't restrained.

"I'm sorry, Mr. Slayton, but we need to make sure you aren't lying to us."

"Just tell me—"

Slayton stopped talking. The door opened behind him again and more people entered. The opposition's number didn't bother him.

He heard squeaking wheels along with the footsteps.

What they brought into the room bothered him...

* * *

Two new arrivals wheeled a cart of equipment along his left side. Leather Jacket turned his attention to the new pair.

"Plug him in and let us know the results as soon as you have them."

"Hey."

"Yes, Mr. Slayton?"

"My offer is still good. Ask me what you want."

Leather Jacket smiled and turned to leave. The blond woman started to follow. Slayton stopped her.

"You're cute. Busy later?"

She smiled without parting her lips and followed Leather Jacket out of the room.

13

A COLD ALCOHOL SWAB TOUCHED SLAYTON'S LEFT ARM. HE snapped his head around. Another woman, thin, brown hair, purple eye shadow; more dark clothes. He was being interrogated by a wannabe Goth club. *The nineties called, you dorks; your outfits were dumb back then.*

She pressed a needle into his arm. Slayton's world turned blurry, and a warm flush crawled through his insides. The flush began at the top of his head and wormed its way to his toes. But he didn't lose consciousness. The scruffy male who joined the woman prepared an IV drip with assorted needles and tubes. He found a vein in Slayton's left arm and inserted the needle for the IV.

The pair worked without speaking. The woman slipped a pulse oximeter onto his left index finger. Slayton followed the connecting wire to a heart monitor near the IV stand. His pulse and heart rate popped up on the display with a greenish glow. Scruffy and Goth Queen sat behind a folding table in front of laptops and no longer looked at him. He wasn't a human any longer; he was a *thing*.

Slayton's muscles relaxed. Soon the chemicals would hit his brain and force him to tell the truth—if they worked according to design. But he'd used the same stuff on others in the past. He knew the protocol. He had to fight. He had to fight otherwise he'd never see Reema again. Emotion, raw, and unfiltered, had to overpower science. Slayton braced for the battle. He'd fight for Reema. She'd protect them both.

Scruffy spoke.

"Tell us about Reema Ashraf."

His voice sounded far away, but not so far away he didn't understand his own words.

"She...was...my girlfriend."

"Good. For how long?"

"Two years."

"What happened to her?"

"I...don't..."

"What happened to her, Mr. Slayton?"

"I...don't...*know*."

"Sure, you know. Tell me what happened to Reema."

Slayton's muscles tensed. He was getting warmer by the second; sweat formed on his forehead and other parts of his body.

"She...left."

"Where did she go?"

"She left."

"She dumped you?"

"Left." Slayton spoke in a near whisper.

"Did she tell you why she left you?" Scruffy pressed.

"No." More heat. He started breathing hard. There was a rapid beeping noise nearby. *The heart monitor.* Beeping faster.

Fight!

He groaned as if in pain but sensed no physical manifestation. The battle was mental.

"What did the CIA tell you about why she left?"

"Not...cleared. Need...to know. Didn't have..."

"Where is Reema now?"

"Don't...no idea." Slayton cried out. His back arched. His temperature increased. More heavy breathing.

Fight!

"You've been searching for her a long time, Mr. Slayton."

"No. Started dating...your mother." Slayton chuckled like a drunk.

Scruffy called out, "Increase the dose."

The Goth Queen said something in reply.

"Mr. Slayton—"

"I'm...gonna kill you...Scruffy."

Slayton winced. Another wave of heat filled his body. He was going to burn alive. He needed cold. His heart rate jumped; the sound of the beeping heart monitor intensified.

Dig that crazy beat...

"Where is Reema?"

No!

"Kill you...Goth Queen...Long Neck..."

"Did you get a code from Reema? What did the code say?"

"Leather Jacket." Slayton tried to stifle a yell but the sound from deep down filled the room. "Mutt...Jeff...I killed...your pals."

"Increase."

Slayton's body arched again; he struggled against the

straps. *Fight!* The questions continued. His answers did not change. Then the heat left his body; his pulse and heart rate settled. A sense of calm drifted over him.

Scruffy provided the parting shot.

"Too bad for you, Mr. Slayton."

Don't bet on it...

His vision faded again.

* * *

Two strong men, neither Scruffy nor Leather Jacket, carried Slayton across pavement. They were the two men with pistols Slayton had seen in his hotel room with Leather Jacket. The sun was bright, the breeze cool and refreshing. The two men carried him between them like a drunk bachelor on his wedding day. A van waited for them a few feet away. When Slayton managed a cursory scan, he took in as much as possible. Chain-link fence beyond the van. Trees. Chirping birds. His legs remained shackled at the ankles while his arms were free and across the shoulders of the two men. The shackles scraped across the concrete. Slayton realized the clues told him nothing. Was he still in France? He might be on the other side of the world.

The pair loaded him into the van, but not easily. Slayton made them work by remaining limp. They retaliated by tossing him in like a side of beef. He landed on the floor. As he groaned from the impact, one of the pair climbed inside and dragged him closer to the driver's seat. The man fastened Slayton's left wrist to a metal bar under the seat. Slayton lay on his side. The carpet felt scratchy against his face.

Both men climbed into the seats up front. Slayton

examined the van as much as his position allowed. Side door, back door, locked. No tools. The carpet showed stains in a few spots.

The pair did not speak. The driver followed a preplanned route. The pair were tuned to each other's wavelengths so much they required no communication en route.

Slayton's mind was clear enough to start making a plan.

They drove over an hour, by Slayton's estimation. His wrist ached and no amount of shifting brought relief. The shackles holding his ankles made a racket with every bump. Slayton had no trouble bending his knees to his stomach, but he only did so once.

Eventually the van slowed, and the driver made a right turn. They left the pavement and bounced along a dirt road. The van's tires crunched over the terrain. Then they stopped. The driver pulled the emergency brake and threw the gear lever into Park.

Neither driver nor passenger glanced back before exiting. Slayton no longer existed. He was trash for disposal. The passenger opened the back door and climbed inside. He pulled a key from a pocket and kneeled beside Slayton to reach under the driver's seat.

"You made a mistake," Slayton said.

"Hmm?" The cuffs snapped open, and Slayton drew his bruised wrist to his body. The killer had short blond hair and a chubby jaw.

"This," Slayton said, springing his left thumb into the blond man's left eye. It wasn't hard enough to gouge the eye or cause damage, but a poke in the eye will distract even the best. The blond sprang away from Slayton with a startled yell and made another mistake. As he pulled back, the front of his shirt lifted. Slayton grabbed the Beretta 9mm autoloader tucked into the blond's waistband.

He pulled the trigger. The gun spit flame. Slayton fired again and again.

The bullets turned the killer's shirt red, chunks of bloody flesh flying out of his back, and he tumbled to the floor.

The driver appeared at the open back door with his own gun. Slayton fired once. The Beretta popped loudly in the confines of the van. The driver's head snapped back with a hole above his eyes. He crumpled to the ground.

Slayton set the gun aside. He grabbed the blond's fallen keys and undid the shackles. A quick pat-down search produced nothing of use; a search of the driver yielded nothing as well. No IDs, wallets, phones.

The cool breeze touched his skin as he looked from one dead man to the other. Trees swayed in the wind. Slayton turned his attention to the environment. They were in a forest area. Mountains in the distance. He was in the middle of nowhere with two dead men who'd planned to leave his body based on the orders of another SOB Slayton very much wanted to meet again.

He dragged the blond out of the van and dropped him next to the driver. He shut the rear doors. The keys remained in the ignition, but the stripped-down vehicle didn't have a GPS. Slayton was too worn out to scream curses at the wind. He had no idea where he was, no idea where he'd been, and no way back to where they'd started. A literal dead end.

Slayton climbed into the driver's seat. The engine rumbled to life at the first twist of the key.

He turned the van around and followed the tracks in the dirt back to the road. A left turn would take him further into the forest; he turned right.

Let them think he was dead. Hours would pass before Leather Jacket realized the error.

Back at his hotel, he found his room as he had left it. Time to hit the road and get Reema.

By the time Leather Jacket and his crew figured out what happened, he'd be long gone.

14

Dylan Sharp had a problem and the only person to talk to was the man in charge of covert ops. His boss, Christopher Fisher. As director of operations, Fisher oversaw all covert activities. He acted as go-between for Dylan and the DCI, when necessary.

He waited in Fisher's outer office. The only other person in the room was Fisher's secretary, an older woman who had held the position for decades. She'd served Fisher's two predecessors as well. She carried out her tasks as if Dylan wasn't there. When the intercom on her desk buzzed, she didn't answer. She finally acknowledged Dylan and told him, "He's ready to see you, Mr. Sharp."

"Thank you." Dylan stood, brushed the front of his suit, and opened the connecting door to Fisher's office.

Fisher looked up from paperwork. Dylan sensed Fisher sizing him up through his wire-rimmed glasses.

"Have a seat."

"How's your day going, Chris?" Dylan sat and crossed his legs.

"Depends on the crisis."

Fisher's office was decorated with basketball memorabilia. Not a lot, only a few items—a signed picture, a game ball in a glass case by the window. He also had pictures of his own local team on the wall behind him. "Bunch of old dudes who still think they're fifteen," he often joked. Fisher and his crew played once a week. He tried to recruit Dylan. "We need all the tall guys we can get!" But Dylan wasn't a sports fan. He didn't know one end of a ball from the other.

"I have a plumbing problem in my department," Dylan said.

"Okay."

Dylan explained the situation with Slayton, Reema, and October Blood. He described how Slayton flew to a random location from which he'd travel to get Reema.

"The other side picked him up as if they'd been waiting," Dylan concluded.

"Has Slayton been in touch since alerting you to this?"

"No."

"This is concerning," Fisher said.

Master of understatement. Dylan suppressed a grin.

"Who do you think caused the leak?"

"Including me, there aren't enough people aware of the assignment to do much talking at all."

"How many?"

"Me, Emily Chapman, and Jack, of course."

"Or anybody in the department who snooped."

"I'll concede your point."

"What do you want to do?"

"I'm not able to carry out this type of investigation," Dylan said. "My own connection is a conflict. We need Internal Security. They need to look at us all, see if we've done anything that slipped through the cracks. I trust my people, and I know for sure *I'm* not telling anybody, but we need a review without the blind spots."

"I appreciate your candor as always, Dylan. Of course, we'll have IS look at this. Is your staff aware of the problem?"

"They are not," Dylan said. "I want to keep them in the dark in case—well, you know."

"It's awful to suspect your own people when you've worked close with them for so long."

"But it's also true the ones closest to us can be the ones who go wrong."

"Sadly," Fisher agreed.

Dylan rose from the chair, and they said goodbye. Dylan exited feeling strange. He didn't want to think anyone in his crew caused the leak. But until Internal Security completed their review, he had to place them on the suspect list. And he had to suspect *himself*. Had he slipped somewhere? But where and how?

Slayton was compromised and the leak hadn't been accidental. When Dylan discovered the cause, he'd dish out the consequences without mercy.

* * *

EMILY CHAPMAN ROLLED her husky body off Dylan and plopped beside him on the bed. Both breathed hard. They'd tangled the sheets; both their bodies wet with sweat. Dylan's eyes drooped and he appeared on the verge of passing out.

He better, she thought, watching him.

The first night they'd slept together, years and years ago now, he told her his preferred positions were anywhere *she* was on top. She'd frowned. Not the usual kink, she thought, but then he told her why. He wanted to watch her jiggle. She should have been mad—she wasn't. His "kink" kept her from having to tell him she had panic attacks when a man got on top. She feared weight of any kind keeping her from moving quickly should the need arise. During her second tour of Afghanistan, she'd been caught in a sandstorm, with very little shelter other than a blanket, and the weight of the sand pinning her to the ground, threatening to bury her entirely, assured she'd ride cowgirl the rest of her life.

As he caught his breath and hers returned to normal, she slipped out of bed to pee. Returning, she rolled close and swung a leg over to hook her body to his. "Again?" She ran a hand through the thick hair on his chest.

"I'm beat, baby."

"Don't tell me no, mister." She nibbled an earlobe and made sure her breasts pressed against him.

"No more tonight," Dylan said.

She snuggled close and listened to his breathing level out. Once he began to snore, she checked the nightstand clock. After midnight. She waited ten more minutes before easing away from his warm body and out of bed.

She tiptoed around the bed to a corner chair, where she found her pink bathrobe. She threw it on and pulled the belt tight. She had started leaving the spare bathrobe, and other items, at his place when their relationship turned serious.

Dylan had passed out by design. She had crushed a pair of Tylenol PM capsules into powder and sprinkled the result into his dinner. Emily did not need much time to complete her task, but she was glad he couldn't pop awake by surprise and find her gone. And then discover her snooping through his computer.

She walked down the short hallway to Dylan's office. His briefcase and work bag sat on the chair in front of his desk. Like all CIA employees, he kept his work computer containing classified data at headquarters. If needed, he had secure remote access software on his personal laptop. And she had his password. Collecting his laptop from the work bag, she fished a USB stick from a pocket of her robe.

Emily sat on the carpet with the laptop and lifted the lid to turn it on. She inserted the USB while the computer booted. When the process finished, she connected to the work server and entered his login details. His password allowed access as usual; he hadn't changed it in the last six months.

A program on the USB began its magic while she waited. Only the flashing red light on the USB stick indicated activity. She kept glancing at the hallway. Dylan wasn't supposed to wake up, but the butterflies in her belly wouldn't quit. The program only needed five minutes. The program made a mirror of everything in Dylan's files. Specific mission files did not concern her. She wanted to know about Dylan's communications with Jack Slayton. Dylan kept a detailed diary of Z Section activities, memos to himself, and added to the notes daily. The diary was his personal record of ongoing activity and his thoughts regarding developments. Anything related to Jack would be there.

Slayton had survived the Biarritz abduction; he was in the wind. She needed to discover his location, so the crew hired by Spencer Wolf had a chance to track him again.

When the program finished, the red light on the USB turned solid, then blinked out. She disconnected the stick, turned off the laptop, and returned the computer to the work bag. She dropped the USB back into her robe pocket.

Back in the bedroom, she tossed the robe on the chair, tiptoed around the bed again, and slid under the sheets. Dylan still snored.

She had a hard time getting to sleep.

Her thoughts spun with what would happen if Dylan discovered her treachery.

She hated spying on him, but didn't have a choice...

15

Dylan cooked breakfast while Emily showered the next morning. When she joined him in the kitchen, he did a double-take. Her pink silk bathrobe was too small—it stopped short of her hips and left enough exposed to make him take a second look.

She stepped closer to see what was in the pan. Eggs and bacon. Basic, but perfectly fine. She had to look up at him when they talked, and noticed he was extra groggy. He admitted things at work were tougher than he let on, and the stress was affecting him. She expressed the expected sympathy and understanding. Next time she'd use only one capsule of Tylenol PM. If there *was* a next time. She didn't *want* a next time.

They started work promptly at nine a.m.

She sat in her glass-walled office and studied the copied material. Dylan had made no notes about Jack since his call about being followed around Biarritz. Which meant he hadn't checked in after his abduction and interrogation. Had he truly escaped the crew ordered to kill him? If he'd dropped out of sight, it was because he wasn't alive anymore but died elsewhere than intended.

But she still needed to report to Wolf and let him know.

She broke away at lunch. Dylan, occupied with a phone call, didn't join her. She picked up a drive-through hamburger and phoned Spencer Wolf from the seat of her car. The bag of lunch remnants sat on the passenger seat. Her parking space faced the busy road in front of the restaurant.

"What did you find?" Spencer Wolf said after they exchanged hellos.

She and the Eagle Alliance boss had a long history, going back to their time in the Marines.

"Nothing that's going to help," she said.

"Tell me anyway."

"Slayton reported our spotters finding him in Biarritz, and the search of his hotel room. Dylan notes Slayton wanted to capture one for questioning. No contact since."

"Slayton is running on his own, then."

"Unless he died elsewhere after taking out Cannon's men."

"The police in the area would have found his body. Once they discovered the other two, they scoured the area. They noted vehicle tracks going in and out. *Somebody* drove the van away, and it had to be Slayton."

"I didn't know that. I agree."

"Keep your eyes open. Cannon and his people are searching for other clues."

"Slayton has personal contacts," she said. "Outside the agency. You can look there."

"Can you send me his dossier?"

"As soon as I return," she said.

"If he calls Sharp, get back to me as soon as possible."

"I will."

"No more tricks till then," Wolf said.

They ended the call and Emily returned to HQ. After accessing Slayton's dossier and notations on known contacts outside the CIA, she sent the file to Wolf. Then she resumed her daily tasks and hoped nobody noticed her trembling hands.

* * *

DYLAN RETURNED to his desk after lunch in the commissary. The private office once again proved its worth. The quiet was welcome as he read an email from Slayton. When he finished, there was no way to hide the distress on his face.

I'm not telling you where I'm going...

Dylan's sense of dread multiplied. He read about the confrontation with Mutt and Jeff and the chemical interrogation. Then he read the account a second time. Slayton suggested Dylan check for reports of two men shot dead somewhere near Biarritz. Maybe the cops could identify them and find out where they originated.

Slayton stated his trail was clear as far as he saw, and he was on his way to Reema.

We'll find our own way home. I'm not trusting agency transport for now.

Dylan needed to update Fisher in person, no doubt. He phoned the boss's secretary and told her it was urgent.

* * *

SLAYTON DROVE out of Biarritz in a rental car. He kept an eye on his backside while thinking.

Doubts about Reema crowded his mind.

How had she changed? How had *he* changed? Were they still the same people who surfed in Ocean City? Had time and circumstances pushed them apart in ways they didn't yet know?

There was no sense worrying, he decided. He'd have the answer as soon as he saw her, and vice versa.

He checked the rearview mirror often, turned off onto side roads, visited tourist stops. He never saw the same car more than he should have, and his gut told him the way was clear. No traps awaited. But Slayton knew he wasn't safe. The enemy would try and find him again. As long as he stayed on his own and didn't involve the agency, they stood a chance of getting home. He replayed in his mind for the umpteenth time Reema's phone call to Dylan. What did she mean about the Eagle Alliance starting a terrorist group? And how did the fact his tormentors were *American* play into the statement?

Reema was the priority. Getting her home was the goal. Anything else remained secondary. He'd let Dylan and the headquarters crew figure out the mystery. His task was clear.

He arrived in Espellete around dinner time and parked at the Euzkadi Hotel. Reema had insisted on staying there during their first holiday. The hotel had a pool, a feature other hotels in the area, at the time, lacked. She wanted to lounge poolside in her bikini. Slayton would have been a fool to deny her the opportunity. And he didn't regret it when she modeled the bikini for him before visiting the pool.

As he sat in the parked rental, he let go of his doubts.

Enough stalling, he decided.

It was time to go knock on the door and see what happened next.

* * *

Slayton tapped a code on the door. It was a simple dot-dot-dash rhythm Reema would recognize if she waited within the room. He stood a moment with no answer. Slayton checked his watch. It was dinnertime, after all. Had she gone out to eat?

Should he wander around to some of their favorite spots and see if she was there?

He tapped a knuckle on the door a second time, repeating the code. Another wait. His pulse beat hard. Slayton took a deep breath to try to settle his nerves. No dice.

And then nothing he did mattered because the lock clicked, and the door opened and there was Reema standing before him. A sight he thought he'd never see again. Her clothes fit loosely. She looked thinner than before. He tried to talk but words didn't come out.

But she managed to talk. "Hurry!" she whispered.

Reema opened the door, he slipped into the room, and she shut the door and threw the locks. She faced him with a gasp and covered her mouth with her hands. She looked him up and down. She didn't believe he was there any more than he believed she was. But they were standing together. For the first time in three years.

Finally, he found his voice.

"Hi."

Tears filled her eyes. She rushed to him, flinging her arms around him in a tight embrace. Reema buried her face in his chest and her body shook with sobs. Slayton embraced her slowly, uncertain. He grunted as she tightened skinny arms around him. Like she needed to hang on for life.

She was fragile, bony, and her dress was too big for her. He started, then stopped, rubbing her back. No words of comfort came to mind. Now wasn't the time to talk. He had nothing to say, anyway, so he remained quiet. And he held her close.

They stood in each other's arms for what seemed like hours in the quiet room. He heard her sobs and felt her heartbeat. He gently pushed her away; she tried to hold on but then lifted her eyes to his.

"I never thought—" She wiped her eyes.

"I know."

"I can't believe you're here."

"Me too."

"I wondered if you'd come."

"Nothing was going to stop me."

"How are we getting home?" she said.

"I have a car downstairs. It's been a busy few days, believe me." He told her about Biarritz.

"But how did they know—"

"Later. You ready to go?"

"Give me five minutes and I'll follow you anywhere."

He didn't tell her where they were going, and she didn't ask.

16

His name was Rylen Cannon; he liked dark clothes and wore a leather jacket.

Three words described Cannon—tall, dark, and deadly. The Eagle Alliance used him for "special projects." He made prisoners tell their deepest secrets or put targets six feet under. Until Jack Slayton came along, his success rate was ninety-nine percent. But Spencer Wolf had made it clear Slayton wasn't a run-of-the-mill jihadist.

"He's done this too long to be easy," Wolf said. "But he needs to go. Him and his Iraqi girlfriend know things they shouldn't. This isn't national security. It's our survival. Can you do the job?"

Cannon named his fee, which Wolf agreed to pay without argument, and began work.

Cannon wanted another look at Slayton's hotel room, so he returned in hopes of finding a lead to where he might go. The CIA man's disappearance meant his own men were dead and Slayton had escaped. Cannon had to admit he faced a formidable opponent this time.

He used a pocket device to override the electronic lock

on Slayton's hotel room, as before. This time the room was empty. Housekeeping had not arrived to tidy up, nor had the desk sold the room to another visitor. If Slayton had left any clues to his next move, they'd still be present.

Entering the room, Cannon shut the door. He waved a bright pen light around, then began his search. He highlighted the floor. Each corner, behind the nightstand, under the bed and the back of the dresser. He found only a room with the usual debris not yet touched by cleaning staff. No clues to suggest Slayton's current whereabouts. Even the best had their sloppy moments. Despite the circumstances of his escape, Slayton had not reached his. Cannon switched off the pen flash and returned it to his pocket. Exiting the room, he let the door slam shut behind him and peeled off the latex gloves from his hands. He stuffed the gloves in a back pocket for later disposal.

As Cannon walked down the hall, his phone rang. He held it to his ear. "Yes?"

"We have a name."

A woman's voice, the one Slayton named Long Neck. Her real name was Monique. She was one of Cannon's best —an expert computer hacker.

"Tell me." Cannon skipped the elevators for the stairs and hurried down. His steps echoed.

"It came from Wolf. Slayton has outside sources he uses, and the nearest one is a man named Adrian Falco. Slayton lists him as a document fixer and a man to see for last-minute transportation. If the Ashraf woman needs a new passport—"

"Got it. How sure are you Slayton will go to Falco? I'll waste a lot of time if he doesn't."

"He's two hundred kilometers from Biarritz in

Bordeaux. I'm sending directions to your phone. It's a two-hour drive. And the only thread we have to pull on."

"No other options?"

"Not in France."

Cannon reached the ground floor and pushed through a door into the lobby. "All right, fine." He hurried across the tiled floor to the exit. The mission hinged on the Ashraf woman being between Biarritz and Bordeaux. Cannon figured the move was likely.

"Thanks, Monique. I'm on my way. The rest of you get home and standby."

"Take it slow, chief."

Cannon promised to do so.

* * *

Spencer Wolf finally had to speak to the big boss.

And Max Hudson did not look pleased.

Wolf approached the bench where Hudson sat in the shadow of the Lincoln Memorial. They had a full view of the reflection park. The public as well as tourists made their presence known with noise and chatter. They were both overdressed compared to everyone around them. If anybody wanted to guess, they'd think of them as politicians getting away from Capitol Hill. Wolf sat on the hard bench and cleared his throat. He had no way to hide the tension in his body language.

"I'm not sure," Wolf opened, "we should be talking under Mr. Lincoln's gaze."

"We are a lot like him, Spencer. All we want is to keep this country in one piece and we will do so by any means, legal or otherwise. Mr. Lincoln would understand."

Hudson grinned at Wolf's frown.

"A leap in logic considering we created October Blood? No, Spencer. It makes perfect sense. Look at our history. After every war, we disarm ourselves. We reduce our defenses to the minimum because we no longer face a threat. And there is peace for a time. But then what? A new threat grows. We aren't prepared. The enemy achieves easy victories, and the politicians go into their Rambo act. They blame the intelligence community, the very organ they cut and defunded once the *previous* threat ceased.

"October Blood wasn't only done for money," Hudson continued. "It was to make sure the US never decided it won the War on Terror and quit being vigilant. Because no matter what, there will always be another threat. We should control the threat while we have the chance. Or *had*. I'm not hearing anything good through the gossip mill. Please explain."

"You're right. I'm not here to share good news." Wolf kept his voice low but was confident in his tradecraft. Nobody had followed him. He knew he wasn't under watch. Wolf explained the failure to neutralize Jack Slayton, and the CIA man's independent effort to find Reema Ashraf.

"Are you saying we *lost* him?" Hudson asked.

"No. I put Rylen Cannon on the case. He's following another lead provided by our insider. He has high confidence the lead will settle the situation."

Hudson let out a breath. "We need to do better. This is not good."

"No," Wolf agreed.

"Stay on task," Hudson said, "and let me know what happens as soon as you learn anything."

Hudson rose to leave. "You should stay a while, Spencer. Relax. The fresh air will do you good."

Wolf scoffed in reply as Hudson walked away. He

remained on the bench, though. He watched the tourists; the pigeons; he didn't glance at the memorial. Lincoln's skullduggery during the Civil War to keep the Union together, the dirty tricks, the imprisonment of opposing voices, the "special police" force, proved successful. Wolf's, so far, had not. He didn't want to acknowledge Lincoln's judging gaze.

But the fresh air *was* nice.

17

SLAYTON WATCHED THE ROAD. REEMA SAT QUIETLY BESIDE HIM.

Two hours, twenty minutes to Bordeaux, according to the in-dash GPS. Two hours, twenty minutes to begin getting used to each other again. They'd not said a word for over thirty minutes. Slayton decided if they maintained the silence, they'd never talk about anything. But not talking wasn't the goal. They had *much* to discuss.

"Are we going to say anything?" He shifted in his seat. The question made him uncomfortable. He hoped he didn't sound aggressive. Or angry.

"I don't know what to say," Reema admitted.

"Look...um...can you tell me what happened? We thought you'd been killed."

"Jack—"

"Please, Reema. Tell me what happened."

She took some time to collect her thoughts but then began. She told him everything, from her capture by the bandits to the rescue by Faisil.

"He brought you back to the headquarters?" Slayton said.

"It was all tents at the time, but yes."

"Then what?"

She told of her long recovery, the need for constant medical attention in the early days. She talked about Hafsa, the woman her brother asked to keep an eye on her. And, she added:

"I found out who's actually in charge of October Blood."

"You said something about a PMC?"

"Yes."

"You can prove this?"

"The proof is on a computer at the base camp."

"It's *where?*"

"Sorry I didn't have time to grab it on my way out. Somebody was trying to put a bullet in my back." Her voice rose. "I told Sharp he needed to hurry and make a move on the base, but he was more interested in telling me I was dead."

Slayton paused. He had to proceed carefully. She'd been through the works. Talking about it wasn't easy for her; hearing her words wasn't easy for him.

"What about your brother?"

"He died covering my escape."

"What happened?"

Reema explained, "Kameel al-Rashid was second in command, and he and Faisil kept having arguments. It was always the same argument, too. When are they planning an *opening attack* to announce themselves? Faisil kept putting it off, which made Kameel more and more upset every time he did. He told my brother he wasn't a real fighter, and they needed a leader who had the guts to see the mission through."

She paused.

Slayton waited.

"I sensed the day coming. Kameel rallied with troops loyal to him. Faisil tried to keep the group from splitting. Kameel and his troops opened fire on Faisil and fighters still loyal to him. The entire base turned into a war zone.

"Faisil pushed me into a truck and told me to run. He told me October Blood was never meant to be *real.* He said he was paid by an American private military corporation. If I survived, he wanted me to tell somebody. I didn't get to ask him more because Kameel shot him in the back. I took off. Kameel tried to kill me too, but I made it outside the wall."

Slayton frowned. "How do you know there's proof on this computer?"

"Because what Faisil said made some of his habits finally make sense. He had his private quarters, and every Wednesday he'd lock himself inside and make a video call. If what he told me is true, his video calls had to be with his handlers. Which means there's a record we can track and discover who he was talking to."

Slayton said nothing for a moment.

"You haven't told me where we're going," she said. She sounded tired.

"I have a friend in Bordeaux. He can get you a fresh passport and arrange a flight out. I don't want to use your current passport in case the name you're traveling under is flagged somehow. What name are you using?"

"I made up a name. I got it in Damascus. The hard way," she added.

"Why don't you try and sleep. We have a bit further to go."

"Uh-huh."

Silence again. But when he looked over at her, she'd fallen asleep.

He wasn't sure what to think about her story. He needed time to process the details. But for certain, he wanted her to repeat everything to Dylan. She'd hate to do it; she'd hate him for making her. But they needed the story on the official record in case anything happened on the way home. Anything to prevent her from telling her story in person.

It was the worst-case scenario, but a high probability.

The enemy wasn't going to give up.

They needed to get the proof and bring the rogue elements to justice. *Fast.* And destroy their sick creation before thousands of innocent people died.

* * *

SLAYTON PACED the hotel room while Reema spoke to Dylan on the phone. She repeated her story with a few more details, but the basics didn't change. It wasn't a story she had invented. Slayton cursed himself for judging her words in such a way. Home base would put her through worse scrutiny when they returned, and she needed to be ready. There was a lot she had to prove, and he hoped they didn't spend too much time vetting her details. Any significant delay allowed October Blood to execute a mass casualty event.

Slayton stopped pacing when she ended the phone call. She stared at him and looked sad.

"Jack—"

His hands shook. He wasn't ready yet. "Hang on," he told her. He grabbed his phone from her and dialed Adrian Falco. The document fixer answered on the third ring. Their conversation did not last long. Slayton described what he needed, and the pair agreed to meet the following afternoon. Slayton put the phone away. Reema was standing closer to him. He needed to stop trembling and ditch the sinking feeling in his gut. They no longer had talk of work to distract them from a more important question.

He said, "Do you want to eat or shower or—"

"Jack, do you still..."

Her eyes widened. She feared the answer same as he did. But then he stopped trembling and stopped feeling nervous because he knew *her* answer.

"I never stopped."

Slayton's pulse raced as he tugged Reema to him. Their lips collided in a frantic, clumsy kiss, all teeth and urgency, three years of absence igniting like a fuse. Reema's hands fumbled at his shirt. She leaned too close and her forehead bumped into his chin. "Ow — sorry," she muttered, cheeks flushing. Slayton laughed as he yanked at her blouse, buttons resisting his trembling fingers.

They stumbled toward the bed, knees knocking awkwardly. Reema tripped over his foot, letting out a surprised yelp as they toppled onto the bed.

"Were we this clumsy before?" she asked, but her voice shook. Half-dressed, hearts pounding too fast, breaths shallow and uneven. Slayton's hands kept shaking as he undid the last button and she rose to take off the blouse. He slipped the bra straps off her shoulders, and she arched her back for him to rotate the garment around to the clasp faced front. He had trouble with the hooks, and she finally helped him, one deft movement freeing the clasp. He pulled the bra from under her and tossed it and the blouse aside.

He hovered his lips over her scars — new, stark against her skin — and kissed softly around them. She took deep breaths to slow down her racing heart. He went to her jeans next and slip them down to her ankles only to be blocked by her shoes.

"Dammit."

She laughed again. He pulled off her shoes and socks and then tossed the jeans on the floor.

She was too thin. Thin and bony. And the scars. It hurt him. She'd been through more than she'd let on and he didn't know what to do or say. Her eyes froze on him as he hesitated. There was fear behind her eyes; fear and doubt. Neither spoke. She pushed him onto his back and started helping him out of his clothes. Slayton closed his eyes and felt his body respond to her light touch.

Their mouths met again, but the rhythm was off, too desperate. Reema's nails grazed his scalp; he flinched, then sucked in air.

"Breathe," she gasped, pressing her palm to his chest. They froze, foreheads touching, panting like they'd sprinted a mile. Her eyes, wide and vulnerable, locked onto his.

"We're okay," he whispered.

"I know."

They started again, slower, tentative. He rolled on top of her and traced her jaw, her neck, each kiss deliberate, searching for sync. Reema's fingers slid down his spine, hesitant, then firmer. Their bodies shifted, awkward at first — his knee bumped her thigh, her elbow grazed his side — but they laughed softly, adjusting. Slayton paused with his mouth at her earlobe.

"Don't stop," she urged, her voice a mix of need and reassurance, pulling him closer. "*Please* don't." Her legs parted, guiding him. He moved with her, slow, careful, their rhythm unsteady but building. Her hands gripped his shoulders. They found a fragile, shared cadence, moving together, bodies aligning like a memory resurfacing.

He sank into her depth with a gentle thrust. Reema peered into his eyes, nodding; he found a rhythm and she matched.

She arched her back and lifted her thighs to take him deeper. When her thighs tightened around him, he slowed. Her body convulsed under him as her climax hit from head to toe. She shook beneath him and bit off a cry, chest and neck flushing red. Slayton went over the top, too. He felt the pressure building, and then the sudden burst as he exploded inside her. They trembled, clinging to each other, the world narrowing to their shared pulse.

After a few minutes he rolled to her side, wary of her fragile frame, both breathless. Reema's eyes sparkled with a mix of exhaustion and mischief.

"We need to practice more," she murmured, a small grin tugging at her lips. She ran a hand through his chest hair. If she noticed the spots of gray, she kept it to herself. "But ... good start," she added.

Slayton laughed and brushed a strand of hair from her face. He wasn't sure how to respond yet.

She wrapped her arms and legs around him. He held her close.

Neither needed to say a word.

18

It was easy to find Adrian Falco's address. He lived and worked in a plain gray building, square with a flat roof, at the end of a street. Alley on one side, street on the other, an anomaly because other shops and restaurants on either side of the road were connected, identifiable only by signs and color scheme.

Falco lived above his shop, according to Slayton's dossier. Cannon only needed to wait for him to close and for the lights to snap on upstairs. The man in the leather jacket left his car down the block and watched Falco's shop from an alley across the street. Falco ran an antique store as a front; the window display showed several pieces for sale.

Cannon examined the alley beside Falco's store. A flight of steps ended at a side door to the upstairs apartment.

Falco closed and locked the shop door and took the stairs at a slow pace. He was older and carried more than a few extra pounds. He reached the apartment door, breathing hard. The door wasn't locked; he went inside. The lights blinked on. He kept the curtains facing the street closed.

Cannon crossed the street with casual steps, at a proper crosswalk. He reached the opposite side and followed the sidewalk to Falco's store.

According to Slayton's notes, the document fixer made a good income from the store. He sold locally and through a website. His forgery and transport business were his primary source of income. Passports, birth certificates, any identity paper somebody needed. Transportation options ran from airplanes to boats—any size, to any location. Somehow, Falco had avoided attention from the police or Interpol. Cannon wasn't easy to impress, but to remain in business as long as Falco was an admirable achievement.

Cannon had a simple plan. Kill the man, take his place, and wait for Slayton to show. He almost hated to ruin the old man's operation. He'd have used him for his own missions requiring clean papers. But Cannon didn't think Falco would be willing to give up Slayton. There was no sense in trying to question him first.

Cannon climbed the alley steps. Light peeked from the crack under the door. A TV blared at high volume—was Falco hard of hearing? Cannon tested the knob. Locked. He went to work with a pair of lock picks pulled from a pocket of his leather jacket. He eased the door open and stepped through.

He entered a small, empty kitchen. The light and TV noise came from an adjoining sitting room a few steps to the right. Cannon eased a suppressor-fitted .22 autoloader from under his jacket. Then he began to ease the door closed by hand.

The hinges let out a loud squeak.

* * *

DYLAN SHARP HATED POLYGRAPH TESTS.

But there was no other way to get to the truth.

Polygraph interviews were a way of life at the CIA. Internal Security tests employees on a regular basis. Dylan didn't like the sensors taped to his skin but understood the necessity. The wires connected to the sensors would record his reactions into the computer. IS needed every detail. He had to answer honestly and study the results after. He hoped the questions helped him think of any moments where he himself screwed up.

"We'll start with baseline questions," said the poly operator. Dylan only nodded. The poly tech was a young man in a gray suit who looked fresh out of college. Dylan wondered if he was old enough to shave. He laughed to himself. The problem with getting older and being around younger people was younger people seemed much younger than their actual birth dates indicated.

The baseline questions were standard yes-and-no fillers. Is your name Dylan Sharp? Were you born in Seattle? Are you a polar bear who shape-shifted into a human? By the time the real questions began, Dylan was more than ready.

"Have you ever betrayed the United States?"

"No," Dylan said.

"Are you passing information to foreign actors who pose a danger to the United States?"

"No."

"Did you begin this investigation to cover your tracks because you *are* in the process of betraying the United States?"

"No."

Other questions followed a similar pattern over a half hours' time. The poly operator was smart. He often reworded the same questions to catch Dylan off-guard. Dylan tried not to resent the interrogation—the effort was his idea, after all. But the kid made him mad once or twice regardless.

After the poly ended, Dylan joined a woman in another office. She was older, middle-aged, with a short haircut. She asked different questions and filled a page with notes. A digital recorder also captured their conversation.

"Tell me what you do during the week?"

"You need special clearance from the DCI for me to tell you."

"Who do you see outside of work? Do you date anybody who is also a CIA employee?"

When Dylan explained he and Emily Chapman had been dating a while, he cut off his remarks mid-sentence.

The woman raised an eyebrow. "Why did you stop talking?"

Dylan had the words in his mind before he spoke to them. The impact of their meaning hit him like a piano falling off the roof of the Empire State Building.

"I began seeing Emily around the same time I took charge of the October Blood case. Almost three years ago."

The blond woman made another note.

A trickle of sweat ran down the back of Dylan's neck.

* * *

Adrian Falco moved fast when he had to.

As the hinges squealed, Rylen Cannon left the doorway. He shifted into the darkness of the kitchen. Falco's shadow moved across the floor as he left the TV room. When the doc fixer appeared, he raised a revolver in Cannon's direction.

The suppressed Browning .22 Buck Mark in Cannon's right fist spit once, and again and again as Cannon worked the trigger. Falco never fired a shot. The first .22 lead slug drilled the old man through the chest. Falco screamed; his gun forgotten. His body twisted in reaction to the repeated bullet hits. Cannon closed the gap between them with fast steps. Falco's feet hit a table leg and he fell. Cannon stood over the bleeding and screaming man and shot him again. Falco stopped screaming.

Cannon replaced the partially spent magazine in his .22 Browning with a full one. He put the gun away.

Not the best; not the worst. Job done. Now he had to wait for Jack Slayton and the Ashraf woman and take care of them the same way.

But, Cannon hoped, without a pair of squeaky hinges to give him away.

19

Slayton cruised past Falco's shop. He glanced at the storefront. He cursed and drove on. He made the next left and then another left and parked curbside behind his friend's shop.

"What's wrong?" Reema asked.

"The shop."

"Sign said it was open."

"The sign is the wrong color. If he was ready for us, the sign would be blue instead of orange."

Slayton reached into his jacket for his phone. He dialed Falco and watched the back of the shop. The line rang four times, and then Falco's voicemail answered. Slayton ended the call and set the phone in the center console. Withdrawing his pistol from under the jacket, he checked the chamber for a seated round. He put the gun back.

"Stay here. I'm not bringing you into a trap."

"If it's a trap, I'm going with you."

He opened his door and said, "Stay," and stepped out. She exited too. He gave her a pointed look.

"I need you alive," she said.

He blinked. They watched each other a moment. Slayton said, "Stay behind me," and crossed the street. Reema hustled to keep up with his jog. They reached the empty back lot of Falco's shop. The older man's car sat parked with nobody inside. A good sign. But...

Dammit, the sign color isn't right.

Slayton glanced at the door to the second-floor apartment. No indication anybody had damaged the door. Falco wouldn't be upstairs during business hours anyway. Slayton approached the rear door on the ground floor. No sign of forced entry—the knob was locked. Reema stopped beside him. Her eyes questioned him; he had questions of his own. *Am I wrong?*

"Are we going in this way?" Reema asked.

Slayton shook his head and indicated they should go around front. Reema followed him. He peeked through the glass. No sign of Falco.

"Get your gun ready," he told Reema.

She unbuttoned her purse and reached inside for her Glock-19. Slayton went to the door and pulled. The bell above chimed. Slayton moved left; Reema right. Display shelves and larger pieces filled the space. Large counter dead center. The walkway up the middle was no-man's-land.

Behind the counter, more displays, then the doors to the back storage rooms. The lights were on, and music played at low volume. But the color of the sign was wrong. And Slayton had another warning. The place didn't smell right.

He took out his gun again.

"Adrian? You're not smoking one of your cheap cigars. This place should stink."

No reply.

"Where you at, buddy?"

Movement on his right. Slayton shifted to look. Reema advanced around displays, keeping close to the right wall. She held her pistol in a two-hand grip. She stopped and dropped to one knee. Her eyes remained locked on the area behind the counter. Slayton faced forward. He didn't see what caught her attention. He left his position and moved closer to the left-side wall. He lowered himself to his belly. *There.* Behind a set of old chairs was somebody's boot.

The snout of a suppressor-fitted pistol appeared beneath one of the chairs. Leather gloves concealed the hand clutching the gun. Slayton fired. The loud pops of the P-10C filled the room and tore a chunk out of the chair.

Reema fired a shot of her own as the gloved assassin rolled away and rushed the front counter. Slayton hesitated as his finger tightened on the trigger. *Leather Jacket!* He fired as the assassin reached the cover of the counter. Slayton fired twice more, rolled right, fired again. The shots from Reema's Glock smacked through the front of the counter, tearing into the fiberboard. Slayton moved forward. The assassin fired at Reema, then moved to the other side to try for Slayton. Slayton took cover behind a hutch. The .22 slug zipped overhead. Slayton prepared to charge the counter. Before he had a chance, Leather Jacket tossed an object over the top. *Grenade! No, smoke bomb!* The canister popped and hissed white smoke. Slayton fired into the growing plume, then charged through. Leather Jacket vanished through the door marked employees only. Slayton fired once but only nicked the door.

He yelled for Reema to go back to the car as he reached the door. He flung it open and ducked to the side as a trio of rounds from LJ's .22 zipped through space. Slayton bent low and charged. LJ was almost at the rear door; he turned and fired. Slayton hit the thin carpet and rolled left into the wall. The exit door swung open and let in a brief stream of outdoor light; the light cut off as the door slammed shut again.

Slayton ran down the hall. Reema called after him, but he ignored her. He eased the door open, taking in the outside view through the ever-widening gap. No more LJ. He stepped outside. Leather Jacket had vanished, run off. He put his gun away.

Reema stopped beside him, breathing hard and sweating. She wiped her brow. Slayton grabbed her left hand and they hurried to return to the rental.

He hated to run without checking for Adrian's body, but his friend was undoubtedly beyond help. And the gunfire had police on the way—he heard sirens in the distance, growing in volume. They had at get away and not look back.

Tires screeched as Slayton stepped on the accelerator. He turned right at the first corner they came to, speeding as far from the scene as possible. Slayton weaved around slower cars before Reema told him to settle down.

Slayton slowed to the flow of traffic. He banged his fist into the steering wheel.

"Are you hurt?" he asked her.

"No. Who was that man?"

"Somebody who shouldn't have known how to find us there."

"So how did he?"

"I'm thinking about it, babe. There's only one possibility."

"The leak is worse than you thought?"

"The only way to find out about Falco was my *dossier* at HQ."

"They looked for somebody you knew who could provide papers and transport."

"Yes."

"Papers we still don't have," she added.

Slayton's mind raced for a solution. He continued driving, which helped focus his thoughts. Every few seconds he had to refocus because his mind flashed to poor Falco. *I'm sorry I was too late, bud.*

Remaining in Bordeaux wasn't an option. How many witnesses heard the gunfire and saw his car leave the scene?

But where to next? They were stuck in France unless they wanted to take their chances with a commercial flight. Asking the CIA to send them a jet was suicide.

Wait...Paris!

"Let's go to Paris," he said.

"What's in Paris?" Reema began working the in-dash GPS for the fastest route.

"*Who* is in Paris. A mercenary named Jarvis. Another old pal. And he's not mentioned in my files."

The GPS voice told them to get on an upcoming motorway.

20

CANNON SAID, "I DON'T KNOW WHERE THEY WENT. ALL I KNOW IS I lost them when I escaped. I didn't expect the woman to have a gun too."

Spencer Wolf, on the other end of the line, remained quiet, but not for long.

"What kind of car were they driving? We can check the freeway speed cameras."

"Couldn't tell which one was theirs. I didn't hang around."

"Are you suggesting this is a dead end?"

"You for sure shot your wad with your inside source," Cannon said. "Slayton will figure out how I knew, and he'll report to his boss. Delete the dossier or whatever you have. Slayton won't go to anybody he's connected to again."

Wolf said, "What's the most likely scenario? What would you do if you were in Slayton's place?"

"I'd head for Paris. It's where all the out-of-work mercenaries hang out. He'll find one who can get them out of France."

"Think you can catch up?"

"I have a few connections of my own," Cannon said. "I'll hit the road and tell them to be on the lookout. We may get lucky."

"Good enough. Keep me informed."

Cannon promised to do so and ended the call. He hit the motorway with renewed energy. Running hadn't been his idea of a proper performance. He expected more of himself. But facing two guns changed the odds—in favor of Slayton and the woman. Reality required he retreat. He'd failed in another way. Slayton had known something was amiss. Cannon couldn't have prepared for what Slayton expected with Falco dead.

But with luck and timing, he'd soon have Jack Slayton and Reema Ashraf in his sights again. The payback was a short time away.

* * *

Slayton and Reema reached Paris without incident and checked into a small hotel off the tourist routes. They'd spent the night searching seedy bars for Jarvis Van Varren but had nothing to show for the effort. Jarvis was nowhere to be found. Once he locked the door, Reema asked if the hotel was safe. What if the other side checked the smaller hotels looking for them?

It was an honest question. As they'd made the rounds, one bartender took them aside. He mentioned another pair of tough-looking goons searching for *them*. The bartender, a friend of Jarvis's, figured Slayton was okay if he knew Jarvis, so he offered the warning. This time, Slayton knew the other side was grasping at straws. They'd predicted the move to Paris by chance. Slayton and Reema still needed to keep an eye out. Leather Jacket wouldn't be far behind.

"We're fine here." Slayton took off his jacket and hung it in the closet. He also hung his shoulder rig but placed the P-10C on the nightstand.

"How are you sure?"

"The owner is a friend. The desk clerk is his oldest son. The opposition can show them our pictures all they want but they'll never get a clue we're here. Well, short of watching the place."

Reema decided the explanation was good enough for her and went to take a shower. All the walking they'd done had worn her out. Bar crawls weren't what they used to be, she told him.

If she was waiting for Slayton to join her, he left her disappointed. He sat at the desk with his phone and began making calls. He wanted to reach people he hadn't seen in person, but of the ten calls he made, only two answered. And neither had any idea where to find Jarvis.

Was he on a job?

Worse, was he dead?

Slayton decided they'd give it one more night. Then he'd call Dylan and work out another option. A Hail Mary for home could be their only choice.

He stretched out on the bed and dozed off. Reema nudged him awake and told him to get out of his clothes if he was going to bed. She didn't have anything amorous in mind. She simply couldn't get under the covers herself with him on the comforter. Slayton rose and undressed as Reema burrowed under the sheets. The lights remained on. He crossed the room, nude, Reema watching or not, and hit the switch. He returned to the bed and fell asleep as fast as the light had gone out.

* * *

Reema wasn't excited when Slayton told her they'd hit the bars again. She agreed to "one more try" only because Slayton promised to call HQ if they rolled snake eyes again.

She grimaced as they walked through the entrance of the first spot. She didn't bother to read the sign; all bars looked the same to her. She swore only to drink at home from now on. Why mercenaries between jobs congregated in Paris remained a mystery. She didn't see anything of value in the city. There were nicer places.

The bar was dark, crowded, and loud. No music—she was grateful for that, at least. She recognized a few faces from the night before. Hard men with scary eyes. Not all had every limb or finger they were born with; some showed scars. A few had covered over the scars with tattoos. Their quick examinations of her reflected either no interest or boredom. They had more important matters to discuss with each other. There were jobs under discussion; hushed, intense conversations, and she wanted none of it. She wanted *out* of Paris as fast as possible. The jumble of voices was louder than any music had a chance to overcome.

The visit turned violent when Slayton jostled a large man playing pool. And the two of them were outnumbered, outmatched, and unarmed.

The man at the pool table was big and broad with close-cropped blond hair and a bony chin. He leaned in to make a called shot. A passerby with an empty beer glass moved between Slayton and Reema, causing Slayton to shift. His left hip bumped the man at the pool table as he made his shot. The cue stick thrust past the white ball with only a light touch. The ball moved to the side and stopped.

The blond man cursed. Three other players at the table told him the shot counted, no do-overs. The man with the stick turned to Slayton and gave him a shove. He shouted in German.

Slayton pushed back. "Don't speakee the lingo, kraut."

Reema knew Slayton understood German perfectly. But one couldn't negotiate their way out of such situations.

The German dropped the stick on the table and balled a fist. There wasn't a lot of room to fight. But as soon as Slayton landed a hit across the German's bony jaw, people scattered and gave them space to groove. They shouted encouragement. Some placed bets.

The German swung; Slayton ducked. He struck with sharp blows in return. The German doubled over, and Slayton smashed a knee into his face. The blond went down and out.

His three buddies at the pool table advanced with their cue sticks held as weapons. Slayton struck one in the face with a high kick. Another dove at him and took Slayton to the floor.

Reema screamed.

The third merc snapped his eyes to her and said, "You with him?"

Reema answered by grabbing a beer bottle from a table and throwing it at him. The man ducked; the bottle sailed over his head, crashed against the wall. The man charged at her.

Reema met his rush with a kick. The force of the impact only stopped him long enough for him to smack her with the cue stick. She felt the blow on her left shoulder; he followed by sweeping her legs out from under her. She hit the floor and yelped. The man tossed aside the stick and leaned down to grab her. Reema rolled out of the way, but not far enough. Stool legs stopped her progress. The man grabbed a fistful of her shirt and lifted her halfway off the sticky floor. Then a hairy hand attached to a thick arm landed on the merc's shoulder.

"Nuh uh, brother."

Reema blinked. The new arrival sported a bristly goatee and round bald head. He looked thick and full of muscle under a tight T-shirt and camouflage pants. The goon dropped Reema and turned to face the new threat. The bald man swung once. It was all he needed. His fist hit with such force the merc flopped back against a table, tipping it over. Bottles and glasses crashed to the floor and shattered. He came to rest on his back.

The bald man went to Slayton. Slayton and the German struggled against each other to the soundtrack of the cheering crowd. Sweat covered their faces as they strained against each other. The bald man grabbed the merc's shoulders and hauled him off Slayton as if he were picking up a pillow. He sank a hairy fist into the opponent's belly. The goon bent in half. The bald man cast him aside and he crumbled onto the floor. He reached down to pick up Slayton, dusted him off with a loud guffaw, and squeezed him with an arm across his shoulders. Slayton's face didn't register the gesture; he looked stunned, out of it, and his face bled a little.

"Get this man a beer!" the bald man shouted. The crowd booed. "What kind of dump is this?"

* * *

TURNED out it was the kind of dump where the owner didn't tolerate fighting. He told Slayton, Reema, and the bald man to leave. Other patrons moved the unconscious Germans off the floor and righted the tables.

Reema stopped at a corner store for a bottle of water

and paper towels. She joined Slayton and the bald man at a park bench. A few wipes with a handful of damp towels and Slayton returned to life. He gave the bald man a smile.

"Jarvis, meet Reema. Reema, this is Jarvis Van Varren."

"Hi," she said. They shook hands. His skin was still sweaty. "Thanks for the rescue." She wiped her hand on a towel.

"You picked the worst thugs to deal with," Jarvis said. "That was Andreas Neuner and his buddies. They're a team. Very violent soldiers, but good to have on your side."

"I doubt I'll ever have the pleasure," Slayton said.

"I hear you're looking for me."

"Where you been?"

"Gotta eat! Just come back from a job. What's going on?"

"I need a passport for Reema and a flight to the US," Slayton said.

"Okay. I can make it happen if the money's right."

"How much?"

"Five thousand US for the passport. The flight will be more. Ten thousand."

"Jesus, Jarvis!"

"It's tough right now. My pilot won't budge on the price. He's got a nice plane, though. He doesn't fly junk."

"At ten grand a pop," Slayton said, "he better have a gold-plated toilet."

Jarvis laughed. "He might!"

"Two thousand for the passport. It doesn't have to be perfect."

"The hell it doesn't."

"Twenty-five hundred," Slayton said.

"Because it's you, thirty-five. Best I can do."

"Deal." They shook. Slayton wiped his hand on his pants.

"I need a few days," Jarvis said.

"We don't have a few days. I can give you two."

"You're asking a lot."

"Jarvis—"

"If we hadn't shaken on thirty-five hundred, I'd go back to five thousand!"

"It's urgent," Slayton said. "I wouldn't make the demand otherwise."

"Okay. We'll be ready in two days. Sounds like you're in a bad spot."

"You wouldn't believe me if I told you."

"We can talk about it later, or not, who cares? I ain't seen you in a long time. You both okay to eat?"

"Sure."

"I know a place close by where they don't mind if you got blood on your face!" Jarvis laughed heartily.

21

Emily Chapman sat in a small room cooled with A/C. They had the A/C on for a reason. If she began to sweat despite the chill, they'd take it as a sign of deception. One of many, of course—she was well aware of the "tells" one displayed under interrogation. But then she checked her thoughts.

This wasn't an interrogation, per se. They were fishing for a leak. *The* leak. Dylan told her it was routine, but he had to have initiated the exams. It made sense for him to do so. Right now, she wasn't a suspect. All she had to do was make sure they didn't think of her as a suspect afterward.

A woman sat across from her to ask the questions. In these politically correct times, the agency made sure to pair women with women. They needed to avoid potential conflicts and "microaggressions." Harassment, coercion, the list went on. The list was so long, Emily stopped caring about the categories.

The poly operator looked at Emily as one examined a dead roach.

"We'll start with some baseline questions..."

Emily was already bored. She'd heard the rap too many times already.

The baselines turned to probing questions and she sat straight and concentrated.

"Have you ever betrayed the United States?"

"No."

"Are you engaged in any unlawful activity which may compromise national security?"

"No."

"Are you meeting privately anybody who may be a threat to this agency or national security?"

"No."

And on and on.

Emily wasn't lying. And it helped her pass the poly.

She didn't believe she was doing anything wrong.

She was only afraid of what would happen if and when Dylan found out.

* * *

Four years ago.

"Did you read the latest from the Senate Intelligence Committee?"

Lunch with Spencer Wolf. He had more hair then and the paunch hadn't begun to show.

"Which part?" Emily said. When dining out with a manager or other colleague, she always ordered a meal she could eat with a knife and fork instead of her hands. But she and Wolf had almost died together in Iraq. He'd saved her life later in Afghanistan, too; he knew her better than most people in her life. With him, her protocol didn't count. She'd ordered a juicy double-cheeseburger with bacon and didn't care about messy hands.

"The part detailing how the bean counters want cutbacks to anti-terror funding. They included the PMCs. They say the current preventative operations are having such a positive effect we could cut a few billion and not miss the money."

"I read it," Emily said. "It's a joke around the office. Nobody believes the president or Congress will agree. The money isn't going anywhere."

"What if they *do* agree?"

"Then we'll cut back and withdraw assets and get stuck with our thumbs up our asses when the next attack comes," she said. Emily picked a short piece of bacon from between the slices of meat and popped the crispy strip into her mouth.

"Isn't it our job to prevent that?"

"*My* job," Emily pointed out. "You're temporary." She laughed.

"I don't think it's funny."

"You're right, but what do we do? These things happen. It's a phase."

"Phases like this do more harm than good, Emily."

"Well, I'm out of suggestions, Spencer. I can't manage my workload and worry about the bean counters, too."

"We have to do *something*. Even I'm not sure what. But we shouldn't wait and see. We need to put ideas together. I'm going to see what my boss thinks. We can't let money be the reason the US gets attacked again. Or, worse, we get stuck in another bullshit war because the president has a hard-on to show the world how tough he is."

* * *

EMILY LEFT the post-poly interview thinking of her long-ago chat with Wolf. It was the first conversation leading to the genesis of October Blood. Hudson liked to think it was *his* plan; but it was truly Wolf's baby.

No, they weren't doing anything wrong. October Blood assured the budget didn't get cut. It also provided a place for the wackos to go so the CIA had a way to keep track of them. It was easier to identify the next break-out jihad asshole when you knew where to look. Having a place for them to flock to was much better than letting them run wild. More spending, more operations, fewer dead Americans. Great plan. But then Ground Branch had to step in and mess up the plan with the raid in Syria.

She walked the hall to an elevator. The colleagues she passed and rode with in the elevator kept to themselves.

She had to get word to Wolf. And she had to do so *before* Internal Security went to phase two. After the polys finished, phase two began with surveillance on all suspected parties. Once she had eyes and ears on her, she'd have to stick close to Dylan. She'd have to pretend Wolf, Hudson, and the Eagle Alliance didn't exist.

* * *

DYLAN once again sat in his boss's office. Fisher waited, but Dylan had a hard time getting the words out.

"Spit it out," Fisher commanded.

"Emily Chapman."

"What about her?"

Dylan explained his polygraph and interview. He explained he began seeing Emily at the same time Z Section picked up the threads of the October Blood case. He didn't outright accuse her of being the leak, but the concern covered his face.

Fisher listened with sympathy. He looked sad as Dylan finished talking.

"Now's not the time for sentiment," Fisher said. "You need to look up where she worked before CIA and start poking around. *Quietly*, Dylan," he added. "We need to know."

"What if I find out it's her?"

"What if you don't?"

Dylan nodded.

"There's only one way to find out. Now, go. Get to work."

Dylan left the chair.

22

Jack Slayton never felt so happy boarding an airplane in his life.

Jarvis came through with the passport for Reema and a private jet. The two days passed without trouble. The plane was a Cessna Citation, full leather seating, television, food and drinks. No solid gold toilet, but he hadn't expected to see one anyway. It would make the trip much easier. Reema fell asleep in her chair after the first hour. Slayton watched a Formula One race on the satellite television.

He'd alerted Dylan to their departure and the Z Section boss promised to meet them at Dulles.

The private jet had been a requirement on which Slayton refused to budge. He knew of instances where an enemy blew up or sabotaged a commercial airliner full of civilians only to kill one or two specific passengers. The chance was more than Slayton wanted to risk.

It didn't matter anymore; he finally had a chance to relax. The exodus was in progress and soon Reema would set foot on home turf for the first time in three years. Three *long* years. The exit was settled, but he still wondered about their future.

He muted the car race and watched her sleep. Her original call to Dylan played through his mind again. Slayton realized the plane ride was the only time he *could* relax. Half their enemy was at home. How could he forget? The battle was only beginning.

But for now, he wanted to enjoy the peace.

* * *

DYLAN MET Slayton and Reema at Dulles. The passport supplied by Jarvis, complete with forged entry and exit stamps, posed no issues. Their luggage cleared inspection too. Dylan escorted them to a Suburban with two security officers inside. They drove to a walled estate outside DC. A tall wall surrounded the property, the grounds immaculate. It was the "Charlie Safe House" as the agency called it, part of a system of several CIA safe houses in and around DC. They used them for a variety of purposes. Debriefings of operatives returning from deep cover. Housing defectors who needed time to adjust. Special meetings with overseas intelligence personnel. The houses were secure and comfortable.

"How's this for first-class?" Dylan said. The Suburban cleared the main gate and traveled the access road to the house. "We got everything here to debrief in comfort. You're also well-protected. If anything gets beyond the high-tech security, and we're talking systems even I don't understand, there are ten shooters who'll take care of problems. They're all ex-SF. Trained fighters."

"Good," Reema said. Slayton didn't reply.

A pair of officers waited at the porch. Male and female,

they wore formal attire and smiled when Reema stepped out of the Suburban. Dylan introduced them and explained the pair would do most of the talking with Reema over the next few days. Slayton went with them to her assigned room. She had a private bath and balcony and a queen bed. When they told Slayton he was no longer required, he wanted to argue. But he knew they had to get the process going. Reema's eyes went wide at the prospect of him departing.

"I'll be close by," he assured her. He kissed her and went to look for Dylan.

He found Dylan in the oversized kitchen. Dylan handed him a bottle of beer and suggested they get a breath of fresh air. *Now what*, Slayton wondered. He noticed Dylan grab a tablet computer from where he'd placed it on the center island. He brought the tablet with him.

They sat on the back patio, on sculpted ergonomic chairs, a table between them. A wide umbrella stood overhead. Dylan explained the umbrella was "smart"—rigged with the latest countermeasures to jam signals coming in or out. Electronic surveillance was effectively neutralized. They could talk freely.

Slayton opened the conversation.

"How long will they keep Reema here?"

"As long as it takes. We have three years to account for."

"She's only going to repeat what we already know, and we'll waste time," Slayton said.

"I don't like it either. But it's *procedure*. The *book*. I can't break the rules any more than anybody else."

Slayton settled down with a swig of cold beer. "All right."

"You look worn out," Dylan told him.

"You don't look too good yourself," Slayton said.

Dylan stared into the yard ahead. The trimmed grass, trees, and the tall wall beyond marking the perimeter. "Yeah." He didn't elaborate and Slayton was in no mood to ask any longer. Dylan continued: "Everything she says will go to the top, Jack. We'll get a handle on this. The opposition stateside might spook and run—"

"But in running, they may also reveal themselves."

"Fingers crossed. Now. Tell me what happened in France."

Slayton explained his kidnapping, the crew who interrogated him, and his escape. Dylan listened without comment.

"You tell me about the leak," Slayton said once he concluded.

"We've been busy," Dylan said. He explained the Internal Security effort so far—but left out any mention of Emily. "The staff passed their polygraphs, so now we'll be watched, me included, to see who we interact with."

"Won't mean much if they know they're under surveillance."

"They think the polys are routine. We're fine."

"Are we?"

"We're *good*, Jack."

"We know nothing," Slayton stated. "We're blind."

"Not exactly," Dylan said. "We have an ID on the man you call Leather Jacket."

He turned on the tablet.

Dylan tapped the touchscreen and passed the device to Slayton.

Slayton frowned at the black-and-white photo on the display. It was Leather Jacket, for sure; along with the two men who'd dragged him to the van. The photo captured them walking down a hallway—the hallway to his hotel room in Biarritz.

"We got it from the hotel security footage," Dylan explained. "I did some digging after your email. The cops in Biarritz *did* identify the two stiffs you left them. They were known associates of a freelance operator named Rylen Cannon. Facial scan of the photo confirmed it's him in the jacket. Name mean anything to you?"

"No," Slayton said. He continued to study the picture. He never wanted to forget Leather Jacket's face. *You'll always be LJ to me, pal.*

Dylan said, "He used to be one of us. Green Beret. Ground Branch. The usual resume. Specializes in—"

"Assassination and interrogation."

"Correct."

"Well, he's not very good." Slayton handed back the tablet. "Where is he now? Still tripping over his dick in Paris?"

"He landed in Virginia today. Little out-of-the-way cabin. Nice place. Got his whole crew there—what's left of them."

"I owe him a bullet." Slayton drank some more beer.

"We need him alive. It would be nice to find out who hired him."

"Hack his bank account. I'm not taking him alive."

"Did you hear me say he's in Virginia?"

"Yes. And normally I'm with you on procedure. Not this time. Z Section doesn't exist. We can fudge the rules."

"You get caught, it's murder, and you'll go away for life, or worse. What will Reema do then?"

"She won't have to do anything," Slayton said. "Because I'm not getting caught."

23

The stone face of Abraham Lincoln looked on once again as Wolf waited on the bench for Max Hudson. Tension again filled his body. He had a hard time not tapping his right heel. The situation was out of control.

Hudson finally showed. Wolf watched him approach. He didn't say hello until the well-dressed older man joined him on the bench.

"Why the worried face, Spencer?"

"The CIA has the Ashraf woman. She's at a debrief facility. Very well-guarded. We can't get to her."

"It's too late now anyway. She'd have told them most of the story during the trip home. They only want details now."

"I'm glad you think it's no big deal. Look, Max, the CIA also has a mole hunt going full speed. They know they have a leak."

"The CIA is always on a mole hunt."

Wolf tried to reply but gave up. Hudson either didn't understand or didn't want to.

"How does this affect your lady friend?" Hudson asked.

"No meetings or phone calls till further notice. But she did pass what I just told you—along with one detail I've neglected—before cutting off contact."

"There's more?"

Wolf flushed red. Hudson's attitude infuriated him, but then he altered his thoughts. What if the older man was right? If he found a way to remain calm, couldn't Wolf? It was worth a try.

"The CIA traced Cannon's location."

"Mr. Slayton will travel to confront him."

"He'll figure out a way, I agree."

"They'll kill each other. Or one will kill the other. We must put our faith in Mr. Cannon. You've alerted him, of course?"

"I have," Wolf said.

"Then the woman is the only one we have to worry about."

"All right."

"It's also time to plan an exit strategy, Spencer."

"I'm aware."

"Relax." Hudson patted Wolf's leg. "Problems will resolve themselves. Reema Ashraf was out of touch for three years. They will not take her story on faith alone."

Hudson departed. Wolf watched him walk away. He wasn't feeling nervous any longer. He felt his body loosen, and the tension departed. Perhaps the old man had the situation under control after all.

* * *

Rylen Cannon shifted into Park, yawned, and eased his tired body from the 7-Series BMW. He reached back into the car to push a button. The cabin's garage door rumbled closed. He went inside.

Paris. An utter waste of time. Slayton was a lucky son of a gun.

Monique, a.k.a. Long Neck, met him in the hallway.

"Welcome back."

Cannon scoffed. They wandered together down the hall and turned a corner into the living room. Computer stations with multiple wide-screen monitors sat on either side of the room. One was for Monique. The other workstation was for a man named Charles, a.k.a. Scruffy. He sat at the right-side terminal and rotated his chair to face Cannon.

"Is Slayton in the city?"

"Landed a few hours ago," Charlie said.

"Any idea where he is now?"

"He's a good driver. Shook our surveillance."

"Wonderful."

Cannon went to Monique's computer. Next to one of her monitors sat a handheld phone resting on a charger. It wasn't a normal household telephone, despite its appearance as such. The cordless unit was actually a secure satellite phone Cannon used to talk to Wolf. He picked up and tried to reach Wolf but received no answer.

The phone needed a code to work. In case the worst happened, and Slayton took the phone, Cannon didn't want him tracing the numbers stored within. He punched a combination into the number pad. The backlight highlighting the numbers turned from green to red. The phone was now useless until somebody entered the unlock code. Cannon placed it back on the charger.

He addressed Monique and Charles.

"I want you both to get weapons and keep them close.

Slayton isn't an amateur. Charles, get everybody back here. They'll watch the outside."

"We aren't leaving?" Charles said.

"Do you want to?"

"No. Bastard killed four of our people."

"Then stay. I'm not going anywhere. I missed Slayton in France. I'll kill him *here* instead. Understand?"

Charles said yes.

* * *

SLAYTON WATCHED FROM A DISTANCE.

He had plenty of space in which to work and observed the cabin with naked eyes. Cannon's cabin sat within a thick forest and the nearest neighbor was five miles away. The thick trees and overgrown terrain made Slayton invisible. The nearest city was Roanoke. They were well into the sticks.

He watched Cannon arrive in his BMW; a slice of good fortune Slayton hadn't expected. Whether he was fresh from France or a milk run didn't matter. Slayton had visual confirmation of Cannon's presence inside.

As long as he stayed put, and Slayton had a feeling Cannon wasn't leaving, the hit had a chance of success.

Slayton stayed on his belly as the night turned darker and the temperature dropped. He tried to ignore the chill. Another car arrived and four people exited. Slayton recognized Goth Queen, the driver—but not the three other males. *Good. Whole crew is here.* He remembered the car, too. It was the four-door Lexus he'd seen trying to follow him when he left the airport.

The leak again.

Goth Queen and her three boyfriends scanned the area,

then entered through the front door. Cannon was fortifying. Good. They were all where Slayton wanted them. But also bad, because Cannon expected violent company.

Slayton wasn't backing down despite the leak. He came prepared to unleash hellfire and destruction. His CZ P-10C sidearm rode on his right hip. His lead weapon was much more substantial: the IWI Galil ACE-21, an Israeli compact assault weapon chambered in 5.56mm NATO. Easy to use indoors, with a cartridge powerful enough to get the job done against human targets. The ACE lay in front of him within easy reach. A suppressor mounted to the muzzle promised to soften the *snap-crack* of the exploding ammunition to only a dull *phut* and *click-clack* of the gun's action.

The body armor he wore fit well. The PVS-7 Night Vision Goggle, mounted on a head strap, allowed him to see night as day. It awaited his need. Six M67 frag grenades rode in the hooks lining either side of his combat vest. The vest held spare mags for the Galil as well.

The windows of the cabin flared with interior light.

The temperature dropped further as night drew on.

It was time to move out.

Slayton was eager for the fight.

24

HE CONFRONTED THE FIRST INFRARED SENSOR FIFTY YARDS FROM the cabin.

Slayton was two steps from passing between two tree trunks. He paused, lowered to his belly, and examined the red line between them through the NVG.

He followed the red laser line to the connection point on the left tree. He frowned. Infrared beams connected to a wireless transmitter. Once the beam broke, a signal would flash in the cabin. They'd know an intruder was close and where to send the troops.

He had a suppressor on the Galil rifle, but somebody in the cabin would not be so equipped. If Slayton used one of his grenades, all bets were off. *The neighbors are going to hear fireworks for sure,* Slayton thought.

Slayton scanned the surroundings in the green glow of the NVG. No people or animals so far; he hadn't encountered so much as a squirrel let alone a deer.

He lifted the NVG back to his forehead and resumed his advance.

He circled around the sensors.

Slayton froze when he spotted the first sentry. He dropped to one knee and steadied the Galil against his shoulder. With his left hand, he lowered the NVG over his eyes once again.

The sentry moved at a slow pace. He faced away from the cabin and scanned the surrounding forest. He was expecting trouble and carried his submachine gun at the ready. Slayton decided to stay in place a few moments. The sentry passed and continued on patrol. Slayton wasn't going to shoot the fellow in the back, but he had to deal with the sentries. He wanted them to come to him. All at once.

Slayton eased to full height and backtracked to the sensors. He kicked out and broke the infrared beam. He hurried to a patch of tangled brush and waited with his rifle set to single shot.

He didn't have long to wait.

Two sentries showed up; they approached from different directions. When they joined up, both men spoke with muted voices.

Slayton sighted through the brush at one of the gunners. He fired twice. The sentry arched his back and dropped with a choked cry cut off by his impact with the ground.

Slayton rotated right to get a clear shot at the second, but the other sentry didn't move. He dropped low and spoke into his radio, and Slayton lost his sight picture. Slayton rolled left to get clear of the brush. On his belly in the open, he waited. Two more on the way. He heard them before he saw either but he held his fire. Once he let another round go, they'd shoot back and he needed to score a hit before the big fight began.

Through the NVG he spotted one sentry near a tree

trunk and the other dashing between trees to reach—*her.* Slayton focused on the gunner's face.

No doubt about it.

Hello, Goth Queen. We meet again.

Slayton had a clear shot and didn't waste time. He fired twice and Goth Queen's head snapped back; she collapsed without a sound. The two newcomers scrambled to cover. Slayton tracked one and fired two more times. A trunk near his target spit bark but none of the shots connected.

Return fire snapped back at him.

Cannon's gunners didn't have suppressors on their weapons. The shots echoed. Slayton slid to cover beside a tree, braced the Galil and fired. He missed. The two gunners began advancing. He adjusted his aim and fired again. One fell back as the two rounds ripped through his chest.

The last sentry dove and rolled. Slayton fired and missed again, his rounds punching into the dirt. Slayton cursed. *The longer this takes...*

A blast of forest debris splashed against his face, kicked up by a round from the last sentry. Two more shots cracked the air above. Slayton switched his rifle to three-shot burst mode and rolled left. He stopped, fired once, twice, shifting his aim with each burst. The sentry ran, Slayton tracking and aiming ahead of the man. As the gunner began to dive for new cover, Slayton squeezed. The burst caught the sentry mid-dive and when he landed on the ground, he stopped moving.

Slayton dropped the mag in the Galil and slapped a full load in place. He aimed toward the cabin. Nobody else emerged. But how many were still inside? Or had they already run off?

No. Not after France. They'd want to even the score, same as he did.

Slayton jumped to his feet and moved forward. With each step, he closed the gap and scanned with the NVG to spot surprises before they proved fatal.

Somebody flung open a cabin window, stuck a rifle out, and started shooting.

Slayton dove out of sight. His chin collided with a rock and a stab of pain flashed through him. The rounds zipped by, smacking trunks, snipping branches. The debris thudded on the forest floor. The shooting stopped. Slayton steadied his breathing. Another burst. The shots strafed past. He aimed at the window and fired back, punching holes in the wall. He didn't adjust his aim. Instead, he rolled right. The gunner in the window let another burst go, but it flew wide and came nowhere near Slayton's position.

Slayton grabbed an M67 grenade and tossed. Watching it fly through the window would have been nice, but he didn't score. The grenade bounced against the wall and arced away, landing two feet from the wall. But a big boom is a big boom and whoever was firing from the window didn't want to be on the receiving end. He or she fled the window as the grenade blew and hammered the wall with a shockwave and shrapnel. The glass in the window shattered; the blast left charcoal-like scorch marks on the outer wall.

The shooter leaving the window gave Slayton the chance he needed. He ran to the wall and ducked under the window. He pitched another grenade through and ran toward the rear. A deck extended from the back, and Slayton vaulted a wooden rail and slid under a table. People yelled to each other inside, their words cut off by the grenade blast.

A sliding glass door with no curtain stood between Slayton and the interior. He rolled a grenade, and it stopped short of the glass. Didn't matter. The blast blew the doors away, the glass falling in a wave from the metal frame. The shards spread out like a puddle on the deck. Slayton fired as he entered—a bedroom. No targets. Hallway to his right. He pivoted and fired twice down the hall and moved to a corner. Return fire zipped into the room, pocking the wall behind him.

A silhouette hugged the hallway wall as the gunner approached the bedroom. The silhouette ducked into another doorway midway. Slayton kneeled and waited. The silhouette left the door—Slayton fired. The man screamed as he fell. Slayton ran to the figure, shot him two more times, and stopped in the doorway. He glanced at the dead man through the NVG. *Told you I'd kill you, Scruffy.* Shots from down the hall hammered the doorway, splinters flying, smacking Slayton's combat vest and body armor. He stayed back.

Three grenades remained. He tossed one as hard as he could. The blast interrupted more return fire, and Slayton left the doorway, staying low, the ACE 21 at his shoulder.

He stopped at the corner and looked around. He didn't hear much and saw less. Kitchen at the end, the left-side wall ending short, another room on the opposite side. Two grenades remained on his vest. He tossed one, bouncing it off the right wall near the kitchen. The M67 ricocheted off the kitchen wall into the unseen room opposite the left wall. A woman screamed; the blast cut off her yell. The walls shook. Slayton moved forward. *Exit Long Neck...*

Now for Cannon.

A man leaned out of an open doorway off the kitchen. Slayton hit the floor. He saw a brief glimpse of Cannon's face and fired back. The sheetrock around the doorway in which Cannon hid puffed white dust clouds. Cannon ran. Another door slammed.

Slayton ran to the doorway, checked one side, then moved to the other. A small entryway. Door leading to the garage? He scooted low across the floor and pulled open the door halfway. A burst of auto fire filled the doorway and punched holes in the door.

Slayton, on the floor, remained unharmed. Footsteps shuffled on concrete. Cannon was running.

Slayton exited and hustled to the right, dropping and rolling to come up on his belly. The BMW 7-Series sat in its parking spot, a doorway beyond still swinging closed. Slayton reloaded his rifle and ran after Cannon. The assassin with a thing for leather jackets was making his getaway, and Slayton sensed a pattern. Cannon knew when to cut his losses and scoot away to fight another day.

Slayton lost sight of Cannon for a moment, then saw him again in the glow of the NVG. Slayton ran hard across the uneven terrain to catch up, branches swiping at his head. Cannon turned and raised his submachine gun. Slayton jogged left into tree cover. Cannon's shots came his way in a furious rush. Slayton fired back. Cannon moved out of sight. Slayton lifted the NVG from his face and continued the pursuit.

A motor chugged to life. Two single shots cracked, but neither bullet reached Slayton. He kept running. The motor revved. Slayton reached the spot where Cannon had disappeared. The ground fell away in a slope, thick foliage covering a small cave. Cannon rode an ATV away at high speed. Slayton shot at the fleeing Cannon, no hits. He ran to the second ATV but didn't climb aboard. Cannon had shot out two tires. The ATV leaned to one side on the flat rubber.

The rumble of Cannon's ATV faded. Slayton cursed. But it was not the time to quit. He ran up the slope and ran back to the cabin.

25

Slayton took care re-entering the cabin. Time was short. Neighbors had to have heard the noise no matter their distance.

He went back in through the garage and bypassed the kitchen. In the living room he found what remained of two computer workstations and a body. The woman on the floor was Long Neck. Her eyes remained open, her body twisted, broken, bloody. He ignored her and searched the debris. He wanted to find something of value in the rubble. Slayton's eyes landed on the satellite phone.

The cordless unit had fallen from its cradle to the carpet. If Cannon received client calls on the phone, Dylan's tech team could trace the numbers. If the most recent call connected to who hired him, they'd have a solid lead. He jammed the phone in an empty pouch on his combat vest.

Time to go.

Slayton reached his concealed car a few minutes later. The first wave of emergency responders screamed up the road. Lights and sirens at full blast. Slayton didn't envy them. They were walking into a gruesome scene.

* * *

SLAYTON MADE it back to the Charlie Safe House and took a long shower in his private room.

His ears still rang from the grenade blasts and gunfire.

His chin hurt where he'd landed on the rock.

His body shook as adrenaline wore off.

Still think you get to do cool shit, dude?

He sighed with relief as the hot water cascaded down his body.

Wearing only a bathrobe, he sat on the bed. It was a quarter past eleven p.m., and he called Dylan. He caught the Z Section boss at home and gave him an update.

"Bring in the phone. We'll crack it."

"Okay."

"You don't sound good."

"Worn out," Slayton said. He felt the tiredness at a molecular level. He needed sleep.

"Have you seen Reema?" Dylan asked.

"Not yet."

"She's almost done. Went faster than we thought."

"In other words, I was right."

Dylan laughed.

"I'll catch up with her. What's the verdict?"

"DCI wants action," Dylan said. "Reema tells us the evidence we need is at the command center. Our satellite scans show October Blood still occupies the base. We'll be looking for a specific laptop Faisil used for the video calls."

"If they haven't destroyed it already."

"It's only been a few days, Jack. They have a lot to organize, and it may have slipped through the cracks."

"How long till we go?"

"Planning in progress. Seventy-two hours or less.

Reema will go with you since she knows the layout. And I have a feeling she wants some payback of her own."

"I bet."

"I'll have more instructions for you shortly."

"I gotta go, Dyl."

"Yeah, you sound like you're about to pass out. Get some rest and I'll be in touch."

Slayton ended the call and climbed under the sheets. He'd see Reema in the morning. His head hit the pillow and he fell asleep within two minutes.

* * *

CANNON REACHED his spare apartment in Roanoke and stayed there twenty-four hours. Then he paid a visit to his bank.

He needed access to his safe deposit box and opened the box in the privacy of a room designated for the purpose.

His hands shook with anger; his teeth hurt from clenching his jaw. He had to remind himself to relax the bite. Wolf warned him about Slayton, and the CIA man had bested him a second time.

No more.

His teammates were gone. Loyal employees he'd worked with for years. Wiped out in the blink of an eye. They deserved vengeance.

He collected from the box papers and accessories needed for one of his many cover identities, along with a small amount of cash and a credit card.

He was going to Washington, DC. First stop, Spencer Wolf. Then he'd bring the fight to Jack Slayton.

Cannon didn't intend to lose a third time.

* * *

Dylan locked his legs around Emily as she climaxed. She arched her back and tipped her head back, blond hair cascading down her back. He followed with a grunt and a gush inside her before she collapsed on top with her mouth near his left ear. She kept her face buried in his neck while he nibbled on her earlobe with his lips. When he finally nudged her off, she turned onto her side. He snuggled against her back with an arm draped over her. What normally was a comfort did little to assure her now.

She had to face how she felt about Dylan and reconcile it with her subversion. An assignment to keep tabs on the October Blood situation developed into a genuine relationship. But she now faced a fork in the road.

She hated lying to him.

She hated spying on him.

Good people were going to get killed to keep a secret she wasn't sure was worth the cost.

Emily wondered if she should come clean and damn the consequences. As soon as the president signed off on the mission to Syria, the CIA would have everything. Any possibility of getting through the matter with her career, and life, intact, was now gone. Evaporated like steaming water. She'd exchange testimony for immunity, but what did she tell Dylan?

We weren't doing anything wrong...

We wanted to protect American lives...

Nobody else will see it that way, sweetie.

And what about the Eagle Alliance? They wouldn't leave her alone. She'd replace one target on her back with another. She'd taken money, siphoned from what the CIA paid the PMC, over the years. A felony all by itself. Spencer had taken his share, too. It was part of the perks related to running the op. And there could be a target on her back already. Old man Hudson could decide to cut loose ends and blame the mess on rogue employees and their CIA source. She may very well already be marked for murder. Dead suspects can't tell the truth.

Dylan began to snore. She remained still, restless.

What to do?

Emily started at the nightstand clock and watched the minutes tick by.

Answers eluded her.

* * *

Wolf worked at the office late into the night. He no longer had a family to go home to—he and his ex-wife had been divorced for over a decade, and she had custody of the kids. Going home to an empty condo held little appeal with his life on the line.

The eight-to-fivers deserted the office hours earlier. The smaller overnight staff worked on the lower floor. The cleaning crew had also come and gone. Wolf was the only person on the sixth floor. All was quiet.

Wolf ignored the clock. He was lost in the soft glow of his computer screen. He wanted to find any sign the CIA was moving against October Blood.

As part of the contract with the agency, Wolf had remote access to CIA operations files and plans. He wasn't cleared to read full details, but there were other clues to sift through, clues which included flight plans. The CIA was a bureaucracy; they had to schedule flights and do so with a paper trail—digital or otherwise—like any other government agency.

He found a note about a US-based flight heading for Syria. The flight was listed as *pending approval.* DDO Christopher Fisher did not have permission to let his team go. The president still needed to sign a presidential finding allowing the covert mission to proceed. A covert mission couldn't take place until the president scrawled his name on the piece of paper saying okay, and he wanted to pray the president declined. But it still wouldn't solve the problem. Slayton and his crew weren't dumb—they'd find another way to continue the mission. And the president always signed off if the CIA met the requirements for doing so.

A flight to Syria from the US meant one thing. Reema Ashraf was going back, but this time with a tactical team. Otherwise, why wouldn't Sharp have used assets already in the region?

The flight could not—absolutely *not*—reach its destination.

Wolf had to work fast. There was only one move to make, and the payoff had no guarantee. He picked up the phone and pressed the button to speed-dial a saved number...

26

Dylan Sharp paced the floor in the Z Section control room. His people ignored him—well, almost. He caught a few questioning glances from the analysts, but only when he stepped too close. He'd spent his morning with mission updates and paperwork. There was nothing to occupy his time for the moment, but he had plenty to occupy his mind.

Fisher wanted him to find out which PMC Emily worked for. He thought it would prove or disprove her involvement. She'd passed her polygraph after all.

Three years.

Was Emily spying on him?

Why?

And for whom? October Blood? Or...?

Or indeed.

Because Emily Chapman had come to the CIA after serving in the Marines...and working for a PMC.

He was afraid to look up *which* PMC.

But he had to. He found an open workstation and began searching for the answer.

* * *

Another wait outside Fisher's office.

Dylan fidgeted as he sat, and Fisher's secretary ignored him. He'd arrived twenty minutes early because he couldn't sit still at his own desk. Not after what he found.

Finally, Fisher's inner office door opened. The DDO said a final goodbye to an older man and woman who exited without smiles. Fisher didn't look happy either. He frowned at Dylan.

"You're early."

"Yup."

"Give me a second."

Fisher retreated to his desk, leaving the door open. Dylan waited a little longer, and then Fisher yelled for him. Dylan shut the door and sat in the chair Fisher offered.

"Well?" Fisher said. "Did you—"

"I did."

"And?"

"Eagle Alliance."

"Shit."

Dylan clutched his hands in his lap.

"All right," Fisher said. "What do you want to do?"

"I have an idea."

"I'm listening."

"I have a friend at Eagle. His name is Toby Hart. We can ask him to...sniff a little."

"Do you trust him?"

"We were frat brothers at Yale."

Fisher tapped his index finger on his upper lip.

"Lives are on the line, Chris."

"I know. Our answers may come from Syria too. The flight's approved, by the way."

"I saw the update. Thank you."

"A frat brother, huh?"

"He handles logistics. He's close to the managers. Could be of help."

"It's risky."

"Between Toby and what Reema assures us they'll find, we'll have the matter wrapped."

"Take it slow, Dylan. You never want to rush this sort of thing. Your friend may be in on the scheme."

"Not Toby."

"You're sure?"

"He's the kind of guy you want to play poker against because his face gives everything away. We learned quick never to trust him with anything we wanted to keep hidden. He wears tells like he wears shirts."

"All right. Give him a call and let's see. Now that we've finished the polygraphs, IS will begin watching you. Have your meeting before they start. I don't want a report coming back saying you're talking to a potential suspect."

Dylan found no way to argue the point. He promised to call Toby Hart right away.

* * *

Security protocols dictated no cell phone inside the HQ building. Dylan drove off campus and pulled over on the side of the road.

He dialed his pal Toby Hart, who answered after the first thing.

"What's new?" Hart said after their exchanged greetings.

Dylan provided a general update and suggested they catch up further over dinner.

"If you can break away from your family for an hour or so," he added.

"This sounds like business."

"It is, Toby. And I'm afraid it's tonight or nothing."

"Well—"

"I need your help. I wouldn't ask last minute if I had another option."

"Wow, okay. I'll make it happen. Where do you want to meet?"

"How about Five Guys? Six thirty? My treat, of course."

"See you then."

With a sigh existing somewhere between relief and dread, Dylan put away his phone and drove back to HQ.

* * *

SLAYTON AND REEMA met the tac team at the CIA's private airfield. The team leader was a former Force Recon officer named Jimmy Hong. Hong's unit contained ten tough-looking shooters who wore full battle dress. Slayton shook hands with each, trying to commit each name to memory. He found a seat next to Reema as the jet began to taxi. They'd fly to the classified CIA staging base in Syria. From there, they'd board Blackhawk helicopters for the last leg to the target.

Hong and his team were on loan from Ground Branch. The shooters consisted of a mix of ex-Green Berets, SEALs, and Recon. Slayton's affiliation with Navy SpecWar made him fast pals with the SEAL contingent.

Reema presented a formal briefing mid-flight. She projected the latest sat scans of the October Blood compound and gave a short history of her time there. The first question was from one of the shooters.

"Will twelve of us be enough?"

Slayton had wondered the same thing.

Reema explained the latest count showed only twenty fighters at the compound. "That's about average," she added. October Blood trained units in batches of twenty, Reema explained. They kept the groups small to keep gunners from knowing too many faces. And if they torched the barracks first, there'd only be nighttime sentries to handle.

She said her brother had taken his video calls in his private hut. "They've cleaned out his gear by now. We'll need to focus our search in the main building.

"We want a specific laptop," Reema continued, "so grab any you find. We may end up sorting through a bunch to see if we have the right one."

Slayton said, "And if it's not there?"

"Punt," Reema said. She shrugged.

"What's on the laptops?" Hong asked.

"IP addresses linked to their American sponsors," Reema said. "The proof to back up everything I've stated on record."

Reema's remarks about *American sponsors* startled Hong and his crew. She told them more.

"They never tell us the good stuff," Hong said. His commandos laughed.

Slayton didn't think it was funny.

But he was happy to watch Reema in action, back in her element. He hoped they'd have some one-on-one time once the smoke cleared.

The flight continued and everybody relaxed.

It was an easy trip until the missile alert.

27

THE CABIN LIGHTS SWITCHED FROM WHITE TO RED. THE PILOT announced somebody on the ground launched a missile. "Prepare for evasive maneuvers!"

Slayton, Reema, and the CIA commandos tightened their seat belts; Hong let out a laugh. "Here's where the fun starts!"

His team responded with "Oooh raaaah!"

Slayton and Reema exchanged glances. He hoped he looked as cool and calm as she. He grasped her hand and she held tightly to his.

They hadn't come this far to get blown out of the sky.

But Slayton wasn't flying the plane. They were at the mercy of the pilots. He hoped they were up to the challenge.

* * *

THE RUSSIAN-MADE Tor missile zeroed on its target. Its pointed tip sliced through the air; stabilizing fins controlled its trajectory. The 15kg warhead contained a fragmenting high-explosive charge.

The Tor was a Cold War relic, albeit still in use. In this case, a crew of October Blood fighters aboard a 9K330 TLAR launched the rocket to prearranged coordinates. The TLAR was a radar-equipped tracked vehicle, like a tank, which needed to stay parked to fire. The big machine sat in a cluster of rocks.

The missile closed the distance to the CIA jet. Sunlight glinted off the deadly pointed tip.

G-forces from the sudden steep climb pushed Slayton into his seat. SAMs had range limits. First order of business, gain altitude. Defeat the projectile by forcing it to fall once it reached its maximum range.

Reema gasped as the jet climbed. She squeezed Slayton's hand harder.

The jet leveled, only to pitch starboard. The seat straps holding Slayton and the rest of the commandos dug into them as their bodies shifted. Another hard roll to port. They had not defeated the missile with altitude.

Slayton looked port side to see out the window. There was nothing but blue sky as the pilot continued violent maneuvers.

"Brace! Brace! Brace!"

The explosion shook the cabin. Slayton shut his eyes. Reema screamed. Slayton expected depressurization—it didn't happen. He opened his eyes. The vibration through the cabin felt strong enough to rip the rivets from the fuselage. The jet dove at a sharp angle, more G-forces pressing him into the back of the seat. They were in free fall.

"We're going down!" the pilot announced. "We avoided a direct impact, but the missile exploded and hit us with a shit ton of fragments. We have one engine. Hang on!"

Hong shouted, "Gonna be a long ride down!"

"Oooh raaah!" the commandos shouted back.

Reema turned pleading eyes on Slayton.

He held her hand. "Hang on," he told her.

* * *

Badri Mirza sat in the TLAR turret and watched the jet trail thick oily smoke as it descended. He watched through a pair of high-powered binoculars. He was the October Blood team leader assigned to shoot down the CIA jet.

"Are we tracking?" he asked.

"Yes, Commander," said the radar officer behind him. The TLAR held a crew of four. The engines rumbled as the driver awaited instructions.

It was true October Blood cut off communications with Wolf and the Eagle Alliance. But their new leader, Kameel al-Rashid, kept the email and phone channels open. Al-Rashid enjoyed the increasingly desperate messages Wolf sent. Forty-eight hours ago, Wolf used the secret phone line to call the jihadist group and leave a final voice message.

"If you aren't responding, I hope you're listening. The CIA is coming for you." He provided details of the CIA flight. "Our deal stands if you want to get back in touch. If not, good luck. This will be my final attempt to reach you."

Badri Mirza wasn't sure if he believed Wolf, but al-Rashid did, and Mirza followed orders. The plane showed up where he said it would, and Mirza's men launched the Tor to bring it down. Al-Rashid wanted prisoners.

"Start moving," Mirza ordered. The TLAR left the cluster of boulders. Mirza gave direction as he kept the smoking jet in sight.

He didn't ride with only the TLAR crew. Three tube-framed, low-slung, four-wheel ATVs, each containing armed fighters, followed the TLAR. A cloud of dust trailed in their wake.

* * *

THE CIA JET hit the ground hard. But it didn't crash. The pilot found the flattest spot of land and aimed for it. With only one engine, he managed to touch down. But the ground wasn't as flat as it looked. When one of the back wheels struck a narrow crack, the landing gear sheared off in a scream of tearing steel. The port wing sank to the ground, snapping off the fuselage. The jet began a slow 360-degree turn on the desert floor, gouging the earth, a giant cloud of dust flying skyward. When the creaking, groaning aircraft finally settled to a stop, nobody inside moved.

Slayton wiped sweat from his face as he gasped. Reema did the same. The cabin was dark except for outside light streaming through the windows.

Hong yelled, "We live!"

Only a single commando offered a dazed "Oooh raaah," in reply.

Slayton began unstrapping from the seat. "Everybody out!" *Don't panic. Breathe. Think.* He stood and helped Reema to her feet. "We need to get the gear out too!"

Hong and his men scrambled from their seats. Hong snapped orders, his commandos moving fast to carry out instructions.

The pilot came back to check on them. He and the co-pilot looked uninjured. The pilot announced he was setting explosives to destroy the plane once they exited. It would be on command, he added, when Slayton asked how long they had until the explosives went off.

The co-pilot joined them, and they opened the side door. The tilted angle made movement tough. The crew and passengers made it outside without incident. The rear cargo hatch, not damaged in the landing, opened by hand since the jet no longer had power. They began unloading bags of gear.

Smoke poured from the port engine, filling the air with choking fumes. But Slayton, Reema, and the CIA commandos ignored the smell and smoke. They had much more to deal with than smoke.

Both pilot and co-pilot grabbed emergency radio equipment from under the nose of the jet.

Clear of the wrecked aircraft, the group began a march south where one of Hong's men spotted rocks. They went toward the rocks, crossing the hard-packed ground quickly. Scattered shrubs covered bare sections of the ground, the dirt cracked and dry under the hot sun. The rocks varied in size with nooks for cover. Once they settled within the cluster, the pilot kneeled in front of his control pack and typed a code.

"Wait," one of the CIA men said. "We got incoming. Dust cloud to the north."

All eyes turned in the indicated direction. The dust cloud wasn't a good sign.

Slayton moved to Hong, who put binoculars to his eyes for a better look.

"What do you see?" Slayton asked.

"Armored vehicle and three smaller vehicles. They're not moving very fast."

"We need to get ready," Slayton said. "We can't outrun them."

Hong lowered the binoculars. "Hope your shooting eye is sharp, Mr. Slayton."

Slayton grinned.

28

Slayton suggested the pilot wait till the convoy drove closer to the jet before detonating. "The blast might take out a few."

The pilot nodded. He and his co-pilot only had pistols. Their faces looked pale; this wasn't their element. Slayton told them to stay low and only shoot if they had to. And if they did have to, it meant everybody else was dead or wounded, and none of them were going to make it out alive.

A second cluster of rocks sat to the left of their position. Hong yelled for two of his men. He referred to his commandos by call signs and addressed the two as Hot Fuzz and Profile. He told them to run the thirty yards to the second cluster and set up a crossfire.

"Two hundred yards and closing!" reported Hong's spotter, a sniper nicknamed Prop Shaft. The sniper balanced his rifle on top of a rock.

"Hey, Prop, wanna get high?" Hong asked.

"Always!"

"Top of the big rock behind us."

Prop Shaft gathered his high-powered rifle. Another commando gave him a boost, and he climbed to the top of the big rock. It was flatter on top, with enough space to accommodate two or three prone snipers. Prop Shaft spread out on his belly and lined up on the incoming enemy.

Hot Fuzz and Profile reported they were in position at the second cluster.

Hong said, "Short Fuse, Blast Off, I want a ring of Claymores out front."

The two CIA men, carrying only heavy packs, jumped into action.

Slayton watched the two men lay out the mines. He knew the Claymores were no good until somebody stepped close. They were the last second "fuck you" option in case the October Blood fighters overran them.

Fight to win. Prepare to die.

He felt calm. It amazed him how calm he could be in such situations.

Slayton gave Reema's shoulder a squeeze. She had her M-4A1 tucked tight to her shoulder.

"They're getting close," was all she said.

The commandos nicknamed Short Fuse and Blast Off laid the Claymore mines out in a crescent. The steel ball bearings packed within the square-shaped explosives would tear apart anything they encountered.

"One-fifty and closing," Prop Shaft the Sniper reported from the top of the rock.

Slayton wiped his sweaty right hand on the seat of his pants and re-gripped his M-4. He watched the approaching enemy through a space between two large rocks.

Reema watched from behind her own gap. Her throat was dry, and she had to work hard to concentrate.

Faisil's last words rang in her mind.

"Run, Reema!"

But she wasn't in Syria to run away. She was there, Jack beside her, to finish what she started and avenge her brother. They needed to survive this fight, get the computers, and dismantle the conspiracy.

Steady, girl.

Focus.

Reema licked her lips and then let out a gasp. "Jack!"

"I see them. Get ready."

Hong yelled, "Here they come! Light 'em up, boys!"

Hong's men didn't "oooh raaah" in reply. They sighted on targets. The time for jocular expressions had passed.

* * *

THE THREE ATVs broke away from the slower TLAR. With their high-revving rear engines, open tubular construction, and beefy tires, they raced toward the rock formation.

They passed through the smoke cloud of the wrecked CIA jet. And when the remains of the plane exploded, more hot flames and chunks of debris flew toward them.

The drivers reacted. They turned right to evade and put distance between them and the flaming wreckage. The debris damaged none of the ATVs, but strewn pieces of the jet now covered the desert floor.

Badri Mirza watched from the TLAR and shook his head. He dropped back through the top hatch and pulled the steel overhead lid closed. Using the plane as an anti-personnel weapon might have been a brilliant idea. But he would not have counted on the blast to deliver casualties. At most the smoke and flames better marked the crash site.

Mirza watched through the forward windows. The Americans were so cute thinking the rocks provided protection. He not only had surface-to-air Tor rockets aboard, but two surface-to-surface as well. They rode in the four-rocket pod atop the TLAR. A flick of a button and he'd turn the Americans and their little "sanctuary" to rubble.

But Kameel al-Rashid wanted a firsthand report of the men in combat. They'd trained in rotating groups since the inception of October Blood. The fighters currently at the camp had yet to see real action. This battle would be a good test for the new fighters.

The TLAR came abreast of the smoking CIA plane. Mirza ordered the driver to halt.

Time to watch the show. If the ATV crew failed, he'd use the missiles.

* * *

SLAYTON BRACED his rifle on the rock and waited for one of the ATVs to get close enough to shoot.

The sniper on top of the rock behind Slayton, Prop Shaft, triggered a single shot. The crack of the discharge set off a ring in Slayton's ears. But the CIA sniper scored a hit on the driver of the lead ATV. The tubular-framed off-roader lurched left, away from the other two. The passenger tried to grab the wheel. Slayton and Reema and the other CIA shooters opened fire, sending a hail of lead at the wayward vehicle. They shredded the dead driver and struggling passenger with 5.56mm slugs. The ATV remained out of control until one of the front wheels hit a rock and tipped it onto its side. The vehicle tumbled several times before coming to a rest.

One down, but nothing else will be easy, Slayton thought. He shifted his aim.

Prop Shaft let another shot go as the remaining two

ATVs veered off. The passengers in both returned fire with what looked like AKMs. Serious firepower no matter the vintage. Slayton dropped his head and grabbed for Reema. The incoming fire struck haphazardly, sprang off the rocks. Chips from the granite spit in all directions. Shards of rock peppered the back of Slayton's neck.

The ATVs cruised by on the left and right of the rock formation. The two CIA men at the neighboring cluster took their turn to fire but missed. Prop Shaft tracked one; he fired a single shot. His intended target was one of the big wheels, but the projectile missed and only kicked up a small chunk of dirt.

The ATVs came around again but traveled away from the rocks. The men in the passenger seats rose to fire over the rear deck. More incoming rounds bounced as the Americans ducked.

Slayton worked the M-4's trigger carefully, trying to connect with one of the gunners.

Brass from Reema's rifle landed on Slayton's clothes. He ignored them.

Prop Shaft kept up a steady rate of single shots, but the zigzagging ATVs made aiming tough for everyone.

The ATVs whipped around and charged back at the rocks. More incoming AK fire smacked their position. Somebody behind Slayton screamed. Prop Shaft's rifle cracked. Slayton traced a line of rounds up the front of the ATV in the lead. The driver snapped the wheel to turn away. Slayton's next shot tagged the passenger in the neck. As the gunner slumped in his seat, another shot from Prop Shaft split the driver's head open. The ATV careened out of control.

One more.

Slayton reloaded his rifle.

29

HONG CROUCHED BESIDE SLAYTON.

"How's your man?" Slayton said.

"Took one in the arm," Hong said.

"We have nowhere to fall back to."

"I'm aware," the CIA team leader said.

"What do you think those guys in the missile truck are thinking?"

"I'm betting they wish they had more than SAMs to fling at us."

"How they knew about our flight plan is what I'd like to know."

A blast made them jump. Blast Off detonated one of the Claymores. The front tires of the last ATV exploded under the impact of the steel balls, and the vehicle rolled over. The driver and passenger attempted to escape. Gunfire from the second set of rocks, from Hot Fuzz and Profile, smacked them down.

All eyes focused on the TLAR vehicle sitting immobile near the wreckage of the CIA jet.

"Now what?" Reema asked.

"I'm afraid of the answer," Slayton told her.

Prop Shaft yelled from the top of the rock, "They're opening another launch tube!"

Slayton fought the urge to raise his head. What did they have in there?

"Not good," Hong said.

The missile spit from the mounted pod in the middle of the TLAR. The rocket headed for the sky as it trailed white smoke and the motor shrieked. The rocket then curved downward and dove on the neighboring rocks where Hong had sent Hot Fuzz and Profile.

"No!" the CIA team commander yelled. The rocket exploded on the secondary position. The explosion turned the hiding spot for Profile and Hot Fuzz into a ball of fire. Chunks of rock rained down; the team covered their necks and heads. Reema yelled when a piece struck her.

Slayton cursed.

"Here they come," Prop Shaft announced. The TLAR missile vehicle began a slow crawl forward.

"Damn thing looks like a tank," Reema said. "We don't have anything—"

"It won't matter in a few seconds, hon," Slayton told her.

"No," Hong said. "They want something else. That rocket was a demonstration."

"Prisoners?"

"We'd be a real catch, wouldn't we?" Hong said.

Reema said, "Jack, if they find out I led you here—"

"They'll finish what they started with your brother; I get it."

She looked at him. He didn't break her gaze. He said, "I have an idea..."

* * *

The TLAR stopped midway between the burning jet and the rocks. The left-side cabin hatch opened, and a man rose from the opening. He aimed a bullhorn in their direction.

Reema gasped.

"Who is he?" Slayton asked.

"Badri Mirza. Second in command to the man who murdered Faisil."

Hong said, "Standby, guys."

The commandos remained focused behind their weapons. Slayton wasn't sure what they could do short of a desperate last stand. Take out Mirza, face a quick end with the next rocket. It would be up to Dylan and the agency to figure out what to do next.

Slayton set his sights on Badri Mirza's neck. He wanted to cave in the man's nose with a bullet.

Mirza spoke through the bullhorn.

"Unless you want to suffer the same fate as your friends, we demand your surrender."

Prop Shaft announced, "I can take him, boss."

"Hold," Hong said. To Slayton: "I hope you're right."

"Just have the Claymores on standby and raise your arms."

"Are you mad?" Reema asked.

"Decidedly so."

Hong yelled for Prop Shaft to get down from the rock. The sniper complied without question. Hong stood up. "I forgot to bring my white flag," he added.

The October Blood officer said, "All of you lower your weapons."

The team complied.

Blast Off stayed low with his hand on a Claymore detonator.

The TLAR vehicle rumbled forward again. Two gunners jumped out and ran forward. Mirza directed the Americans to step out from behind the rocks. Hong and Slayton started to move as the two gunners stepped within range of the last pair of Claymores. Blast Off pressed the detonator.

The blast cut the two gunners down in a flash of fire and torn flesh.

Reema fired once. Badri Mirza's head snapped back. He dropped the bullhorn and tipped over, his body stopping against the edge of the open hatch as if he was still standing.

Slayton and Hong picked up their rifles and ran across to the TLAR. Hong flung open the side door. The driver threw up his hands. Slayton hauled him out, shoved the man to the ground, and shot him twice in the chest.

Hong examined the interior. "We can fit four in here."

"Put the rest in the ATVs that still run," Slayton suggested.

"We used up a lot of ammo."

"Take their weapons. I'm sure they have some left."

Hong waved for the rest of the team to come over.

* * *

THE OCTOBER BLOOD base appeared imposing at first glance. No expense spared. The L-shaped main building was where the command staff worked. They used the latest and greatest computer equipment. Across from the building sat a row of three barracks. Next to the barracks, a cluster of ATVs and trucks were carefully parked.

A wall of reinforced concrete squares, wrapped in wire

mesh, covered the exterior. Guard towers stood at three corners. The fourth corner, beside the main building, contained a tall communications tower. The tower fired off brief burst transmissions to various recipients in the region. Burst transmissions barely registered on western snooper satellites. All detection meant was a signal coming from a particular spot. Western intelligence would need to send eyes or cameras to see what or who was sending the signal. *If* they detected the transmission to begin with. The Eagle Alliance provided the necessary countermeasures to prevent detection.

A steel door marked the only entrance and exit on the east side. Against the wall on the opposite west side were the two huts used as private quarters for the top dogs. An open space was between the main building and the barracks. They used the area for morning assembly and inspection.

Inside the building was all business. Work areas scattered across the open interior. Large glowing monitors on the walls. Other workstations sat on folding tables. The building's big secret waited at the 90-degree corner of the L: a heavy trapdoor in the floor leading to an escape tunnel.

The details flashed through Slayton's mind as he rode with Hong and Reema in the TLAR missile vehicle. The rest of the CIA commandos rode on the salvaged ATVs. They were short two—four if you included the pair killed in the rocket strike. The wounded commando and team medic remained at the rocks, with the pilots.

Slayton drove. The steering and gas were simple enough. Reema and Hong, both of whom had a good command of Russian, studied the fire controls.

"They had two SAMs, and two surface-to-surface

missiles," Hong reported. "We have one of each left. What do you want to do with the SSM?"

"What would you do?" Slayton said.

"Knock out communications first."

"Then when we see the big antenna, let her fly."

Neither Reema nor Hong argued.

30

A COMMANDING VOICE, GROWING IN AGITATION, DEMANDED A reply from the TLAR. His voice filled the noisy cabin.

"I bet we missed a check-in code," Slayton said.

"Here goes nothing," Hong stated. He fired the last SSM rocket. The vehicle jostled from side to side as the missile left the roof pod. They heard the shriek of the rocket motor. Slayton let off the brake and the machine rolled forward.

Chatter on the cabin radio cut off mid-sentence. Hong directed his commandos to go forward. "Pay attention to the guard towers!"

The SSM struck the concrete wall protecting the base of the antenna. A geyser of flame blew upward. The debris produced by the fiery impact accomplished the same as a direct hit. The metal legs at the base of the antenna groaned and crumpled. The tower toppled against the top edge of the wall and split in half. The other half stabbed into the sand.

"Get us to the wall!" Hong shouted.

"Giving her all she's got!" Slayton shouted back. The

roar of the full-throttle engine almost drowned out the exchange.

The guards in the tower at the northwest corner, closest to the building, opened fire. They directed their salvos at the ATVs as the speeders approached. The drivers zigzagged; at the last second, the ATV in the lead spun perpendicular and skidded. The commando in the passenger seat rolled a grenade under the base of the tower. The driver kicked up sand and left a huge cloud in his wake as he sped away from the walled terrorist base.

The grenade exploded and splintered two of the tower's wooden supports. The structure fell sideways like a downed tree, guards and all. The top booth with its 360-degree viewing platform slammed into the ground. The two guards died beneath the rubble.

The remaining two guard towers were next. The men up top fired on the ATVs. The commandos fired back. Another drove close enough to perform the grenade maneuver again. And again, on the last tower.

As the towers tipped over, Slayton stopped the TLAR inches from the concrete wall. He picked a place where the back wall of the main building met the outer wall at the same level. Weapons at the ready, Slayton, Reema, and Hong scooted out the upper hatch and onto the top of the TLAR. Slayton jumped from the TLAR onto the roof. October Blood troops rallied in the center of the compound. An officer shouted orders and told a handful of fighters to prepare for the assault. They were the last words the man spoke. Slayton snapped his M-4 to his shoulder and sent two rounds through the officer's chest. The other terrorists scrambled out of the line of fire. Slayton and Hong kept them busy with scattered single shots. And then the CIA commandos blasted through the steel gate. They drove through the cloud of smoke with weapons blazing.

Slayton turned from the battle below and stayed low as Hong wired a shaped charge to the center of the roof. He finished, and the trio took cover behind an air conditioning unit. The explosive detonated with the press of a button. The charge blasted a near-perfect circle in the roof. Slayton and Reema dropped stun and high-explosive grenades through the smoking hole. Explosions echoed within. Hong anchored a zip line to the A/C unit. He threw the remaining length of rope to Slayton, who dropped it down the hole. Slayton grasped the line and slid into the unknown with Hong close behind him.

They dropped into near darkness, but the hole in the roof spotlighted them as they fell through. Landing on the pile of chunky sheet rock threw off their balance. Slayton and Hong quickly moved away from the shaft of light. Slayton lurched right, facing one way; Hong left, facing the other. Slayton rolled onto his belly. He faced the 90-degree corner, Hong the front entrance.

Thick dust hung in the air. Men screamed. Bodies on the floor didn't move. The shaft of light allowed Slayton to make sense of the interior despite the darkness.

A few October Blood fighters didn't scream, but they fired in Slayton's direction. He heard Hong firing but didn't look back. Slayton aimed at the muzzle flashes, shifting his aim. Two gunners fell. Most of the gunmen clustered near the 90-degree corner. As Slayton yanked another grenade from his vest, he yelled for Reema to hurry. He tossed the high-explosive M67. The blast filled the room with a flash of light accompanied by screams. Then silence.

Reema slithered down the rope. Slayton and Hong

pivoted with their weapons, searching for left-over targets. There were none.

Slayton, Reema and Hong followed one wall. Slayton flicked on the light mounted on his M-4. The beam showed more thick dust. He coughed. His eyes itched. *Move forward.* A work area at the corner grabbed Reema's attention. She ran around Slayton, despite his protests, to the tables.

"They're not here!"

Slayton heard Reema speak but didn't comprehend. He swept the beam of light over the bodies on the floor and fired bullets into three who looked to be faking. But there was no faking the trapdoor he found. A set of wooden steps led into more than darkness. They led to pitch black.

"Jack!"

He ran to her. Hong called out something. Slayton let the other CIA man wait.

"What is it?"

Reema tossed around odds and ends. She pulled at cords connected at one end to power strips on the floor, but nothing at the other.

"They took the computers."

"Down there?" Slayton shined his light on the trapdoor.

Hong yelled, "Hey! I found this."

Slayton examined the item Hong handed over. It was another secure satellite telephone, same as the one he'd found at Cannon's cabin.

"We need the codes for this," Slayton said. "Try and find them. I'll go down the trap." He ran for the open door in the floor.

"Jack!"

Slayton was already descending. "See you at the rendezvous!"

* * *

Hong said to Reema, "Did they keep passwords somewhere?"

Reema scoffed with disgust. "I'll check here. See what you can find where the phone was."

Hong moved. "It's probably blasted..."

The floating dust continued to irritate but they worked through the discomfort. Fighting outside remained fierce, but Hong stuck to his task. He feared for his men, but knew they were tough enough to handle the opposition.

And if not, it didn't matter what he or Reema or Slayton found.

31

Slayton's boots touched solid ground. The abyss ahead called to him. He shined his light around. The tunnel, dug out of the rock below the sand, didn't have an end from where he stood. He turned off the light, put his hand out to feel the wall, and held his M-4 in his right. The sling supported the rifle up front.

The air was hot. Sounds from above faded—only a large explosion penetrated the din. He hoped the commandos were all right.

No sharp voices; no running footsteps. For all Slayton knew, the open trap was a diversion. It was no ambush. If anybody had escaped via this route, they meant to get away. And *fast*. Making a stand wasn't their goal. Neither was a counterattack.

But where did the passage end?

Slayton continued forward. Sweat trickled down his back. He fought the temptation to use his light again. Once was all he dared risk. But he also fought the urge to turn around. Walking into darkness, into literal unknown, made his nerves jump. He'd rather have been back in the firefight.

Forward. A few more feet. *Pause. Listen.* Another careful advance. The tunnel so far hadn't turned or—

He felt the breeze on the exposed portions of his skin.

A gust of wind dried the sweat.

Slayton stopped. A frown creased his face. A noise—loud, growing in volume. Not made by nature.

Made by—

A *helicopter!*

Slayton switched on his light. He ran ahead, as fast as he dared, the wind becoming stronger as his legs pumped and carried him along. A sliver of light ahead. The end! He ran faster. The light grew into a circle. The wind blew harder and the whipping of rotor blades grew louder.

The opposite end opened into a tall and wide cavern with an opening at the top—like a volcano. Slayton stopped, framed in the opening. He watched the small chopper rise through the opening. He lifted his rifle, fired twice; flipped the selector switch to full-auto, and burned through the magazine. Too late. The chopper flew away, out of sight, with no damage Slayton's naked eyes could discern.

He hurried to reload, then ran back the way he'd come.

Kameel al-Rashid had escaped with the evidence crucial to Reema's story.

We failed.

Then another thought occurred to Slayton.

Maybe not.

* * *

THE CREW HAD no time to rest.

Three commandos dead, two wounded. Hong and those not wounded loaded the casualties onto trucks found near the barracks. They borrowed two of the vehicles and put the battleground behind them in a growing cloud of dust.

Reema drove while Slayton and Hong sat in the back. They examined the sat phone and the ledger of codes recovered from the command building. The jolts over rough terrain didn't distract them. The second truck with the other commandos and casualties rode behind them.

"We have to try every one of these codes," Hong said.

"And it may still be the wrong book," Slayton added.

But it was their only chance. Perhaps the phone contained evidence of the American connection to October Blood.

"We can ignore the ones with letters. The phone uses a number code. You notice what I already see?"

"It's a US phone."

"Delivered by the people Reema talked about."

"I found a similar unit on another excursion," Slayton said. He didn't reveal where the excursion took place. "We'll have to hand it over to the lab guys. They already have the other one."

Hong only nodded.

"I'm sorry about your men," Slayton said.

"Me too," Hong said.

They returned to the rocks, where the first part of the battle began. There they found the pilots, team medic, and the wounded commando from the first engagement. And they recovered what they could of the CIA men killed by the SSM rocket. An hour later, they reached their extraction point. The two-vehicle convoy encountered nothing but natural terrain during the trip.

Slayton and the others didn't relax until their Blackhawk lifted off. Next stop, the CIA desert station, where they'd hop another jet for home. It was going to be a long trip no matter how fast the jet flew.

* * *

DYLAN FOUND he was starving when he entered the Five Guys hamburger restaurant.

He wasn't sure he'd be able to eat after hearing Slayton's update from Syria, but nature overruled his thinking. As always.

He found his buddy Toby Hart waiting at a table with his back to the wall. Hart had a pile of empty peanut shells on the table; he cracked another from a paper container as Dylan reached him.

"Dyl!" Hart said, rising. He brushed off his hands on a napkin and extended his right. Dylan shook hands and returned the jovial greetings, but he forced his smile.

"Thanks for coming out, Toby."

"My wife says I owe her one, so let's order and get your problem sorted. I can read it on your face, something is wrong."

"If you can help me out, I'll pay for you and your wife to take a vacation in Mexico."

"Hell, *now* you're talking!"

They ordered and made small talk, catching up.

After forging their friendship in college, they'd gone their separate ways career-wise. Dylan joined the CIA; Hart took a job as a forensic accountant for the DEA. He left the anti-drug agency after five years to work for the Eagle Alliance. As their overseas logistics coordinator, he knew how to search for irregularities. Most importantly, Dylan trusted him. But there'd be no beating around the bush.

Dylan needed to go for the jugular. And see how his old friend reacted to the request.

A kid behind the counter called their number. They collected their food and drinks. Nobody else in the restaurant wore shirts and ties, but they didn't receive any undue attention. Dylan appeared more casual with his tie loosened and top button undone.

Returning to the table, Dylan joked that he hoped Toby hadn't eaten too many peanuts. Hart assured him he could eat a horse. "You'll see when you pay for our all-expense trip to Mexico."

Dylan forced a laugh. Toby might not be so eager once he heard what Dylan needed.

32

"We're hearing rumors," Dylan began, "disturbing ones, and I wanted to talk to you about them."

"Rumors about *me*?" Tony said.

Dylan shook his head.

"Eagle?"

"Afraid so."

"What kind of rumors?"

"Is Eagle funding a terrorist group?"

"Are we *what*?"

The surprise on Toby's face wasn't something the man had the ability to fake.

"Do you know anything about a terrorist group called October Blood?" Dylan asked.

"You haven't answered my question, Dyl."

"Answer mine first, and I promise I'll explain."

"The name has crossed my desk, yeah. No active operations against them. They're on our watch list. They haven't done much. Been active around two years."

"Three. I had somebody undercover in the group. She

claims the Eagle Alliance is supplying money and equipment."

"For *what*?"

"I've been asking myself the same thing."

"And?"

"Three years ago, the Senate Intelligence Committee talked about cutting the anti-terrorism budget. Doing so would affect contractors like Eagle before it affected the agency. What if somebody created a new threat to show it wasn't the time to cut budgets, but *increase* them?"

"It would have to be somebody high up," Toby said. "I mean tippy-top high up, and they'd have to be nuts."

"Problem is," Dylan said, "it's not impossible. Find the right personality to lead, pass some money—"

"I don't want to ask how you're so confident in your statement. You're talking about more than rumors, buddy."

"No comment."

They paused to eat a few moments. Dylan's fries were getting cold. He sensed tension between them, but there was no going back now. He needed to convince Toby and then ask him to help.

Toby said, "If you had an undercover in place, what are you talking to me for?"

"Because we have no hard data yet."

"No evidence?"

"Nothing I can take to the FBI. We have a leak in my department too, and it's compromised our effort to solve this from the start."

"Really."

"*Somebody* is trying to stop us, Toby."

"What you're asking—"

"Not what you think. I know you're not involved."

"Not where I was going. You want me to be your *friend* at Eagle."

"Yes."

"You have no proof whatsoever?"

"We're working on a few things, but it's taking time," Dylan said.

"Did you find the leak?"

"Not yet."

"I have two jobs?"

"Yes."

"Jesus, Dyl—"

"You can say no."

"Are you kidding? And stay awake all night wondering if my employer is conspiring to defraud taxpayers and putting innocent people at risk? Really? I can say *no*?"

Dylan swallowed a lukewarm french fry and chased it with a sip of soda.

"I coordinate moving people and things," Hart said. "I look over the books and costs and make sure the math adds up. I've seen nothing untoward."

"Your experience at DEA should remind you how bad guys hide their stuff, in the books, or don't use books at all."

Toby sighed. "True."

"What do you say?"

"How much time do I have?"

"As long as it takes to do this right."

"Okay, I'll poke around. Don't forget about Mexico."

"I won't."

Dylan hoped he hadn't put a target on his friend's back.

* * *

Dylan returned to CIA HQ. Only a few staffers occupied the Z Section ops center, the overnight crew he didn't see often. After reminding them their boss did exist with a walk-through hello, he went to his private office. He wanted to look at the evening reports. Jack's update made him put out an alert for Kameel al-Rashid, based on a description provided by Reema. He doubted anything had turned up so fast, and he wasn't wrong. Operatives in the Middle East acknowledged the alert, but nothing more. If al-Rashid remained in Syria, he'd be tough to find. And there was no reason to believe he'd leave the desert. Reema had no idea where he might go. He could vanish into a cave and never show himself again.

Hours passed. Dylan checked the clock. Quarter to midnight. HQ was quiet at night no matter where you worked. The calm contrast of nighttime, as opposed to the chaos of daytime, made him wonder if dayside played up the drama of their tasks too much.

He wanted to head home but there was still a detail nagging at him. He also wanted to stay busy since Emily hadn't said much to him the last two days. She tried to be her usual self, but she looked distracted to him. Consumed with thoughts she either could not or *would* not articulate to him. When he asked, she claimed she was only tired, not sleeping well. She didn't appreciate his snarky remark about their late-night trysts being the cause.

He hated to admit it, but he welcomed the rift. He didn't know what to do with her right now.

What bothered him, as he sat at his desk, was Jack's report. The missile attack on the jet. The leak struck again. And almost succeeded in wiping out the two people who might crack the October Blood case.

Using his computer, Dylan looked up the flight log for

the Syria mission. Somebody else had accessed the data, too. The same somebody had also leaked the information. His pulse raced as he checked who'd opened the file. Dylan didn't want to see Emily's name.

What he found made him pause. He read a name unknown to him. Not somebody who worked for the CIA.

Who the hell was Spencer Wolf? And why was he looking at CIA flight plans? He *only* checked the Syria flight. Dylan noticed he used a password associated with contractors conducting agency business.

Was this the clue he needed? So easily handed to him?

Dylan closed the file and clicked on his web browser. He went to the Eagle Alliance website and searched the company personnel files. It took less than a minute to put a picture of Spencer Wolf on his screen. But it took longer to think about what to do with the new information.

Check for known connections, of course.

Dylan's hands shook as he did a search for Spencer Wolf, adding "Eagle Alliance" after his name in the search bar.

He clicked on a LinkedIn profile bearing Wolf's name. He took a deep breath while the computer signed him in because of his own profile on the site.

He found Emily on Wolf's network list.

No surprise. He'd already determined she'd worked for the PMC.

But then—

Oh, no.

How long had they known each other?

Dylan examined Wolf's resume and compared it with Emily's. Where had their paths crossed before?

Bingo.

They'd served in the Marines at the same time before either of them worked for Eagle. Same unit.

Could she...?

He needed more. *Much* more. Logging onto CIA computers was a privilege Wolf had based on his work with the government. It was not evidence of a crime.

All he had were suspects.

He needed to prove they were guilty.

Dylan finally went home after midnight, but he didn't sleep well.

33

The next morning, tired and preoccupied, Dylan checked in with Christopher Fisher.

The DDO took the news stoically.

"Follow up," Fisher said, "and be ready for the worst."

Dylan agreed.

Returning to Z Section's ops center, he looked for Emily. Her office was empty. He learned she'd called in sick, then checked his voicemail. She'd left a message. Now he could make moves and not have to lie to her about what he was doing.

He visited the tech lab after lunch. He wanted to know if the crew had made any progress unlocking the sat phone Jack recovered from Cannon's cabin. He advised them Slayton was bringing in another shortly.

They had, according to one tech who told him. Only one number was ever called. The tech provided the number. Dylan went back to his office and searched for where the number connected. An architectural firm downtown. He called, but only a voice mail greeting answered. But he had an address too. He wanted to check the office in person.

Dylan let his mind wander as he drove. He tried not to dwell on Emily. His first instinct was to confront her and demand the truth.

Worse, he found himself questioning their entire relationship. Was she working under orders to spy on him, and found dating the path of least resistance?

But what did she stand to gain?

Focus. Deal with her later.

The address he wanted was nowhere near the headquarters of the Eagle Alliance. He had a feeling he'd find a throwaway office, a shell company. A place where incoming calls rerouted to another phone. But he had to make the effort to find out.

He found the office building next to a financial planning company. All three looked generic, nothing in their design stood out. Steel and glass. There was only street parking available, and Dylan didn't find a place to leave his car for another two blocks. He returned on foot.

The security guard posted behind a lobby desk only gave him a nod as he passed through the entryway. Dylan went around the corner to the elevators, pressed a call button, and waited. The overhead lights reflected off the brightly polished tiled floor. The ugly dark-yellow paint on the walls created an unpleasant aura.

The elevator arrived and he entered. He pressed the button for the fifteenth floor.

The frayed carpet on fifteen didn't help the first impression. White walls, buzzing fluorescent lights. Dylan walked down the hall looking for suite 1527. He found it at the end, a pair of locked doors blocking the way. A window beside the right door allowed him to see inside, and the empty suite confirmed his suspicion. Nobody worked there, but somebody was paying the rent and phone bill.

* * *

"WHAT'S the latest on the Somalia operation?"

Toby Hart watched Spencer Wolf direct the question to a woman seated on his left. The conference room overlooked the parking lot and trees at the edge of the campus. The length of the windows on the left wall let in plenty of sunlight. Toby Hart sat three chairs from Wolf's right and watched the man. He could not forget the conversation he shared with Dylan the night before.

Hart turned his attention to the woman—her name was Nora, and she shared the overseas department with Hart and others—as she answered Wolf's question. She consulted a folder of notes as she spoke. Eagle was working an operation in Somalia to take out a branch of al-Qaeda at the CIA's request. The mission called for both land and maritime operations. The AQ cell had begun using pirate tactics to loot shipping vessels and take hostages.

"Our teams engaged in a firefight last night with AQ," Nora reported. "Two of our people were wounded. All enemies KIA. Maps recovered have led to hiding places for the boats the pirates use. It's too soon to say if we've made a dent in stopping them." She stopped talking and looked at Wolf.

"Good news anyway," Wolf said, "when we need some."

Wolf's appearance and body language interested Hart. His suit was pressed and his tie straight; he looked the part of Eagle's second in command. But...the color of his face wasn't right. He looked pasty, anxious. Hart noticed him fidgeting in his seat as if he had trouble getting comfortable. Not his usual habit or appearance. He was a man with more on his mind than the state of overseas missions. Hart began to wonder for real if Dylan was right.

If Wolf was part of the October Blood scheme, who would he conspire with? Where would they find a secure location to talk? Of course, Hart knew a variety of locations existed for clandestine meetings, even out in the open. Two or three people could hold a secret meeting anywhere as long as they used proper safeguards. Hart narrowed his thinking to another option instead.

Wolf called for "anything else," but when nobody offered further business, he dismissed the meeting. Hart returned to his office to think about his idea.

The basement. *The conference room in the basement!* The one used for classified discussions on a regular basis.

Perfect place to talk and not risk monitoring. A scheduled use of the room would also not raise eyebrows. Hart turned to his computer and looked up the booking sheet. He knew it might be a dead end. Wolf could have had any number of meetings in the room. But was one not like the other?

He found a reservation in Wolf's name from a week earlier. No reservations involving Wolf in the two weeks before or since. The second person listed for the meet was Max Hudson, who owned the company.

"It would have to be somebody high up...tippy-top high up..."

Hart recalled Hudson's visit the day of the meeting. The joke had been "better look busy" but the old man didn't tour the offices per his usual visit routine. He showed up, had his meeting, and departed.

Like Wolf fidgeting in his chair and his pasty complexion, it was out of character.

But also, nothing to hang a conspiracy on.

Hart noted the date. By itself, the meeting meant nothing. The change in pattern, however, did.

The date.

What if the date of the meeting was the important part? What if the date corresponded with the events—the compromised missions—Dylan talked about?

He had to tell Dylan and let the CIA man decide for himself.

34

Kameel al-Rashid landed in Berlin with a grim set to his face.

They'd almost—*almost*—interrupted the timetable. Had Spencer Wolf not tipped them to the incoming attack, the CIA might have succeeded. The irony amused Kameel. Wolf was trying to protect himself, but in doing so sealing his own doom. Kameel had plans to expose the entire conspiracy. October Blood would earn its first victory and send the United States government into disarray. Then, the *real* jihad began. Faisil Ashraf was no longer around to ruin Kameel's ambitions.

The crowd at customs did not disappoint. What he also expected was the sharp-eyed efficiency of the German customs agents. They were out in force to deal with the flood of travelers. The uniformed inspectors weren't letting anybody simply walk into the country. Kameel came prepared. Proper passport under another name, photo to match his *slightly* altered appearance. He'd cut his hair, shaved his beard and mustache, and added contact lenses to change the color of his eyes. The missing beard revealed the jagged scar along his jaw, a knife wound that never properly healed. He needed to act like it wasn't there. He needed to ignore anybody staring at it. It was a war wound; he should be proud to have it on display. And the man who gave him the scar hadn't survived.

He reached the table. One agent inspected his carry-on, and another examined his passport. Their scrutiny did not create anxiety.

"Your name?" the agent holding the passport said.

"James Asami."

"Your purpose in Germany?" The agent turned cold blue eyes on Kameel's face. He was looking at the scar. Kameel tried not to let the stare shake his confidence.

"I'm a real estate investor."

The agent raised an eyebrow. Kameel had not answered the question to his satisfaction. He added more detail.

"I'm here to look at properties to buy."

"First time in Germany?"

"Yes."

The agent nodded, placed the passport on his podium, and slammed home an entry stamp. He handed back the passport.

"Enjoy your stay."

Kameel thanked them both and took his carry-on through. He walked deeper into the Berlin Brandenburg Airport. Signs directed him to baggage claim. He didn't suppress the grin spreading across his face. He'd made it.

While waiting at the baggage claim carousel, he scanned the noisy crowd for his contact. A pair of October Blood operatives had been in Berlin for two weeks. His arrival indicated the start of their first major offensive.

By the time he collected his luggage, he found the man

sent to pick him up. He did not remember the man's name; he was young and appeared nervous.

"It is well," Kameel told him. "Remind me of your name, brother."

"Saleet el-Dar."

The young man tried to keep his voice from shaking. Kameel set his suitcase down to squeeze the young man's shoulder. "Allah has blessed us, Saleet. Let's go. Our destiny awaits."

"I'm parked outside."

"Lead. I will follow."

Before Kameel grabbed the suitcase, Saleet snatched it and started for the exit. Kameel followed behind. Saleet and his associate scored the highest out of the trainees who went through the base camp. It's what earned them the assignment.

But Kameel chided himself for his lapse in memory. He should have remembered Saleet's name. He blamed the stress of his escape from Syria. But it was a blunder a real leader wasn't supposed to make.

He sat in the passenger seat. Saleet negotiated the heavy traffic with ease. The stop-and-go allowed Kameel to reflect on how far he'd come in a short amount of time.

Kameel al-Rashid joined October Blood after a decade in al-Qaeda. He'd gone into hiding after US forces killed Osama bin Laden. He didn't rush into ISIS knowing they were next on the Great Satan's hit list. Instead, he bided his time till another chance came along. His next *chance* took the form of Faisil Ashraf. Ashraf claimed to have a vision for a new organization. He wanted to make those who came before look like children throwing sticks and stones. Faisil made big promises and had the money to back up the hearty talk. But therein lay the root of his treachery.

Faisil and Kameel began training and recruitment. Kameel, in charge of instruction, drove recruits to their breaking point and beyond. When Faisil offered him the post of second in command, he jumped for it. All was well for a time, but then he discovered Faisil's American connection. The true source of the money and equipment. And the trickery—October Blood existed in name only. There were no plans to carry on the fight. Kameel's dream of contributing to true jihad shattered like a mirror dropped from a roof. Worse, he discovered the truth in response to Faisil blocking him from video meetings.

Faisil took weekly video calls but never included Kameel. As second in command, Kameel felt he should be part of the discussions. If anything happened to Faisil, he needed to know what he knew. The then-October Blood leader refused. Kameel decided to get creative and eavesdrop. Acquiring a small video camera, he planted the device in Faisil's private quarters. Kameel watched the video later and listened with growing anger to the audio. The conversation revealed Faisil's true intentions.

October Blood was a fraud, a group funded by American mercenaries. Faisil Ashraf had no intention of sending out fighters except to be set up for targeted kills. There was then only one option for Kameel. Taking over. And taking over required him to first kill Faisil Ashraf...and his sister.

He'd never approved of Reema Ashraf's presence at the base. His protests went nowhere. Unfortunately, Faisil's last second sacrifice saved her from a bullet. Kameel put more bullets into Faisil's body instead. And he was going to get even by taking what they'd built and turning it against them. He wanted to use their own words and video to convict as well. Everything was on the laptops. Faisil made recordings of every video call for his own protection. Now, Faisil's protection was Kameel's ultimate weapon.

But he still faced the unresolved matter of Reema Ashraf. She was *out there* somewhere; eventually, she'd find him and try to kill him.

He'd deal with her when she showed herself. For now, he was safe. From *her*.

The CIA?

Well, they were another story.

35

Saleet carried Kameel's suitcase and carry-on in the elevator. Kameel planned to stay at the hotel for the next seventy-two hours. Then he'd switch to another safe house in the city.

Saleet knocked on the hotel room door in a specific coded pattern; after a moment, the door opened. Kameel smiled when he saw the face behind the door.

Kameel and Tareef Mansur embraced with gladness and happy greetings. They'd served in AQ together, and Kameel picked him to lead the mission into the US. Saleet made mint tea for them, and they sat to talk.

Kameel surprised them by saying he was changing the mission plans.

"I'll be directing from here," he said, after a sip of the mint tea.

"Wait," Tareef said. "You were planning—"

"I got into Germany. I may not get into the United States." Kameel took time to explain what happened with the American raid. Tareef and Saleet took the news somberly, and Kameel saw a fire spark within Tareef. He'd want vengeance for the loss of comrades-in-arms. He'd channel the rage into action when he reached the US.

"The CIA will be looking for me," Kameel concluded, "so it's safer if I stay here."

"The videos—"

"We can feed them over the internet from here. Won't be hard to make the arrangements."

"What about our brothers in the US?" Tareef said.

Saleet sat and listened.

"They are waiting and ready to receive you."

"You'll see us off tomorrow?"

"Yes, my friend. I will not hide while you take the risks. Allah helped me get out of Syria. He will travel ahead of you, too."

Tareef nodded. Saleet said nothing.

Soon they began talking of other things.

* * *

DYLAN LEFT work early for once, and in his car found a voicemail from Toby Hart on his cell. Emily still claimed to be sick and planned to see her doctor in the morning. They only had a short conversation about the matter. Emily refused his offer to bring over medicine. She'd even said no to her favorite takeout.

He sat in his car and listened to Toby say, "Hey, dude. Call me back ASAP."

Dylan's pulse jumped. He dialed his friend. Toby answered while on the road, in traffic.

"You have something?" Dylan asked.

"I have a date."

"Does your wife know?"

"Har, har. No. The date of a basement conference room

meeting at Eagle HQ. I want to know if this date corresponds with some of the problems you described."

"Okay."

"A week ago, Wednesday, the twenty-fourth."

"Tell me about the meeting."

Toby explained the classified matters often discussed in the basement. He mentioned Spencer Wolf—*that name again!*—and Max Hudson and explained their roles in the PMC. Toby also talked about the irregularities he noticed not only in Wolf's behavior, but Hudson's as well.

Toby Hart said, "I know it's not much—"

"It helps."

"Does the date—"

"Yes, Toby. If I had to guess, the meeting was an emergency. I can't explain more now, but thank you."

"Want me to keep looking?"

"No, but standby. I may need you for something else."

"Did I earn Mexico?"

"Pal, you earned Acapulco if you want it. Talk to you later."

Dylan ended the call and sat for a moment to catch his breath. Yeah, the twenty-fourth was important. It was two days *after* Z Section received the message from Reema. And the only way Spencer Wolf and Max Hudson knew was because of the leak in Z Section caused by Emily Chapman.

Dylan started the car. The hell with being "sick," he needed to confront Emily. Now. He only had circumstantial evidence at best. A collection of coincidences. Nothing the FBI or any court of law would accept. What he needed was a confrontation...and a confession. A double agent. Make the mole work for *him*.

If he ever meant anything to Emily, maybe she would admit the conspiracy and help end the plot. If not, Dylan had no desire to ponder what she might force him to do next.

* * *

A PAIR of steely eyes watched Spencer Wolf approach another man seated on a bench. They were meeting in the shadow of President Lincoln. "Shadow" was apt. As evening replaced daytime, flood lights took over, making it easier for the observer to hide. Spencer Wolf wasn't terrible at tradecraft, he knew how to watch his back, but the observer was better.

* * *

WOLF TRIED to avoid Max Hudson's stare. This was not going to be a good meeting. Had any of them been? He shifted on the bench to get comfortable; it was impossible. Hudson, legs crossed, arms folded, didn't appear bothered.

"Start," Hudson said.

"They raided the October Blood base," Wolf said. He explained the attempt to wipe out the commando team. He admitted he had no clue about the outcome of the attack. As far as Wolf was aware, the team was on the way back to the US.

"So, the CIA may, or may not, have collected evidence with our names all over it. What about the group itself?" Hudson asked.

"They put out an alert for Kameel al-Rashid. The alert claims he's the leader of the group."

"Did al-Rashid kill Faisil?"

"We can assume."

"I don't like assuming the answers to these questions."

"We talked once before about who knows too much—" Wolf swallowed. "We may need to—"

"Emily Chapman is the greatest threat," Hudson stated.

Wolf nodded.

"And her boyfriend."

"Uh-huh."

"Kill them both."

Wolf tried to read Hudson's face. The old man's shaded expression bore no clues. But Wolf was certain of one thing. Three people can keep a secret only when two of them were dead.

Wolf departed first and moved faster than usual back to his car. He'd parked curbside on Constitution Avenue. He cut through a park, using the trees for cover, skirting a baseball diamond. When he reached the sidewalk, he checked the street to see if it was safe to go around to the driver's door—

"Don't make a sound."

Wolf's momentary panic settled once he recognized the voice in his ear.

Rylen Cannon.

"The gun in your back has a suppressor on the barrel," Cannon said, "so I can kill you right here if I need to."

"But you want to talk instead."

"Get in the car."

Wolf nodded. He used the fob in his pocket to unlock the car. Front and back lights flashed; the horn chirped. He walked at low speed to the car, and he and Cannon opened their doors at the same time. Both climbed inside.

36

Cannon held his gun on his lap, still pointing at Wolf. Light flashed inside the dark car with every passing vehicle.

"The man you sent me to kill turned the tables," Cannon said. "Now, tell me you didn't send him."

"Why would I send a man to kill you?"

"You tell me."

"I did *not* sell you out, Cannon. What happened?"

Cannon explained the attack on his cabin, the loss of his people. "It was Jack Slayton. He knew where to find me."

"What happened to your phone?"

"Nobody cares about your fancy phone."

"But—"

"I locked the phone, Spencer. If Slayton found it, and the tech people cracked it, you'd be in a bag by now."

"Don't be so sure," Wolf said. "It would take a while to trace where the number bounces off—"

"Enough. Are they back in the States? Slayton and the Ashraf woman."

"I don't know."

"Don't play games with me, Spencer."

"I'm not! There's been another mission since what happened to you. They *may* not be back yet. If you want to know for sure when Slayton and Ashraf return, follow their boss. Dylan Sharp is his name. Also—"

Wolf explained the relationship between Dylan and Emily Chapman. And how developing events dictated they both die.

"How convenient," Cannon said when Wolf finished.

"Well, we're covering both ends—"

"Shut up, Spencer."

Wolf swallowed.

"You're paying triple, yes?"

"Yes! Of course, no argument."

"Where do I find Sharp?"

Wolf told him.

Cannon exited the car and faded into the night.

Wolf let out a breath, as if he'd been holding it underwater, only surfacing before his lungs burst. He gripped the steering wheel with both hands while he waited to get his breathing under control.

Well, one thing for sure was Rylen Cannon might solve all the problems.

But Wolf was betting a lot on one man.

Slayton unlocked the door to his place and the stuffy air inside hit him with a *thwack*. He went through the place turning on lights and opening windows. Last, he turned on the ceiling fan in the living room.

Slayton turned from the wall switch to look at her. She was looking at him, still holding her gear bags, uncertain.

"You can set those anywhere."

She put them against a wall where he'd placed his. "You moved," she said.

"Last place jacked my rent above what I was willing to pay," he told her. "Are you hungry?"

"Do you have anything not expired?" She smiled a little.

Slayton laughed. "Probably not. But I will find something. Go shower and it will be ready when you come out."

"Um..."

"What's wrong?"

"Where's the shower?"

He showed her.

They'd been back in the US for a couple of days but remained at Bolling Air Force base in DC for debrief. The CIA went over the Syria mission backward, forward, inside and out. It was an exhausting process. The lives lost on the mission weighed on Slayton, too. Losing as many as they had, with nothing to show for it, made their deaths more tragic.

While Reema showered, Slayton took stock of the food situation. He indeed found many items in the fridge past their useful dates. He found a carton of eggs still good.

"Hey, Jack!"

He turned down the stove and leaned into the hallway. Reema had part of her head exposed by the half-open bathroom door.

"Got a spare bathrobe?"

Slayton said yes and found one in his bedroom closet. He passed it to her and she shut the door again.

When she came out, hair wrapped in a towel, they both laughed. The white terrycloth robe was too big for her.

Slayton served scrambled eggs and toast— "We lucked out on the bread; I had a loaf in the freezer,"—and she tapped salt and pepper on hers. He also made tea. Decaf. He didn't want to be up all night. Then again, he was so tired it might not have mattered.

They ate without talking. He showed her how to work the television while he showered. When he emerged in another bathrobe, he found her zonked on the couch. Slayton switched off the TV and went to turn down the bed. She awoke at his touch and groggily followed him down the hall, his hand in hers. Anything they wanted, or needed, to say would wait till morning.

* * *

DYLAN SHARP DIDN'T BOTHER to knock.

He let himself into Emily's apartment with the spare key she'd given him. Long ago. When he felt they had something. All they'd shared—no, not shared. His feelings were real. Emily's were lies.

Tonight, the lies stopped.

He caught her in the kitchen, looking in the refrigerator, bent over to search the bottom shelf. She gasped, straightening, her eyes wide. She was not sick. Dylan ignored her expression.

He said, "I know everything, Emily. We're going to talk whether you like it or not."

Emily pressed her lips together. Her bottom lip began to quiver.

"You're going to start crying? *That's* your go-to move?"

"Dammit, Dylan! No. It's not!"

"It's cute you're the one getting upset."

"Wait! Stop!" She put up both hands in surrender. "I'm not going to do this standing in the kitchen."

She turned sharply and walked away from him. He followed, and she sat on the couch. Turning off the TV, she sat down hard and crossed her legs. Dylan lowered himself into a chair. He did not cross his legs. He needed to be ready to move if she made any threatening gestures. He may not have been a field man any longer, but the instincts remained.

"Start talking," he said.

"How did you find out?"

"Never mind how. I *did.* Now I need a reason."

"A reason to turn me over to the FBI?"

"You know what I need, Emily."

"Okay, yes, it started as a job. I needed to get close to you, but not romantically. That—"

"Was a bonus?"

"Was something I didn't *expect.* I *did* fall in love with you. Made the job ten times harder."

"But you managed," Dylan said.

Emily scoffed. She sniffed and reached for a Kleenex box on the coffee table.

"Yeah, I'm a good spy. The Marines taught me well."

"And Wolf."

"Him, too." She dabbed at her eyes and blew her nose.

"Why?" he asked. "None of this makes sense."

"We did it to protect Americans."

"And exactly how was it going to work?"

"Wolf's idea. And some of mine. We figured we could keep track of the young radicals who wanted to fight, and control where they went. They'd be easier to identify and kill. You remember the sandbox. You remember how many we lost. I wanted the crazies in a box, so they'd be easier to shoot.

"But then Hudson got involved. He wanted to do it for the money. Keep the threats alive and the contracts coming. And they've been siphoning off the contracts to fill their own pockets. I took some money, too," she added.

"Delicious," Dylan said. "And you didn't mind sacrificing two fellow officers to make this dream a reality. Should I tell you who died in Syria or does it not matter?"

She choked, sobbed. Dylan waited. His heart hurt. The pain had settled in his chest.

"It wasn't supposed to happen!" Emily said. "None of this would have happened if the CIA hadn't found October Blood so fast. And if Reema Ashraf hadn't gone undercover."

"You are *not* blaming this on *her*, Emily."

"Wolf and Hudson had a meeting and decided. What was I supposed to do? I was in it up to my neck. I *had* to go along."

"Uh-huh."

"I'm sorry."

"And it's all fixed, right?"

"No! I'm sorry I did this to you. You don't know what I've been going through."

"Yeah. I'm sure. Like you said, you're a good spy. We lie for a living. For you, it was a lifestyle."

She sobbed quietly. Or tried to. Every once in a while, she uttered a loud gasp or groan of pain. He sat and let her. He had to think and think fast.

She'd admitted everything and tied the loose pieces together. Not in a bow—he was sure there was more to the story. But his tactic had worked. And how he wished he'd been wrong. He wished she'd denied it all.

What next?

"Stop crying."

She glared at him. "What?"

"I need you on the record."

"You want me to rat on Eagle?"

"You like breathing?"

"Dylan—"

"If you're going to come out of this with your skin intact, you need to testify. Help me get Wolf and Hudson."

"If I live long enough."

"What you mean?"

"Come on, Dylan! Conspiracy 101. The secret's out. And I know *too much*, get it?"

The only way three people can keep a secret...

Dylan knew the punchline as well as anybody.

"I'm going to make a suggestion counter to my best judgment," Dylan said, "because frankly, I never want to see you again. But I need you alive, so you'll stay with me tonight and we'll see Chris Fisher in the morning."

"Okay." She sniffed. Splotches of red covered her face.

"I'll watch you pack."

She hurriedly filled a suitcase in her bedroom, the case open on her bed. She threw clothes and accessories inside. Then she opened the nightstand drawer to reach for a pistol. Dylan intercepted and snatched the gun from her hand.

"We may need it," she said.

"For sure." He tucked the Beretta APX 9mm behind his back and helped himself to the pair of spare magazines also in the drawer.

She angrily finished packing, adding toiletries, underwear, makeup, and a hair dryer. When she began to zip the case, he shoved her aside and did it himself, taking the case off the bed.

"Go ahead of me. No sudden moves."

She stared at him. Shoulders slumped, defeated, she turned to go out.

He followed.

37

THE RED DOT OF A LASER SIGHT LANDED ON EMILY'S BACK.

"Down!"

Emily screamed as Dylan crashed into her. He forced her onto the parking garage's oil-stained concrete deck. Three suppressed shots smacked into the wall and elevator doors ahead. One bullet whined off the concrete to pop and overhead fluorescent bulb. The glass from the tube tinkled onto the ground. Emily squirmed beneath Dylan; he already had a location for the shooter.

He let go of Emily to spin around, staying on the floor, grabbing the Beretta APX from behind his back. He stabbed the pistol forward to aim at the figure shifting between parked cars. The killer stopped and aimed his rifle. A stone pillar partly concealed the killer's body, but he had a foot exposed. Dylan aimed for the foot and pulled the trigger. It was a small target, and he didn't expect to score. What he did was let the killer know he wasn't the only one with a gun. The single shot did the trick. The killer scrambled for another position as the bullet careened off the floor.

Dylan grabbed Emily and hauled her up. Spots of oil

stained her gray sweatpants, but at least it wasn't blood. Dylan urged her forward. They ran fast, Dylan lagging behind, with her suitcase in his left hand. His right gripped the Beretta. He looked around as he waited for the killer's next appearance. Their shoes scuffed and squeaked on the smooth floor.

"Stay low," he told her.

"I know what to do!"

They squeezed between two cars. Dylan bumped his elbow on a side mirror. He stifled a grunt as pain flashed through his arm. He glanced back. *There!* The killer cut across the aisle. Dylan fired twice. The first shot missed, but the second nicked the heel of the killer's left shoe. The man tumbled to the ground and rolled out of Dylan's line of fire.

Dylan turned and ran ahead. Emily waited beside his car, keeping low. He reached the car and dropped beside the driver's side back fender. A pop of the key fob unlocked the car. Emily scrambled inside. Dylan chucked the suitcase in the back. The red laser sight found him. He fired three blind shots. The red dot went away, but he still hadn't scored a hit.

Dylan dropped behind the wheel and jammed the hot Beretta under his left leg. The motor grumbled to life. Emily made herself small below the window glass. Dylan backed out and hit the gas, steering for the exit. He powered down his window.

The killer appeared behind another car as they sped to the street ramp and took aim. Dylan fired out the window. Four rapid blasts. He caught only a brief glimpse of the assassin as he ran away again. Dylan raced up the ramp and onto the empty street. Speeding through a red light, he made a few more turns as they traveled several blocks. Emily slammed against the door as she remained low with no seat belt. Dylan then straightened the car after one final turn and slowed a little.

Emily sat up and buckled her seat belt.

"Where are we going now?" she asked.

"Somewhere." Dylan breathed hard.

"Not much of an answer."

"Somewhere your friends can't find us."

"I didn't think—"

"Be glad you thought to grab your gun."

"I noticed you didn't hit anything with it."

He bit back his initial response; she wanted the joke to lighten the tension. He grinned instead. "Guess I need range time."

He signaled for a freeway on-ramp and increased speed as he reached it.

* * *

SLAYTON TAPPED his cell phone screen to disconnect. He frowned.

Reema said, "Still can't reach him?"

"No." It was his third attempt.

"Put the phone down and finish eating."

Slayton shrugged and did so. He'd risen before Reema and made a quick trip to the store for more food, and they'd cooked breakfast together. It felt good to be domestic. It felt like they'd never been apart. But now they had to get back to work, and Dylan was MIA.

He'd try the office line next.

But Dylan called while they washed dishes.

"Hey. Sorry. Been a long night."

"We need to meet."

"Not at the office," Dylan said. "I'll text you an address.

We'll tell you what happened on our end and go over your stuff."

The phone beeped. Slayton looked at the address in the text message.

"Where is this?" He didn't recognize the location.

"Emergency safehouse."

"The one—"

"No, different one. Get your butt over here and I'll explain."

Slayton said they'd leave right away.

The route took them into Maryland and a neighborhood up a hill. Large homes suggested a neighborhood of opulence and privacy. The last turn took them down a cul-de-sac ending with a gated property. Large house, wide patch of land. Brick wall perimeter. Slayton stopped at the gate and reached out to press a button on a call box.

A buzzer sounded. The gate swung open. Dylan's voice over the call box speaker said, "Head up to the porch," and Slayton called out, "Copy," as he drove through. He stopped the car and waited till the gate swung closed.

The single-story house stretched lengthwise before them. A yard crew worked the grass and flower beds they passed. But the men weren't simple landscapers. They possessed the steely eyes of sentries.

* * *

THE PROBLEM with the safehouse was how easy it was to see from the tallest part of the neighborhood.

If one kept driving to the top of the hill, to a spot designated as a hike and nature area, the house was visible. And its grounds. Rylen Cannon sat on a slope, concealed by trees and brush. He watched the safehouse through high-powered binoculars.

He hadn't meant to kill Dylan Sharp and Emily Chapman at the garage.

In the time it had taken for Sharp and Chapman walked to the elevator, Cannon placed a tracking device on their car. *Then* he opened fire after catching Sharp's attention with the oh-so-obvious laser sight. Only Hollywood, and poor shooters considered laser sights cool. But the gimmick did the trick, and now he had all four in one place. He watched Slayton and the Ashraf woman exit their car. Sharp met them on the porch.

Cannon scanned the grounds. Because now he needed a plan to deal with the security team. Six men, junior-level operatives gaining experience for better posts.

For now, Cannon watched and waited...

38

"I LIKED THE OTHER PLACE BETTER," SLAYTON SAID.

Dylan grinned as Slayton took in the expensively decorated safehouse.

"It's protected," Dylan told him.

They entered the large living room where a blond woman sat on a couch. She stood as Dylan approached with Slayton and Reema.

Slayton wanted to say hello to Emily, but he sensed the tension between her and Dylan. He stayed quiet as he and Reema found seats of their own.

"Tell him," Dylan told Emily. He sat next to her.

Emily explained her involvement in the conspiracy, and her leaks to the other side. She didn't leave anything out.

"Now what?" Slayton said. He tried to suppress his anger, but a red flush crawled up his neck. He wanted to knock Emily on her ass. "She's on our side again?"

"She's agreed to testify against Wolf and Hudson," Dylan said.

Slayton turned his hostile gaze on Emily again. "You tried to kill me."

"I'm sorry."

"You'll be as sorry as the poor bastards trusted with the job if I have anything –"

"Enough!" Dylan shouted. "We've come a long way to this point, and it's the only way to win. Our priority is finding al-Rashid and ending this conspiracy, not fighting each other."

"All right," Slayton said.

"You sure?"

"I'm cool."

"I suggest we take a time out and continue in a few minutes."

"Let's start now," Slayton said instead. "We've wasted enough time, and you're right. Al-Rashid is still out there."

They moved to the dining area, where Dylan served drinks. Slayton, Reema, and Emily sat not trusting each other. Slayton's hard look was the most intense of the three.

Emily started over with Dylan running a digital recorder to capture her testimony. She explained again the history of the conspiracy.

It wasn't long before Reema interrupted.

"I need to know something," she said.

Emily looked at her.

"Why Faisil? He was never a radical. He *hated* the jihadists. How did you get him to run October Blood?"

"He was perfect," she said. "We needed somebody of stature and education, somebody who wasn't a useful idiot, you know? When we told him he'd be a sort of clearing house for the crazies and could help keep a lot of them either out of circulation or send them to their deaths, he agreed. It was his way of solving the extremist problem. He never told you?"

Reema shook her head. "We never spoke in private. He

always had his goons around him. I didn't even know the basics of the Eagle connection till the day he died."

Emily explained more about the scheme, and toward the end, Dylan asked a question of his own.

"Who tried to kill us in the garage?" Dylan asked.

"It was Cannon," Emily said.

"Good," Slayton said. "Another person I want to see again."

Dylan opened his mouth to say more, but Slayton cut him off.

"I'm done being nice, Dylan. You see what they put in motion. You think the government will let this get out? The scandal would be huge. This will be covered up, Congress will pass more oversight on PMCs, and nothing will happen. The only way these clowns will see any justice is if *we* bring it to them. Especially because this monster they created is now out of control. *Lives* are on the line, Dylan. And you're treating this like it's a parking violation."

"I know what's on the line, Jack."

"Then *act* like it."

"Let's take a break," Dylan suggested for the second time.

Slayton didn't argue. Dylan stopped the recorder.

* * *

THE BREAKS HAPPENED LONGER than Dylan intended, off and on well into evening. Slayton could not sit at the same table with Emily Chapman for long periods of time. Slayton went out to the back patio. The landscapers he'd seen earlier left after six. Another crew replaced them. The replacements patrolled the ground like the sentries he knew them to be. They were subtle, staying near the walled perimeter. Three on, three off, rotating every two hours. It seemed like a cushy post. Slayton wondered if he should ask about a rotation. A rest, some gardening, and nighttime strolls sounded nice.

He stared at the city lights in the distance. He wished he could calm down. Here he was face-to-face with one of the people who started the mess; despite his assurance of being okay, he wasn't. All Slayton wanted to do was get his hands around Emily's neck and squeeze. And Dylan was either thinking with his dick or subscribing to "fair play." In Slayton's experience, fair play did not exist in reality. When an enemy wants to kill you, it did not matter if she was amazing in bed—she's an enemy. The only good enemy was a dead one. Why Dylan was fooling around when they had all they needed to *wipe out the enemy* Slayton didn't understand.

The patio doors slid open behind him. Slayton grimaced. He wasn't ready for company, not even Reema. But it was Dylan who stopped beside him.

"Nice view," Dylan said.

"Uh-huh."

"We should talk about the phones you brought back."

"What did you find?"

Dylan told him about the shell company.

"Anything else?"

Dylan shook his head.

"Everything ties to Wolf," Slayton said. "I don't know why we need to pursue the phones further. Wolf used them to communicate with Cannon and the terrorists. They're useless as clues. We know what's on them."

"What's really on your mind, Jack?"

An angry flash crossed Slayton's face. "Syria was a waste. All we had to do was wait for you to confront your girlfriend. A bunch of guys died for nothing. You remember them, right?"

"I remember. But, Jack? If we 'kill 'em all,' we break the law. We must take this to the FBI."

"You're making a mistake."

"I have a plan for pulling Wolf into the open. I'll need your help to make it work. Here's what I'm thinking..."

The explosion came from the left. A bright ball of flame. Slayton and Dylan didn't spend time looking for more details. They ran into the house. They were under attack.

And Slayton couldn't wait to get the enemy under his gun.

* * *

CANNON WAITED TILL DARK.

While waiting, he prepared a Milkor MGL. It was a heavy, bulky weapon firing 40mm grenades from a six-round cylinder. With a pistol grip for firing and forward grip for stability, Cannon's MGL was also topped by a red dot sighting system.

Cannon wore dark fighting fatigues and was loaded for war. A pair of H&K MP5K submachine guns in a double-shoulder rig under each arm. His combat vest contained extra grenades and spare ammo. His sidearm was a trusty Glock-17. But he didn't think the fight would get so bad he'd need to rely on the handgun.

To blow the wall, he had a hunk of C-4 and a timer. Once the wall went down, the fight would start.

Carrying the C-4 charge, he started down the hill. Working through the forest didn't slow him down, and he stopped at the west side wall. He wasn't worried about electronic countermeasures. Anybody who ran to investigate would get a face full of 40mm high explosive and good night, Gracie.

He applied the C-4 to the base. Voices on the other side — "We got an alarm!"—told him he'd indeed tripped a sensor. But it only made the opening better if he took out more than one with his first salvo. Cannon ran to cover. When the C-4 detonated, the explosion sent a fireball into the night sky. Cannon charged ahead with the MGL in hand. The ball of flame faded, leaving a pile of rubble to climb over. Cannon fired two 40mm shells at the figures running toward him. The explosions tore holes in the grass, throwing chunks of dirt in the air. And body parts, as the CIA security men fell to the shock wave and shrapnel.

Cannon paused, looking ahead. More shooters ran his way from the left. About 100 yards away. The patio. Two figures ran into the house. They weren't armed. Cannon turned left and fired the MGL. The hiss and whistle of the speeding 40mm charge landed midway. The blast took down both shooters. Cannon turned to the house and let another grenade go. The projectile landed near a wall and exploded. The blast showered the side with shrapnel and flame and set the roof's overhang edge on fire. Rifle fire crackled—a sentry on his left survived. But he wasn't moving, he was flat on the grass. Cannon sighted through the red dot optic and triggered the MGL again. This time, the grenade blast finished what the first had started. The CIA security man didn't move again.

One grenade left. He aimed for the house and fired the last round. The explosion blew a flaming hole in the upper corner of the roof. More flames enveloped the house. Cannon dropped the MGL and grabbed his twin MP5Ks. He ran for the patio. Two more sentries appeared on the opposite side of the concrete. They fired as Cannon dove behind a squared-off hedgerow. He swung his right-hand MP5K over the top of the hedge and fired back, then set the sub gun down and plucked a grenade from his vest. This time he used the M67 variety, standard issue for the US military. He pulled the pin. The safety spoon popped with a *ping*. He tossed the explosive over the hedge. Then he grabbed another and moved to the other end to roll it toward the patio doors. Both M67s exploded at the same time. The screams of the men didn't drown out the shattering of glass and protesting metal as the door frames buckled. Grabbing the MP5K he'd set down, Cannon fired another stream over the hedge and ran into the house.

39

Dylan punched a code into the keypad on the wall, then pushed forward a thick metal door. They entered the "gun room" in the basement. Slayton, Reema, and Emily followed him inside. They helped themselves to automatic rifles and ammunition magazines. Standard issue was the order of the day. They had the choice of M-4 carbines, HK416s, and SIG-Sauer M-17 pistols. Slayton had his P-10C, but an extra gun never hurt. He jammed an M-17 behind his back after locking a mag into an M-4.

The house shook as an explosion rocked the walls and rattled the foundation.

"He has artillery?" Reema yelled.

"Dylan, get the women out of here!" Slayton said. "I'll cover. Follow me."

Slayton took the lead out of the basement, emerging at the top of the stairs to check each direction of the hallway. Then he waved the others up. He ran through his mind what he and Dylan saw on the patio. Cannon attacked from the west side wall. His easiest point of entry into the house was the patio.

He led Dylan and the women to the front entryway and told them to scoot. This time Dylan took point. He and Emily ran for the front door. Reema gave Slayton a wide-eyed, frightened look. He kissed her, told her to go. As Reema ran to join the other pair, another explosion hit. Chunks of the ceiling fell with a crash, and smoke trickled in from above. The roof was on fire.

A third explosion shook the house, and glass shattered. Cannon had broken through the rear. Slayton yelled for the others to run. Dylan and Emily raced outside. One last look from Reema, and she followed.

Slayton jumped to his feet and headed for his next confrontation with the killer named Rylen Cannon.

And only one of them was walking away alive this time.

* * *

SLAYTON FLICKED the M-4's selector switch to full-auto. He entered the sitting room near the broken patio doors, scanning left to right. Movement behind a couch! He swung left again and fired a short burst. The impacts tore the couch cushions to ribbons and made Rylen Cannon reveal himself. The freelance killer triggered a pair of MP5Ks as he rose and flung himself further away from Slayton. He hit the floor and rolled toward a table. Slayton tracked him, fired, and knocked a leg out from under the table. The table collapsed on Cannon. As Slayton moved in, Cannon fired; Slayton dodged left, striking his foot on a chair. He crashed on the carpet and crawled forward.

The roof continued to burn. Smoke drifted across the ceiling. But the open patio doors filtered the smoke outside.

Ping.

Slayton tensed. A grenade sailed overhead, bounced off

the wall behind him, and landed in an adjacent room. Slayton covered the back of his neck. The blast flung debris into the sitting room along with a flash of fire. Slayton felt the heat. Cannon had the aces with the grenades. Their roles from their fight at the cabin were now reversed.

A burst of auto fire from Cannon's sub guns ripped into the wall near Slayton. He rolled left, then eased forward again to stop behind a couch. The M-4 was getting too big to maneuver through the furniture. He slung the rifle across his back and took out both pistols, the P-10C in his right hand, the M-17 in his left.

Slayton crawled around the side of the couch and squeezed between a coffee table and chair. The M-4 bumped the chair and caught. He shifted to pull it free.

Ping.

The grenade rolled across the carpet inches from Slayton's face. He struck with the barrel of the M-17, like hitting a tennis ball with a racket. The barrel slammed against the M67 and sent it to the other side of the room. The blast shattered a window, blew a hole in the wall, and set curtains on fire. The flames licked the ceiling.

Slayton jumped to his feet and pivoted left. Cannon was partly concealed by the fallen table. Slayton fired in rapid succession. Flame spit from the barrel and brass flew across his field of vision. The table splintered as the 9mm rounds punched through the wood. Cannon uttered a single scream. The P-10C's action locked open, but Slayton still had ammo in the large-capacity M-17. He stowed the P-10C and switched the SIG to his right hand. He worked his way around the table to get a full view of Cannon's body.

The freelancer lay on his side, bleeding from several wounds, face twisted with pain. Slayton applied pressure to the M-17's trigger—but then he saw what Cannon gripped in his hand.

Ping.

Cannon let the grenade fall in front of him. Slayton lurched to the left, knocking over a chair, leaping over another couch near the coffee table. He landed on the table, crying out as the hard wooden edge dug into him. But the grenade blast drowned out his cry. Slayton rolled onto the floor. Pieces of the tipped-over table and bloody chunks of what used to be Rylen Cannon landed beside him.

The curtains, now consumed with flame, continued to spread fire to the ceiling. Thick smoke filled the room. The open patio doors did nothing to stop the flow. Slayton coughed, groaned, and stood. There was no sense checking on Cannon's body. He stuck the SIG in his belt and raced to the front of the house. More smoke outside, the glow of flame from the roof. Slayton ran the length of the long driveway, clutching the M-4 in both hands. He hoped Dylan, Reema, and Emily weren't too far away.

* * *

SPENCER WOLF DIDN'T WANT to leave his house. But he had to keep up appearances.

Cannon was their last hope, and Cannon failed. It hadn't taken long for rumors of the battle at the safehouse to reach him. The scant details provided did not encourage him. Nobody was talking about a dead Z Section leader or his subordinates.

But he had to maintain an "all is well" aura. There was still work to do and Eagle missions to oversee. He'd have to live with the jitters until the end. If Hudson wanted him dead now, there wasn't anything he could do short of turning himself in to avoid getting shot.

As he drove to a breakfast meeting with Toby Hart, he wondered if Emily Chapman had turned. What, after all, was she doing at the safehouse? What had she told Sharp?

He checked the rearview often and made a few extra turns. He and Hart had to talk over a few logistic problems related to the Somalia anti-pirate mission. Hart said a breakfast meeting would beat the dreary walls of the office. Wolf agreed only because to do otherwise would hurt his effort to maintain a proper poker face. Plus, in public, he might be safer from the inevitable assassin's bullet until he figured out what to do.

He reached the Denny's Toby Hart suggested. The overseas coordinator waited outside in his car. Wolf parked beside him. They shook hands on the way inside and waited for an escort to their table. Hart had a backpack over one shoulder and told Wolf he'd brought all the material they needed to discuss.

They sat across from each other. The waitress took their orders for coffee while they consulted menus.

"You doing okay, Spence? Look a little pink."

"I was up too late watching an old movie."

"Which one?"

"*Key Largo*. Bogart and, um—"

"Robinson."

"Right."

"I *love* that movie," a new voice said.

Wolf snapped up his head. He forgot the menu in his hands. The speaker hovered beside the table. The new arrival said, "Take a hike, Toby."

Hart scooted out of the booth and the new man took his place.

40

"Hello, Mr. Wolf."

"Good morning, Mr. Slayton. You had breakfast?"

"You buying?"

"I owe you something, I guess."

"You guess?"

Wolf consulted the menu further. "With Cannon gone, I'm facing a choice between one consequence and another. One's a bullet. I don't know what the other will be."

"A bullet," Slayton said. "But from my gun instead of whoever Hudson replaces Cannon with."

"Nobody can replace Cannon. I think I'll get a Denver omelet."

"Emily is telling the FBI all about the scheme. Kameel al-Rashid is on the run. We're convinced he's no longer in Syria. Where is he planning to go, or strike?"

"I have no idea, Mr. Slayton. My arrangement was with Faisil Ashraf. Al-Rashid murdered him and took over and cut us off."

"I've seen crazy stuff in my career," Slayton said, "and a lot of guys who thought they could get away with anything.

But this...is the worst. You've risked lives for money, and you're looking at me like you'll never face punishment."

Wolf looked up over the menu.

"I know how the government works as well as you do, Mr. Slayton."

The waitress came with their coffee. If she noticed Slayton wasn't the same person who entered with Wolf, she gave no sign. Wolf ordered his Denver omelet. Slayton selected bacon and eggs with hash browns and toast.

"I get the sense," Slayton continued after the waitress departed, "you're going to talk."

"Should keep me from bullets. Yours or otherwise. For the time being."

Slayton grinned. The expression made Wolf pause. Maybe he shouldn't be so cocky. He faced a man with a grudge, and he had a creeping sense Slayton might find a way to kill him anyway. His usefulness, after all, would reach a natural conclusion. Slayton would have nothing to lose. He had plenty of time and patience, too. Wolf took a deep breath and sipped some coffee. Slayton's eyes never left him.

Yeah. He'd talk and ask for protection. But he didn't need protection from Hudson. He needed protection from Jack Slayton.

He wasn't sure his situation had improved much, but it was worth a try.

* * *

Tareef Mansur and Saleet el-Dar arrived in New York City and settled at a nondescript hotel. The October Blood operatives wanted to be out of the tourist area and off the radar. Tareef felt more nervous than expected. If the Americans were looking for Kameel, they'd be looking for people connected to him. They'd find Tareef in Kameel's background—not only the al-Qaeda connection, but Oxford, too. But he couldn't dwell on the problem. The clock was ticking; ticking loud in Tareef's ear, and they had to move fast. If the worst happened, Tareef wasn't worried. Even without him, Saleet and the brothers could achieve victory. But he figured they'd be okay if they stuck to the aggressive schedule.

The pair waited forty-eight hours before trying to meet the others. When they left their hotel, they took a cab to a downtown restaurant.

The cabbie pulled over into a too small space out front. Tareef paid the driver, who then caused a traffic jam trying to get back into the flow. A rash of honking horns and screaming drivers accumulated behind him. The cabbie ignored the noise in typical New Yorker fashion. He powered the cab into a gap in traffic, and the flow of vehicles resumed.

Saleet held the door and Tareef entered first. The restaurant was noisy in the front and back. Customers spoke at high levels as they ate. Food sizzled from behind the floor-to-ceiling menu board. Steam drifted around the wall to the counter area.

"What!" shouted the man behind the counter. He looked at Tareef and Saleet with impatience. "What you want?"

Tareef glanced at the floor to make sure he wasn't about to step on a patch of grease. The smell hung thick in the air. The tiles looked worn with patina, but clean. He approached the counter.

The counterman's white apron contained a collage of stains. He looked grumpy. When Tareef gave him the expected password, the man's face changed. He didn't smile but seemed less pissed off. He softened his voice.

"Yes, brother, welcome. Take a chair. We'll be with you." He hurried to the back.

Tareef selected a table far from the entrance. He sat facing the door while Saleet timidly took the other seat and tried not to look uncomfortable. Saleet maintained his near silence, only speaking when necessary. Tareef hoped the younger man could hold up. But he also remembered having a case of nerves on some of his early missions. Once Saleet had a few more behind him, he'd settle down.

The counterman returned and in rapid Arabic called Tareef and Saleet to the back. He told them to go down a short hallway past the restrooms and turn right. The directions led them into the hot kitchen where four men worked the stoves. At the end of the hall, another man emerged from a back office. The man was older, his face pudgy and round, his head bald. He made the pair comfortable in his office while he served hot tea.

"I am Ahmad," the older man told them. "You'll meet the others shortly. They are the ones you saw in the kitchen. It's lunch hour; very busy."

"Is the equipment ready?" Tareef said. "Do you have everything we need?"

"In the basement, yes. All there. Hotel is good, too. We took pictures pretending to be tourists."

"We need to see the hotel ourselves."

"I will take you. Come, let's go downstairs."

Tareef frowned but did not ask anything more. He and Saleet followed Ahmad out of the office, turning left down a short and narrow hall, into another room. There, Ahmad lifted a trapdoor in the floor which led to a small space. They went down a set of steps. The square room was lined with brick, with a concrete floor. Racks on the walls contained automatic weapons. Metal containers sat on the floor, as did the bomb. The plain metal case containing the bomb rested atop one of the bigger containers. Ahmad beamed. He explained the timing mechanism and the explosive power contained within. When Ahmad flipped the latches and raised the lid, Tareef motioned for Saleet. Saleet was the bomb expert. The bomb would be his responsibility when the mission began. The quiet young man stepped close and examined the device. The timer, C-4 brick, and other critical components had been assembled with expert care. He said so to Tareef.

"What about this place?" Tareef asked as Ahmad closed the lid.

"I don't understand."

"Your security. How is it?"

"I've been here twenty years. I'm as invisible as everybody else in this city."

"And that's good?"

Ahmad laughed. "My brother, in this country, it's better than gold!"

Tareef wasn't sure if it was okay to laugh or not. For once, he looked as uncomfortable as Saleet.

"I'll take your word for it, brother," he said.

41

Slayton had to think about the last time he wore a suit. He could not remember. What he knew now, as he rode in the elevator with Dylan to the seventh floor, was the collar of his shirt was too tight. He felt like he had a pair of hands around his neck.

Their wait in Fisher's outer office, while the secretary ignored them, didn't take long. Fisher opened the door and motioned them to enter. The two men sat in front of Fisher's desk. The DDO stared at Slayton with a mixture of suspicion and anger.

"Mr. Slayton," he began.

"Yes."

"I need to get this off my chest. Rylen Cannon was once a member of his agency, and a friend of mine."

"And?"

Dylan audibly winced. Fisher's face turned angrier.

"I don't appreciate your attitude."

"Look, Mr. Fisher, sir, Rylen Cannon may have been a Boy Scout when you knew him. But when I had to deal with him, he was trying very hard to kill me, multiple times. I'm sorry I didn't ask your permission first."

Dylan shifted in his seat. Fisher glared at Slayton.

Slayton said, "Anything else on your mind? Sir," he added.

Fisher closed his eyes and pinched the top of his nose. "I don't understand what he did. Not at all." He looked at them again. "All right. There's no good call here. The only thing to do is end this conspiracy. Where are Wolf and Chapman right now?"

"With the FBI," Dylan said. "I met with the chief of counterintelligence late last night. They're currently taking statements. Max Hudson, the owner of the Eagle Alliance, is under surveillance. He hasn't run. He hasn't left home, actually."

"Is he aware they're watching?" Fisher asked.

"I'm sure, by now, he knows the scheme isn't a secret any longer."

"What charges are they talking about?"

"Aiding and abetting terrorism, conspiracy to defraud the government, various others."

"We need to do something about our polygraph protocols. How your girlfriend slipped through, I'll never guess."

"She didn't think she was lying, Chris."

"Her words?"

"Yes, sir."

Fisher balled his right fist, then released the pressure. "We got played, gentlemen. The DCI is ordering his own investigation. And I can't say we won't all face some sort of reprimand, or worse. We're beyond a write-up at this point."

The three men sat in silence while Fisher stewed in his

seat. He didn't look at either Slayton or Dylan. His eyes focused on the top of his desk in a blank stare. With a deep breath, he turned his attention back to them.

"Now," he said, "we have a terrorist on the loose, using our money and our equipment. Where are we with Kameel al-Rashid?"

Slayton stayed quiet while Dylan consulted the file he'd brought to the meeting. He already knew the answer. He hoped Fisher didn't disagree with their plan of action and hand the mission to somebody else. Slayton decided he'd go off on his own if he had to.

"Two of Kameel's associates entered the United States from Germany," Dylan said. He handed Fisher a photograph. "The man pictured there is Tareef Mansur, formerly of al-Qaeda."

Fisher examined the picture with a frown. "Connection with al-Rashid?"

"They were in AQ and attended Oxford together." Dylan handed Fisher a second picture. "This was taken at JFK customs. We're not sure who the man with Tareef is yet."

Fisher nodded and handed back both. "Where are they now?"

"New York City. They were spotted this morning at the New Continental Hotel, wandering the lobby. They ate breakfast at the hotel restaurant and left."

"Are they scouting the hotel?"

"Not sure," Dylan said. "Could be. We lost track of them after they left."

"You got a plan for our end, or is the FBI taking over?"

"I'd like Slayton and Reema to consult with the FBI on this."

Dylan stopped talking. Slayton said nothing. Fisher glanced at both expectantly. When they added nothing more, he said, "If we can stop al-Rashid, it'll get the DCI off our backs. I'm well aware since Z Section does not officially exist, you, Mr. Slayton, are not unwilling to go and take your chances. Dylan, did you talk this over with the Feds?"

"Yes, sir, they're willing to have somebody handy who knows the big picture."

"Then you two need to get to work."

Dylan said, "Yes, sir, thank you," and rose from his chair.

Slayton didn't speak, but he nodded at Fisher. Fisher said, "Good luck." Slayton followed Dylan out of the office.

* * *

SLAYTON BROKE the silence during the elevator ride down.

"I wasn't aware he knew Cannon."

"Uh-huh."

"What are you thinking?"

"I think your mouth is going to get you in serious trouble someday, Jack."

"Aside from that."

"Go by the book in New York. Tareef and the other man may only be scouts. If al-Rashid shows up, let the FBI have him."

"Dylan. The man killed Reema's brother. He tried to kill us in Syria. If I get a shot, I'm taking it."

"Then don't miss."

* * *

REEMA SAID, "You promised Dylan we'd check in with the FBI."

Slayton raised an eyebrow at Reema, who sat next to

him. They were in a bright sitting area in the lobby of the New Continental Hotel in NYC. The brightness came from wide windows and reflecting surfaces. It was a great spot to sit and read or people watch, as they were doing. But they were watching for one person in particular.

"We've only been here a day," Slayton said. "If we don't see any sign of Mansur by tonight, we'll see the Feds tomorrow."

"Don't wreck this for us."

Slayton nodded, keeping his reply to himself. It was the first time since they'd returned from Syria where she'd referred to them as "us." He liked the sound. They still needed to talk about their future, and he had hoped she wasn't avoiding the topic. Now that she'd indicated otherwise, he wanted to have the conversation right away. But they had to stay focused on the mission for now.

"There are so many people wandering around," she said.

"It's a shiny new hotel. Everybody wants to take a look."

"A lot of people are at risk if this place is a target," Reema said. "We can miss him in this crowd. We need to see the Feds, Jack."

"Just a few more hours, Reema, please."

Slayton knew he was taking a chance and risking the wrath of Dylan and DDO Fisher. He'd give each a reason never to trust him again. But they *had* to stop October Blood. Slayton wasn't going to let the slow machinations of the law take over. A bullet in the head was the best solution, but there was no room for error. And he also knew he was working from ego instead of good sense. What he hadn't yet decided was whether he cared. He wanted the terrorists dead and information leading to their boss. The showdown would happen one way or another, and soon.

He watched everybody of Middle Eastern origin. He hated to profile but knew one thing for sure. They weren't going to catch foreign terrorists by watching blond women from the Netherlands.

Reema elbowed him. "There."

42

Slayton looked where she indicated and Reema wasn't wrong. Tareef hadn't bothered to change his appearance, which set off an alarm in Slayton's mind. The attack wasn't far away. He had no need to hide because their timetable didn't leave room for delay.

"I want to know if al-Rashid is with him," he said to Reema.

"That isn't a cell phone he's taking pictures with."

"Only high-quality for them."

"He's cutting through that crowd to the doors."

"Let's go."

Slayton rose first and Reema followed. They walked hand-in-hand so as not to appear in hot pursuit. Tareef pushed through the revolving door. Slayton and Reema used one of the regular doors beside it and gave Tareef a short lead. He turned right, keeping close to the building side of the sidewalk. The rush of pedestrians enveloped him, and Slayton and Reema merged to follow.

They walked behind him for two blocks. He didn't

pause, look back, or perform any kind of counter-surveillance move.

"The hell is he doing?" Reema said.

"Meeting somebody?"

"He's not looking back."

"He may not have to. Could be a second team running his counter," Slayton said.

A *Don't Walk* sign at a crosswalk forced them to pause, but Tareef kept going. He jogged across, ignored horns, and reached the opposite sidewalk. Slayton and Reema had too many people around them to push through and do likewise. Plus, such a move would tip off the terrorist. Slayton worked to keep the tan tweed coat in sight. Reema looked left.

"If we take this other crosswalk to the other side of the street, we can follow parallel."

"Come on."

They pushed through the crowd to the second cross-walk and started across—

The blue panel van screeched to a halt in front of them, blocking their way. Somebody flung open the side door. A blond man in a suit jumped out; two more men grabbed Slayton and Reema from behind. Slayton tried to fight, but the hands gripping him didn't budge. The blond man stepped aside while the other two shoved Slayton and Reema into the van. The blond man jumped in last and pulled the door shut. The van turned the corner.

Slayton and Reema were on the floor of the van. The two men who'd grabbed them sat behind. Slayton glanced around with alarm. He didn't like the sense of *déjà vu.* At least this time he wasn't handcuffed.

The blond man scooted in front of them and showed Slayton a badge and ID.

"FBI."

Slayton stared at the man.

"We expected you to check in with us, Mr. Slayton." The blond man put away his ID.

"We just got here."

"You got here *yesterday*."

"What's your name?"

"Special Agent Jack Perry."

"You know we lost our suspect, right, Agent Perry?"

"Stop it. You think we're stupid? We have a team on him and I daresay we know more than you."

"Do tell."

"You're going home. We don't need a cowboy 'consultant' from Langley here who can't follow the rules."

"What about me?" Reema said.

Perry turned to her. "*Or* a cowgirl riding with this cowboy who can't follow the rules."

"You don't know the whole story, Agent Perry," Slayton said. "Tareef Mansur has answers to questions you don't know how to ask."

The FBI man laughed. "Sure."

"This isn't only a New York operation," Slayton said. "Mansur is part of a global network, and we need to know what he knows."

"Okay. Good enough. We'll ask him and stovepipe the answers to you."

"You'll spend months going in circles."

"We aren't stupid, Mr. Slayton."

"No, you follow the rules. The rules aren't going to help this time. Look, my apologies for not coming to see you right away. But we can still work together and finish this and nobody has to get hurt."

Perry regarded Slayton without speaking. Then he turned his attention to the agents behind Slayton and Reema.

"What do you think, Cal?"

Slayton didn't turn to see the other man reply.

"What the hell, let's see what the cowboy can do."

"And cowgirl," Reema added.

Perry said, "How deep does this network go?"

"She's the expert," Slayton said, tilting his head to Reema.

She said, "Worldwide. Mansur is a close friend of the leader, who murdered my brother and tried to kill me, too."

"So, it's personal?"

"Yes," she said.

"I understand personal," Perry told them. "Okay, I won't tell your boss. We'll consider this your check-in, but don't make me regret it. *Either* of you."

"Thank you," Slayton said.

"Don't thank me yet."

"You said you had a team on Mansur?"

"Yeah. He and a partner are staying at a rundown hotel. They keep visiting a halal restaurant and spending a good deal of time there."

"If we can hit both places—"

"In progress. Which one do you want to be at?"

"We'll take the hotel."

"Fair enough. Turn around. Meet Special Agents Calvin Giles and Tyler Bass."

Slayton and Reema shook hands with the other two. Giles was the oldest of the three, Bass the youngest.

"Heck of a grip," Slayton told Giles.

"I lift a lot," Giles replied.

"Okay, listen up..." Perry said.

The van continued through traffic.

* * *

SLAYTON AND REEMA kept close to Perry as the FBI team advanced along the hallway. The FBI SWAT operators had the lead. Four agents decked out in full combat gear, body armor, sub guns and face shields.

Slayton and Reema and Agent Perry carried only pistols but also wore bulletproof vests. The goal was to take Mansur and his partner alive. Reema finally got a look at a photo of Mansur's partner and gave them his name. Saleet el-Dar. She noted he was a younger recruit and it surprised her he'd been chosen for the mission.

The SWAT operators blew the door off the hinges. The blast, within the confined space of the hallway, rattled their eardrums. The noise continued as the SWAT team rushed inside. Slayton and Reema waited outside with Perry.

"Clear!" one SWAT member shouted.

"There's nobody here, Agent Perry!" yelled another.

Perry led the way; Slayton and Reema followed. Slayton slammed back the closet doors and pawed through clothes and empty suitcases. They had been at the hotel.

"You had them covered, Perry!"

Panic covered Perry's face. "My people saw Mansur come back. He must have left another way."

Slayton turned to Reema, who wore her alarm like a sweater. Perry answered a call from Agent Calvin Giles, who was with the SWAT team at the halal restaurant. The conversation lasted one minute.

"I'll tell them," Perry said. He ended the call. To Slayton: "The other team hit the restaurant. Found the owner alone.

Short fight—owner's dead. There's a trapdoor leading to a storage room. Bunch of guns and other stuff. Five of the gun racks are empty."

"Attack in progress," Slayton said.

The FBI man asked, "But where?"

43

Slayton and Reema returned to the New Continental with agents Perry and Giles in tow. They stood around the lobby. No sign of trouble. They split up and walked around. The FBI SWAT operators waited in two vans outside, standing by for the "go" signal. But Perry had nothing to report.

Reema whispered to Slayton, "Is this place a diversion?"

"I hope not."

They kept looking, moving from the busy lobby to the row of shops. Much more crowded as people from the street browsed. Boutiques, high-end jewelry, tourist traps. Narrower off-shoot hallways led to other entrances and exits. Slayton and Reema turned in all directions with growing urgency.

Then an explosion rattled the walls.

* * *

Tareef Mansur was the last to arrive.

He breezed through the front entrance as if he'd been there a thousand times. He didn't need to look for the brothers or Saleet el-Dar. He knew they waited for his signal. The signal was the detonation of the grenade Tareef carried in the right-hand pocket of his coat.

Tareef stood in the middle of the lobby. People passed by some shifting to avoid a collision. He took in the sight around him as if he was visiting for the first time. The crowd moved like a stream. Those at the reception desk stood like an improvised dam.

The infidels installed ornate decorations and furnishings to make the hotel nice. They'd spent a lot of money, more than he'd ever see, on the place. Tareef knew plenty of Muslims had worked hard to build the hotel and set up its attractions. He hated to destroy their honest labor. But they would understand. He was not there to admire the architecture. Tareef Mansur had a job to do. He pulled the grenade from his jacket pocket. Nobody noticed. It amazed him how one needed to worry little about concealment when the moment of truth arrived. Because targets, like the cannon fodder they were, never noticed. Same as they passed by him but didn't *see* him standing there.

He pulled the pin. When he tossed the grenade into the line of incoming guests and shouted "Allah Akbar!" a few heads turned. A security guard talking to two men in suits let out a curse. The men in suits took out guns. And then the blast wiped out the existence of many of those in line. Screaming began and increased in volume as the explosion batted back and forth.

The two men in suits had Tareef's attention. He was aware of Saleet and the four brothers going into action. The crackle and bark of their Kalashnikovs overpowered the screaming. But the two men were clear threats. He wasn't going to let them interfere.

Tareef moved fast, using running bodies for cover. He

drew a handgun from under his left arm. Shoving a frightened man out of his way, he had a clear shot at the pair. The two men in suits were trying to get closer to him. They yelled "FBI!" but Tareef didn't think anybody understood. He fired one shot. A neat red hole appeared in the sweat-glistened forehead of one of them, a blond. Tareef let two more rounds go, conscious of the spent brass landing at his feet, as if they landed in slow motion. The second agent took both rounds high in the chest. The security guard had no gun; he tried to duck under his kiosk. Tareef took off the top of his head with another 9mm hollow point.

The roar of popping Kalashnikovs took over. Tareef ran for cover. Saleet and the brothers split to move through the lobby and shopping row. They gunned down anything remaining on two legs. Blood made the tiled floor slippery. Many fell as they tried to flee, only to struggle to rise and fall when bullets found them. Bodies fell atop bodies and still the brothers marched through.

Tareef ran to a sitting area, shooting a man cowering on the floor. He dropped to one knee. Some of the people would get out through the other exits. He and Saleet and the brothers didn't have the resources to keep everybody inside. He was okay with their escape. Those on the upper floors also didn't matter. They'd have plenty of survivors to take as hostages for the big show. The lobby massacre was only the overture.

* * *

SLAYTON DOVE for Reema as the explosion reverberated. He grabbed her with both arms and took her to the floor. Automatic weapons fire filled his ringing ears. They scrambled away as two gunners with AKMs fired into the stores. A burst missed them as they dove into a dress shop. Another salvo of deadly projectiles chewed into the wall as they hit the floor again. Displays toppled under the fusillade. Two mannequins tipped over with holes dotting their frames. Limbs popped loose on impact. The tail end of the salvo cut off the panicked clerk's scream as bullets slapped into her chest. She fell against the counter and left a smear of red behind on her way to the floor.

Slayton pinned Reema on the opposite side of a rack of dresses. They crawled under the hanging hems.

Slayton's mind raced.

How many?

What happened to Perry and Giles?

Do we have any escape routes open?

Reema squirmed beneath him. She said, "What are we going to do?"

The horror continued.

Slayton wished he had an answer.

* * *

Saleet el-Dar and two of the brothers from the restaurant had the lobby covered. When the FBI SWAT team appeared at the glass doors of the entryway, they knew what they had to do. They brought the AKMs to their shoulders and fired on full-auto. Tongues on flame flicked from the rifle muzzle. Glass shattered; bullets tore into bodies. Their body armor was no match for the steel-core projectiles spitting from the mouths of the AKMs. Saleet didn't count the men who fell, but he saw several pull back.

Tareef yelled for them to start gathering survivors.

Some hotel guests up in their rooms when the shooting started filtered down to escape. They found themselves staring into gun muzzles. The terrorists herded them like cattle through the lobby instead. They followed other survivors down a long hallway. Another gunman let his rifle dangle on a sling while he filmed them with a video camera. Their destination was a conference room at the end of the hall. The gunner with the camera filled his viewfinder with frightened faces and blood.

Slayton and Reema let themselves get tossed into the mix. They kept hold of each other with appropriate expressions of panic. The act hid the fact they carried weapons. The cries of the hostages filled Slayton with rage. There were only six terrorists, all young men. The killers looked pleased and laughed at the sight before them. Slayton figured between him and Reema the odds were about even. But then he stopped his train of thought. The terrorist, in a fight, wouldn't focus on him and Reema. They'd turn their AKMs on the hostages. Slayton had already seen their ruthlessness. He decided to play it cool and see what developed.

44

The hostages passed through the open double doors of the wide conference room. Bare carpet greeted them. No tables, no chairs. The terrorists ordered everybody to spread out on the floor. Lay, sit, whatever; they didn't care. Slayton and Reema found a spot along one wall. Three of the gunmen stayed in the room with them. The others showed up within a few minutes, pushing three large gray cases on a rolling cart. The one with the video camera carried a tripod. Slayton and Reema watched. The terrorists with the cases put everything at the front of the room. The last terrorist arrived and pulled shut the double doors. Slayton turned his attention to him.

The man was Tareef Mansur.

Should have shot him in the back when we had the chance, Slayton thought.

It wouldn't have made a difference, idiot. And you'd be wanted for murder.

"Your attention, please."

The hostages couldn't or didn't hear him. Their cries continued.

"Everybody be quiet!" Mansur shouted now. "Silence, please. We are sorry for the bloodshed, but you will soon understand it is your own government who is responsible."

Mansur waited while faces turned his way. Some still whimpered and sobbed.

"You will be quiet, or you will be shot!"

Mansur took out his gun.

* * *

SILENCE FINALLY DESCENDED over the gathered hostages. The only noise came from the front of the room. The crew who had wheeled in the cases began lifting the lids. Slayton was afraid of what they might bring out.

"My name is Tareef Mansur." The terrorist leader began to walk through the hostages spread out on the floor. He still held his gun. Most shrank away from him. Others glared in defiance.

"Do not worry about my men. You will see they are only setting up a video camera, a projection screen, and computers. We want to show you how your government is to blame not only for today's unfortunate incident, but for many such incidents around the world. Millions of lives have been needlessly ended because of the choices your leaders have made. And not only recently—their decisions happened before you were born. An accident of history brought you here today. But you will be the jury in the most important trial the world has ever seen."

The crew emptied the cases and set up the video gear. The last case they opened with care. Two men standing on either side of the case lifted out a steel box. Slayton and Reema exchanged glances. Both knew the steel case housed a bomb. The terrorists placed the case on the table. The man Reema identified as Saleet el-Dar lifted the lid and fiddled with whatever lay inside. He closed the lid. Then he helped the others finish setting up. They placed laptops and the monitors on a folding table and placed the projection screen in a corner. One of the terrorists turned on a projection unit plugged into a laptop. He adjusted the unit to center a still photo of a garden on the screen.

Tareef Mansur continued his stroll among the hostages. He stepped over arms and legs. He stared down as he continued his speech.

Slayton tuned Mansur out. He and Reema were in the very back of the room. He might kill Mansur and one or two others, but he'd never get across the room in time to stop them from detonating the bomb.

"...you're having a hard time believing what I say," Mansur continued. "But this is what happened. Does this make sense? *Why* is your country so *obsessed* with war? With *being* at war? *Encouraging* war or *starting* war? What benefit do you receive? All you get in return are thousands of dead sons and daughters and for what? So, your leaders can start another when the *next* generation reaches fighting age?

"But now, don't take my word for it," Mansur continued. He had finally worked his way through the hostages to the front. He stood beside the projector unit as one of his men dimmed the lights via a switch. "We are going to bring you a live video feed shortly. But first, I must address the gathering police and FBI on the street. Don't get excited. They are not going to save you. Nobody can save you." For emphasis, Mansur stepped over to the steel box and gave it a loving pat. But he didn't announce what the box contained.

Slayton knew.

* * *

"FBI SAYS they're starting to communicate."

DDO Christopher Fisher spoke the words to Dylan Sharp, who stood near the wall-mounted television in Fisher's office. Other members of the anti-terrorist departments also crowded within. And all eyes were glued to the TV and the live reports coming from New York City.

Fisher added, "They've sent a video statement to one of the TV stations." He listened to the voice on the other end, then cupped the mouthpiece. He announced, "Dylan, change to channel 52."

Dylan took the remote from Fisher's desk and changed the station. Another news feed, but this one showed video inside the hotel. The anchor announced there might be disturbing images, and he wasn't kidding. The hostages looked bloody, beaten, and ragged. But then two faces jumped out of the crowd, and Dylan wasn't the only one who noticed. Fisher spotted the pair too.

"Holy shit—"

"Yeah," Dylan said.

The others in the room muttered about not knowing what was going on. Fisher said, "Dylan's people," and returned to the phone. "Yes, I'm still here."

Dylan tuned his boss out as he watched. The gunmen led the hostages through a pair of double doors into a wide conference room. He frowned. Why were the terrorists giving away key information? The location of the hostages should have remained secret. Unless they didn't care if authorities knew where they were because there'd be no time for a rescue attempt.

He hoped Slayton and Reema had a plan. Or at least a

trick up their sleeve. He didn't like feeling powerless, sitting and watching. But it didn't make much difference. He was useless where he was at. Everything rested on the NYPD, local FBI, and two CIA officers who weren't supposed to get mixed up in the mess.

45

THE LOCAL FBI CREW VIEWED THE HOTEL FOOTAGE AND NOTED the careless inclusion of some of the gunmen. Counter-terrorist agents began identifying the gunmen and searched for related connections. There had to be a local support network other than the restaurant; something to tie the gun crew to the city.

Police, FBI, and emergency crews filled the streets in front and on either side of the building. The FBI negotiators gathered under a large quick tent. They'd set up tables and communication gear under the canopy. Power came from a large, ubiquitous "FBI surveillance" van. The van also contained the computers needed to tap into the national intelligence database.

Police occupied the lobby. They'd cordoned off the area taken over by the terrorists. Their job was evacuation. Get the remaining guests out safe and questioned, in case they had seen anything of value to help the rescue effort.

* * *

THE ONLY CONCERN on Special Agent Jay Kramer's mind was first contact. But he had to wait till the evac finished. He stood under the quick tent, his team beside him, with his arms folded and jaw tight.

"How much longer?"

Kramer directed the question to the woman beside him, S.A. Sylvia Osborne. The fact she stood two inches taller than him and could have used some of the extra pounds he carried on her skinny frame, didn't bother him. They were expert negotiators. A well-oiled machine.

"Another half hour," she said.

"Okay." *It wasn't.* "We'll be all set when they're done." *They already were.* Kramer hated waiting but knew the value of patience in a case such as this. Rushing through would cost lives. The lives he wanted to save.

Kramer adjusted his glasses and scratched his goatee. He had more hair on his chin than his head and dyed the goatee to cover flecks of gray.

Cops exited the hotel with group after group of civilians. The hotel guests appeared uninjured but supercharged with panic. Kramer shook his head. Luckily one of the members of his team was an expert on jihad activity. He'd need the input.

They'd barricaded the media half a block away, but Kramer thought the camera crews were still too close. He wished he had the authority to order the news choppers high above out of the area.

And it was a hot day. He'd removed the jacket he wore with his gray suit. But per regulations, he'd not loosened his tie.

Police escorted two more groups of guests out of the building. Then the NYPD captain radioed. He said they'd cleared the rooms and the only people still inside were the terrorists and the hostages.

Sylvia Osborne acknowledged and turned to Kramer. "Ready?"

"Let's call 'em."

Kramer approached the table, ignoring the spread of gear for his primary tool. The telephone. Each of the hotel's conference rooms had a dedicated extension. Kramer dialed to connect to the room occupied by the hostage-takers. Sylvia listened on her own handset, as did the man on his left. The third member of the team was Melvin Buckholm, the jihad specialist.

The phone rang three times. Kramer tuned out the street noise, including the overhead helicopters.

The other end of the line clicked.

"Is this the FBI?"

Kramer glanced at his coworkers. The man on the other end spoke without an accent. The voice surprised them.

"This is Special Agent Kramer speaking."

"And how is your day, Special Agent Kramer?"

"It will be a great day if we can save some lives and settle whatever matters you'd like to discuss."

"We have much to discuss."

"What's your name?"

"I am Tareef Mansur."

Buckholm, the jihad expert, wrote the name down on a sheet of notebook paper.

"Hello, Tareef," Kramer continued. "How can we help you today? We don't want anybody else hurt."

"Our demands are simple. I represent our leader. He wants to address the nation and expose your government's corruption."

"Is your leader here?" Kramer said.

"No. We have a live stream set up and will broadcast video of his message."

"I see," said Kramer.

"We know you've evacuated the hotel. I hope you noted we did not interfere."

"Your restraint did not go unnoticed, Tareef. And we very much appreciate what you did. Before I can help you, I need you to do something more for me."

"It's too early to ask for a favor, Special Agent."

"Hear me out. I'd like you to release two or three hostages, ones who need medical attention. We'll get them taken care of, and then we can get the TV people here to see about your broadcast."

"Not good enough."

"Tareef, I don't tell the TV people what to do. They need to come in on the conversation, do you understand?"

Mansur went quiet. Kramer stayed focused on the building.

"I understand," Mansur said. "How do I reach you?"

Kramer gave him the number to his phone and assured Mansur he was the only person who'd answer.

"I'll call back in fifteen minutes."

The line clicked in Kramer's ear. He placed the phone back on its cradle. He turned to Buckholm.

"He's the guy we've been tracking," the jihad expert said. "Couple raids today—no joy. Then he turned up here."

"Great," Kramer said. "The agents in charge of following him?"

Buckholm gestured at the hotel. He shook his head.

"Great," Kramer said again.

"He's not stressed," Sylvia Osborne said.

"Very calm considering how many people they murdered."

* * *

Tareef hooked the phone and turned to face the hostages. All eyes focused on him, his side of the conversation. His men watched him too.

"That was the FBI," he announced. He didn't move from the wall where the phone hung. "They would like me to release two or three of you who need medical attention. The most immediate attention, that is."

Excited murmurs rose from the hostages. Tareef raised his hands and asked for quiet. He still held his handgun. The talking ceased. Tareef directed Saleet to make the selections. The younger man left the bomb and ventured into the group.

46

Slayton and Reema watched from the back wall.

"What do you think they said?" she whispered.

"I don't know. Whatever they asked for, looks like Mansur is complying."

"Which means his goal—"

"Is whatever he's doing with the live stream."

"It's a strange request."

"No."

"What do you mean?"

"The broadcast is everything. October Blood isn't interested in a big attack."

"They want a propaganda victory."

"Yes. They're going to expose the conspiracy," Slayton said.

"And do our job for us."

"What will the cost be? The government won't be able to contain the fallout now."

"Maybe it should be that way."

"I'm not so sure."

"Well," Reema said, "we're about to find out the hard way."

* * *

"Special Agent Kramer."

"I'm listening, Tareef."

"We have made our selection. You will send two people, two people only, to collect the injured hostages. My men will place them outside the door. Do not make a move until I direct you to do so."

"We will follow your instructions, Tareef."

Mansur left the line but did not hang up. Kramer plugged his left ear with a finger. He heard voices in the background, some he didn't understand, but he heard some English too.

Two minutes later:

"Send your people now."

"Tareef—"

The terrorist hung up.

* * *

A police officer and a paramedic entered the hotel. Kramer, Sylvia, and the other FBI agents watched from under the tent.

Melvin Buckholm returned from the van. He pulled Kramer aside and consulted scratches on a notepad.

"Got anything?"

"Perry's file. This guy Mansur is former al-Qaeda. Oxford-educated. Long record."

"What do you think?"

"This guy wants to get on TV," Buckholm said.

"That's all?"

"Strange as it sounds, yeah."

"Will they let us see this broadcast first?"

"Hell no. You can ask."

"I can *ask* anything."

The cop and paramedic exited with three hostages. Only one needed the support of the medic to walk. As far as he was from the glass doors, Kramer had trouble making out the extent of the injuries.

"Let's get some TV people over here," Kramer said, "and get them involved."

Sylvia and two other agents left to get what Kramer asked for.

* * *

Tareef Mansur, gun in hand, walked among the hostages once more.

"You can see we are not unreasonable. The rest of you need not fear for your lives. We've asked for nothing more than for our voices to be heard."

Slayton listened to the words. Mansur remained steady and unemotional.

He thought about the bomb. How did it play into the endgame?

If Mansur killed the hostages, any propaganda win would be moot. They'd give the government the opportunity to claim his video contained nothing but lies.

Mansur continued. "The FBI appears to be reasonable as well. Take heart. You may be home before you know it."

Reema leaned close. "He's lying."

Slayton didn't reply.

Did he and Reema have a chance to end this? Wait till

the broadcast, and open fire when the enemy's tasks distracted them?

If they were distracted.

The phone on the wall rang. Slayton jumped at the shrill sound.

Tareef Mansur hurried to answer.

* * *

"Yes?"

"Tareef?"

"Who else, Special Agent Kramer?"

"We have people from the TV stations here. How do you propose to get your broadcast to them?"

Mansur put away his gun and snapped his fingers at his men. They sprang into action at the table. He said into the phone, "We have an internet address. A specific website for our message. They can re-transmit from the site."

"Hang on."

Mansur listened to the hurried discussion. He only deciphered bits and pieces of the conversation.

When Kramer returned to the line, he said, "Give me the web address, Tareef."

Mansur repeated the web address twice, and confirmed Kramer's read back.

"Are you live now?" the FBI man asked.

"Ten minutes."

"I'll call you back."

Tareef hung up the phone. He went to the table and issued instructions.

* * *

Any hope Slayton had of the terrorist crew being distracted evaporated. Only two manned the computers and equipment. The other three held on to their AKMs and watched the hostages.

Wouldn't have worked anyway, he decided.

The FBI and NYPD had questioned the three released hostages by now, he figured. They'd know the full situation and the layout. They'd know about the steel case if any one of them had noticed. Slayton didn't see how they could gloss over the detail.

There was no way into the conference room except the main doors. No SWAT breach through the roof. No blasting through the walls.

But he and Reema couldn't sit still. Not when so many lives remained at risk.

Think, dammit!

Slayton's body tensed. Reema noticed. She touched his leg. He relaxed.

There has to be a way...

Reema gasped.

Slayton covered her with his right arm and pulled her close to him. She buried her face against his neck.

He saw the face on the projection screen too.

Kameel al-Rashid.

The feed was live. Mansur and Kameel exchanged greetings, and Mansur gave him a summary of the events so far. Kameel listened without comment.

The phone rang. Mansur excused himself the answer.

Slayton held Reema close. One of the gunmen turned the video camera to the hostages. If al-Rashid had a feed of the conference room, he didn't want the October Blood commander to see her face in the crowd.

"Hang on, babe."

Reema squeezed him tight.

* * *

DYLAN SHARP SAID, "I'm still here, Agent Osborne."

Dylan and DDO Fisher now stood in the Z Section control room, having departed Fisher's office. They watched a row of large monitors on a wall. The screens showed the activity outside the New Continental Hotel.

Analysts sat before them. They worked their various terminals, taking in the data as it occurred on scene. One of the screens switched from the street view to the feed from the terrorists. Dylan and Fisher watched the calm face of Kameel al-Rashid.

"He's in a hotel room," Fisher remarked. "Can we trace the signal? Find something in this image we can match to a location?"

"Working on it, sir," one of the analysts said.

"He'll know we'll try this," Dylan said.

"Repeat," Agent Osborne said in Dylan's left ear.

"Nothing, Agent Osborne. We have the feed. Be advised we have two operatives among the hostages."

"Copy. Can they help?"

"I don't know. They won't jeopardize the plan."

The FBI wanted the TV stations to run the terrorist's internet feed. It would keep them calm, make them think they had their way. While the feed transmitted, the CIA would attempt a trace. The FBI SWAT team would plan their entry into the conference room. It sounded good in theory.

"Is SWAT on site?" Dylan asked Osborne.

"Yes. They're going over the hotel layout. The three

hostages they let go have been very helpful with other details."

"We have the trace running," Dylan said. "Carry on."

"Wait one."

Dylan paused while Sylvia Osborne left the line.

Fisher pointed out, "Al-Rashid looks anxious."

Dylan let the comment go. Fisher was only filling empty space.

Kameel began talking, his voice coming through the control room speakers. He wasn't starting his speech but instead answering questions from the other end of his feed. They were waiting for the New York TV stations to confirm receipt of the web stream.

Fisher said, "There must be another way to play this. We're giving them too much."

"Second-guessing won't help, Chris. FBI thinks it will work."

"I don't like only being a spectator, Dylan."

"I know."

Sylvia Osborne came back on the line. "TV has the signal. They're going with it despite opposition from the mayor and others."

"We're watching," Dylan told her.

Fisher said, "Time to call the White House," and left the room.

Dylan kept his eyes on the monitors. How the broadcast would play out was top of mind of every person in the room. They could only watch and stare at the video feed.

47

Television screens across New York City and the nation displayed the face of Kameel al-Rashid. The feed wasn't perfect. Distorted pixels crossed the screen at regular intervals. But his voice was clear.

"Greetings, Americans. My name is Kameel al-Rashid. I am the commander of October Blood. You'd call me a terrorist, but your own government are the real terrorists, and I will explain how.

"I will show you, with plenty of video evidence, how your government created an enemy out of nothing. The goal was to perpetuate your so-called War on Terror, the outcome of which is continued fighting, needless deaths, and profits for your military-industrial complex.

"Your government, for too long, has depended on mercenaries to fight your war on my people. You call them private military contractors, but they *are* mercenaries, soldiers for hire, paid to kill.

"Three years ago..."

* * *

DYLAN SHARP PACED the control room. Fisher stood still with his eyes on the screen. He'd not said what transpired with his call to the president. Dylan didn't want to ask.

"He's telling the whole story," Fisher said as they watched.

Dylan stopped short, fixed on the screen, as al-Rashid began showing his video evidence.

The first "exhibit" was a two-way video conversation. Spencer Wolf and the late Faisil Ashraf appeared side-by-side. Al-Rashid made sure to identify the participants. He also explained Wolf's background before the video played.

"I'm impressed with the detail," Dylan remarked.

"The president is going ape shit," Fisher said. "He's barely processed what we've told him so far, and now *this*."

Dylan sensed his boss's anger, and shared it, but saw little to gain by expressing angry emotion. Their job was to clean up the mess. He had a feeling they'd be busy well into the future.

* * *

REEMA PEEKED at the projection screen as the Wolf / Faisil conversation played. She wiped away a tear at the sound of her half brother's voice.

Slayton said, "Is this what we needed to recover in Syria?"

"Yes."

They listened further. The first video ended, and Kameel returned to the screen. He explained more about the conspiracy. His voice rose in anger as he told how many recruits joined the organization and had no idea they were set up to die.

Al-Rashid's face filled the screen.

"I spoke many times with Faisil about our plans," he said, "only for him to rebuff me every time. I don't think Faisil ever *had* an action plan, but he sent our fighters into the world anyway. They were pawns, an excuse to fight. An enemy created to keep your military killing innocent people who only want to live in peace.

"But you won't let us live in peace. Your government is addicted to war, with no plan to ever stop. You spread your death squads around the globe in the name of defending your nation. From whom? Farmers and sheep herders? Think about this, America. You bring this horror on yourselves. We *never* wanted this fight. We only wanted to be left alone. But you won't leave us alone..."

The tirade continued. Kameel paused to catch his breath and play more "evidence" videos. Their own words solidified al-Rashid's point about October Blood's creation.

Reema buried her face in Slayton's neck again. "We have to do something."

The feed carried on...

* * *

Reema played out scenarios in her mind. How she and Jack might take out the gunmen. How they might diffuse the bomb in the steel case...

What if Mansur and his men planned to blow themselves up with the hostages?

Because Reema didn't see how they'd escape alive. Law enforcement surrounded the hotel.

Did they really have *suicide* in mind?

Nothing she considered kept the hostages alive. She and Slayton might get the terrorists, but they'd get some of the hostages in the crossfire.

How many losses could they accept?

"Jack?"

"Hmmm."

"We don't have a choice. We do something soon or we all die."

* * *

ONE OF THE CIA analysts at Z Section held up a hand. Dylan and Fisher went over to her and examined the computer screen.

"What do you have?" Fisher asked.

"The signal. It bounces around but keeps returning to Berlin more than anywhere else. I think it's the origin."

"Can you narrow it down?"

"Trying, sir."

Dylan, still on the phone with the FBI, waved Fisher over. The DDO went to him as Dylan cupped the phone receiver's mouthpiece.

"They're going in."

"I hope it's the right move," Fisher said.

* * *

"AND NOW, America, your leaders must respond to my statements. I expect them to lie to you, and it is up to—"

Slayton nudged Reema.

The image on the projector screen flickered and froze. Tareef hurried to the table; even the gunmen who kept watch over the hostages turned their heads away.

Slayton and Reema rose and took out their pistols.

Front sight, squeeze...

The mantra echoed through Slayton's mind as he

settled the sights on his first target. He fired once, twice; began shouting, "Hostages down!" as he shifted his aim. He and Reema repeated the command. Slayton fired again, the gunman he aimed at turning, and as he completed his turn, Slayton's 9mm slug hit him in the face. Slayton shifted again. Reema's pistol cracked; a terrorist seated at the table dropped from her rapid fire.

Slayton swung the CZ on Tareef Mansur. As Tareef drew his gun and began to extend his arm, Slayton fired twice. The front of Mansur's shirt puckered as the pair of rounds impacted. Mansur's legs gave out and he collapsed, dead before he hit the carpet.

The doors blew open with a sudden explosion. The force of the blast shoved Slayton and Reema off their feet. They landed on the floor, Slayton turning his head to see the FBI SWAT team storming into the room.

More calls of "Hostages down!" but the FBI men had no terrorists to shoot. The team split. Some converged on the hostages, others approached the bodies up front. Slayton felt a heavy weight on him as a SWAT shooter put a knee on his back and wrenched his arms around to zip-tie his wrists. They gave Reema the same treatment. Neither argued and kept their mouths shut. Slayton turned his attention to the still-frozen image on the projection screen. The defiant face of Kameel al-Rashid.

You're next.

48

SLAYTON WAS IN NO MOOD TO TALK, BUT THEY STILL HAD A LOT TO talk about regarding events in NYC.

Getting free of the FBI and out of New York City had almost taken an act of Congress. Slayton and Reema satisfied the FBI about their involvement. But the session took most of the day following the attack. Travel back to Virginia took most of the next day.

Now Slayton and Reema had to explain everything to the CIA. They were in separate interview rooms with Dylan going back and forth.

The decision to send in the FBI SWAT team, Slayton learned, came after the three released hostages told them about the bomb.

"Was it a bomb?" Slayton asked. He and Dylan finally had a moment to themselves, the stern interviewer out of the room.

"Yup," Dylan said.

"What about al-Rashid?"

Dylan shook his head. "Here's what happened. One of our analysts identified the hotel he was staying in by the pattern on the wallpaper. The web signal corresponded; he was in Berlin. Emphasis on *was*. By the time German police kicked down the door, he was gone."

"We can't leave him out there in the wild."

"Nope."

"Think he's still in Berlin?"

"I'd bet on it. Nothing he does will give him a fast exit."

Slayton saw the strain on Dylan's face and felt for him. He felt whipped too. They all three needed a rest. But Slayton couldn't stop until he planted a bullet in al-Rashid's guts.

If the man was still in Germany, Slayton wanted to find him.

* * *

KAMEEL AL-RASHID KNEW when the web feed froze; what he couldn't do was attempt to restore it. He had two monitors in front of him. One showed a split screen allowing him to select and play the video evidence. The other showed him a point-of-view shot of the hostages. He had the ability to see their reactions. And while the web feed may have frozen, the camera shot at the hostages had not.

Any sense of victory he felt vanished as the gunfire began. Worse, he recognized the woman firing.

Reema Ashraf.

She'd gone to the Americans?

Or maybe she'd been with them from the beginning.

He closed down his equipment and packed fast, vacating the hotel with haste. He left the computer gear behind.

They'd ruined his plan. Worse—

They killed Tareef and Saleet.

Kameel left the building and hopped into a taxi. He directed the driver to Berlin Central Station. But he had no intention of boarding a train. He used a locker to store his luggage, then hailed another cab to take him to yet another address. An apartment. Where a contact waited.

Nassaar Mohammed went by "John" and taught at the Berlin University of Applied Sciences. Kameel did not call ahead. Once the cab driver dropped him off, he took the elevator to Mohammed's floor and knocked on the door. He tapped a rapid code and tried to calm his beating heart. He glanced up and down the hall. Nervous sweat coated his body; made his shirt stick to his back.

Nassaar Mohammed answered with his own look of alarm. He was older than Kameel, and very much resembled a university professor. Bald head, pudgy; a man who lived the soft life. He let Kameel inside without comment, closed and locked the door.

"What is it, Kameel?"

"The CIA. They're after me..." He explained the New York City mission.

"Go sit. I will make tea."

They sat on either side of Mohammed's couch. The tea tasted good and finally settled Kameel's nerves.

"Tell me again what happened."

Kameel offered more detail the second time. Mohammed listened without comment.

When Kameel finished, Mohammed said, "What do you want to do?"

"I want to go to the United States and kill the people who killed my friend."

"How are you going to find them?"

"I don't know."

"If they are looking for you, you will not get into the US

easily. They will capture or kill you before you have a chance to avenge your friends."

"I can't let them get away with this. Especially her."

"The smarter move is to hide until you can pick a better time."

"I know. Deep down, I *know* that. But I can't—"

"You must."

"You've been out of it too long, Nassaar. You don't know what it's like anymore."

"You forget, Kameel, how many friends I've lost in the fight, too. I do know."

"What am I supposed to do? They will come to Berlin first or use agents-in-place. Then they will look in Syria."

"You know how to hide in Syria, Kameel. Don't lie to me."

Kameel contemplated the tea still in his mug.

"If you want another option," Mohammed continued, "I have a suggestion."

"What?"

Kameel didn't like the suggestion at first. Slowly, it dawned on him Mohammed was right.

He took the option.

* * *

"How many guns did you bring?" Reema asked.

Slayton glanced at her with a raised eyebrow. "Only my pistol. What do you think we'll need heavy artillery for?"

"You never know," she said. Reema drove the rented black Audi. They traveled through nighttime Berlin in light traffic. They were on a mission to track down Kameel al-Rashid once and for all.

Z Section's best guess was Kameel remained in the city,

but only for a short time. Slayton and Reema had a list of known "people movers" to visit. The kind with the know-how and experience at helping fugitives escape capture. It was no guarantee. But it was a start.

Nighttime Berlin resembled any other major city across the world. Buildings big and small, bright lights and signs. Slayton didn't bother to take note of anything. He'd been there before, and it was nothing he hadn't seen before. Too much of the world left him unimpressed now. Since McDonalds had conquered the globe, world travel wasn't interesting any longer.

Reema reached the autobahn and accelerated. The Audi zoomed along with the faster traffic. Other cars were bright flashes of headlamps alongside them.

Their first target was a man named Lex Hahn. Arms dealer. Smuggler.

Reema continued, "Hahn may have agreed to see us, but he'll have plenty of gunners. He can be paranoid. Thinks everybody is out to get him."

"If he'd deal with a better class of people, he'd sleep okay at night."

Reema kept driving. She slowed for an exit and made a left at the end of the ramp. Slayton's security scan increased. Old storefronts and warehouses. Most closed. Streetlights minimal. Most of the streetlights were broken—not shining at all or flickering rapidly. Unusual for Germany, Slayton decided. He remembered a time when the lack of maintenance would have embarrassed the entire city. Nothing was like it used to be anymore.

"How much further?" he asked.

"Another couple blocks."

Slayton wanted the night over. He wanted a solid lead.

Hopefully we get both...

49

Alexander "Lex" Hahn paced the walkway in front of his warehouse office.

His nondescript warehouse sat nestled among many such structures covering a three-block area. And his wasn't the biggest. No signs identified who owned the warehouse, and his was the only one minus such displays. It didn't matter. Nobody who worked along the three blocks paid attention. One warehouse was the same as another, and if it wasn't the one signing your check, why bother?

If anybody asked, Lex Hahn explained he sold wholesale maritime machine parts. If anybody wanted to look, he had crates full of such gear. The crates were an illusion. He hid the real items he sold under the warehouse floor in steel-lined compartments. The hidden caches contained enough weapons to fight a small conflict. Hahn had simple policy. He sold to whoever had money to pay. He charged a premium and rarely budged from the set price.

He wasn't familiar with the new potential clients on the way to see him. They had checked out, though. He wasn't worried about them bringing a raiding party. But, because he never left such things to chance, he had a small squad of shooters with him. He needed to make sure the pair caused no problems. His crew had moved the crates of machine parts around to use as cover in case a gun battle broke out.

Hahn had enemies, usually competitors. Thugs who wanted to steal his inventory hassled him too.

He rested his hands on the walkway railing. His office sat on the second level, and he overlooked the partially lit warehouse floor. The lack of full lighting created a mass of shadows across the floor below. The shadows offered plenty of places for his men to conceal themselves.

Hahn liked to wear his wealth. His Saville Roe suit hadn't come cheap, nor his gold-rimmed glasses and matching Rolex. Smuggling paid well. He glanced at the Rolex. Another five minutes until the new clients arrived. Hahn ignored the nervous rumbles in his gut. He had to remain calm.

* * *

REEMA TURNED the Audi into the warehouse parking lot. Slayton didn't see much in the brief pass of the headlamps. But he did see two men waiting outside near the open loading bay. One held up a hand. Reema stopped the car. The two men approached.

"This had better work," she said.

"I'll do the talking."

"We don't have much time for talking, Jack."

"I know."

Slayton and Reema powered down their windows. Cold air entered the car. The two men came along either side to examine them. The man on Slayton's side shined a light on his face, then consulted his cell phone. The glow of the screen lit his face. The man was older than Slayton would have expected, his face marked with wrinkles and scar tissue. He put away the phone.

"All right," the man said. "You match your picture." To his buddy on Reema's side: "She all right?"

The man near Reema's door, younger and fitter than his counterpart, didn't hide his leer. "She's fine."

"Not what I mean, smart ass."

"It's her."

The older man leaned into Slayton's window. "Go in. Keep it slow. Stop before you hit the crates."

Reema fed the Audi gas and entered the warehouse. The headlamps highlighted two crates in front of the car. She braked. A gunman stood between the two crates, his submachine gun dangling from a shoulder sling. His eyes took in Slayton and Reema. Slayton reminded himself not to make any sudden moves till everybody calmed down. Hahn was letting them see only part of the crew he'd called to join the meeting.

"Step out," called the gunner.

Slayton exited first. Reema shifted the car into park and followed him. From the second level overlooking their entry, a spotlight flared. The bright beam landed on Slayton's face. He blocked enough of the glare with his left hand to see two men on the upper-level walkway. He didn't bother with the man holding the light, but the second man was for sure Lex Hahn.

* * *

THE SMUGGLER'S voice was loud in the shadowy confines of the warehouse.

"Forgive my precautions. Until we get to know one another, I need to be careful."

"No problem," Slayton called back. "We need your help."

"You're Americans?"

"Yes."

"Why do Americans need my help?"

"We're looking for someone, and there is money in it for you if you know where this someone is."

Slayton explained the reason for their visit without saying who he and Reema worked for. Hahn listened without interrupting. When Slayton finished, he waited for a reply. The gunner at the crates shifted, but Slayton didn't sense aggression.

"I don't know any terrorists in Berlin, sir. Syrian or otherwise. They do not advertise themselves."

"Nobody's asked you to help them out of the country?"

"I sell guns. I don't smuggle people."

"Lex, don't lie to me."

"Your information is not correct. I am shady, but I am not a liar."

"Think hard, Lex."

Hahn paused. The spotlight didn't waver, and Slayton's eyes hurt from the glare.

"You act as if I am a suspect."

"If you were a suspect," Slayton replied, "we wouldn't be talking. I'd have your nipples connected to a car battery."

"I have no information to share, sir. You have wasted enough of my time. I suggest you and your lady friend—"

But what Hahn wanted to suggest, he never had a chance to say.

An explosion shook the warehouse. A flash of flame from the opposite side lit the interior for a moment, then faded. Gunmen dressed in dark combat garb rushed inside with crackling automatic weapons.

The spotlight winked out and left Slayton with spots across his vision. Somebody nearby began shouting orders, and Hahn's men broke cover to engage the invaders. Bullets zipped through the air and chewed into the wooden crates. More slugs pinged off steel beams. Slayton dug out his P-10C, the checkered grip of the polymer-framed pistol digging into his palm. The gunner nearest him and Reema lifted his weapon at them; Slayton shot the gunner in the face. He pivoted right to fire at the unknown attackers as they spread through the building. Hahn's men met their barrage of auto-fire with salvos of their own.

Reema shouted, "Come on!"

She'd already dropped behind the wheel, shifted the car in reverse, her foot on the brake. Slayton fired in rapid succession. Flame pulsed from the CZ's barrel as he worked through the magazine. Then he dove into the Audi. Reema stomped the accelerator. The two men who had greeted them jumped clear as she screeched onto the pavement. A stray bullet nicked the Audi's left fender and whined into the night. With her head craned over her right shoulder, Reema reversed onto the street. She spun the car in a bootlegger's 180-degree turn and the tires screeched in protest. She shifted into drive and stomped the pedal again. A bullet smacked the back window, creating a tight spider crack, and the slug *chunked* into the dashboard.

Slayton reloaded his gun and stowed it back in the shoulder rig. "What the hell was that?"

Reema glanced in the rearview. "They came for us. Got another car closing fast."

"Do something, honey."

Reema only grunted in reply. Her eyes focused on the road.

Slayton fastened his seat belt. Reema cut off the exterior lights and made a tight right turn. She was taking them back the way they'd come.

"They're getting close."

Two shots thumped into the Audi's body.

"Find a spot in the dark," Slayton said. He took out his gun again. "Should have brought more guns."

"Should have brought a bazooka."

"Wouldn't fit in the trunk."

Reema spun the wheel left. She bumped onto the driveway of another warehouse and steered across the lot to the side of the building. No lights—and the building blocked them from the street, too. Slayton and Reema left the car and ran. Slayton clutched his CZ, while Reema drew her own Beretta 92FS. They ran along the wall of the warehouse. Slayton tried doors as they passed them. All locked. And no cover around. The usual German efficiency was at work on the property. The parking lot was spotless.

"Go to the corner ahead," Slayton said.

He cut left across the open space. Reema didn't argue. Slayton dropped flat on the dry blacktop, facing the way they'd come, and trained his gun forward.

The enemy car stopped behind the Audi. Doors opened and shut. Three men with sub guns spread out, and the car moved slowly behind them. They followed the same path as Slayton and Reema. They checked the doors, too.

Slayton took a breath. He was out in the open. When the car's headlamps found him—

Further to the right, the lot ended at a chain-link fence.

Can't get out that way...

Gotta keep them away from Reema...

It wasn't hard to figure out the scenario. Kameel al-Rashid had more resources in Berlin than Z Section had given him credit for. They were watching "the usual suspects" same as the CIA. All they had to do was wait and see who the two American operatives visited first.

Keep them from Reema...

The glowing night sights of the CZ pistol gave him a good picture. He eased back the trigger and the gun fired. One of the three gunmen pitched over as the 9mm hollow point found its mark. The other two opened fire with their subguns, the twin streams flying overhead. Slayton stayed low, but the pavement prevented him from going lower. He fired twice and rolled right. As he stopped, the enemy car with its bright halogen headlamps veered at him. The driver sped up. Slayton was again spotlighted. He fired rapidly as he rolled left. The car shot by, turning before hitting the chain link. The driver U-turned for another pass.

Focus.

Slayton fired twice more as the sub gunners scattered. One ran to the cover of the Audi. The other ran at Slayton. Tires screeched behind him. The engine surged. Slayton hit the onrushing gunner with two shots. The gunner struck the pavement and tumbled. Slayton jumped up, holstered his pistol, and ran for the fallen gunner's weapon.

More gunfire. Reema joining the fight. Tires popped; glass shattered. As Slayton dove for the dead gunner's sub gun, grasping it with both hands, he rolled once again. The enemy car no longer mattered, and its lights shined on the Audi. Slayton and the last man raised their weapons. Slayton fired first. He dumped the burst into the gunner's chest, knocking him back against the Audi. He then slid to the ground.

"Jack!"

Reema stopped beside Slayton and helped him to his feet.

"I got the driver," she said.

"Let's get out of here."

They ran back to the Audi. Slayton dragged the dead gunner away to allow Reema to get behind the wheel. She sped off and flipped the car through a tight U-turn before Slayton had his door shut.

50

THEY WAITED TILL MORNING TO CONTACT A GERMAN FEDERAL agent named Hugo Muntz. Slayton knew Muntz from previous missions in Berlin. Reema gave him a hard time for once again not reaching out when they first arrived.

Slayton made the call after breakfast. He reached Muntz after three rings.

"Muntz," the German answered.

"Hugo. It's Jack Slayton."

"Hello, my friend."

"I'm in Berlin."

A chuckle. "I know."

Of course, you do. "I'd like to talk to you. Can we get a beer?"

"I will forgive your tardy phone call if you have the fifty euros you owe me from your last visit."

"For heaven's sake, Hugo."

"Do you have it?"

Slayton hoped Hugo Muntz would have forgotten the money by now. "I have it."

"Then yes. We will get beer and have a conversation. I will pick you up in an hour."

Slayton also wasn't surprised Muntz already knew where they were staying. He suggested Reema stay in the room and report to headquarters. He met Muntz outside the hotel an hour later. Slayton pulled the passenger door closed. Muntz didn't move the vehicle.

"What?" Slayton said. "Why are you staring at me?"

Hugo Muntz wore a gray suit, but his attire wasn't what anybody noticed when they first set eyes on him. He was tall and wide with a shock of white hair and matching bushy mustache. He smiled with a mischievous glint in both eyes.

"Let's see the money," the German federal cop said.

When Slayton last visited Berlin, a year earlier, he'd met a young lady from Muntz's team who agreed to a date. At the time, Slayton found himself short of funds. Muntz loaned him the money and saved the night, but Slayton couldn't shake Reema's then-ghost easily. Neither the young lady nor Slayton wanted to see each other again after their first evening.

And Slayton didn't want Reema to know, hence his suggestion she sit out the meeting.

He pulled the bills from his shirt pocket.

"Give," Muntz said.

Slayton handed over the money.

"Now," the German said, "we can talk about a bunch of bodies in Lex Hahn's warehouse. And elsewhere," he added.

Muntz put the car in gear and drove.

* * *

The big German was an agent for his nation's equivalent of the Federal Bureau of Investigation—the BfV, or Bundesamt fur Verfassungsschutz.

"Tell me what happened at the warehouse," Muntz said.

"Ask Hahn."

"He didn't make it."

"Really?"

"Tell me what happened at the warehouse."

Slayton explained the reason for questioning Hahn, and the attack from the unknown subjects. He ended with him and Reema fighting off the extra carload.

Muntz grinned. The glint in his eyes gave Slayton a bad feeling. The German fed was about to spring something on him.

"What are you grinning at, Hugo?"

Muntz refused to answer and told Slayton to sit and enjoy the ride.

"We're going to the morgue," Muntz said with a straight face.

* * *

Slayton shivered despite the jacket. The morgue attendant pulled three of the six cooler drawers open. The bodies shared similar features. Bony faces, dark hair, dark complexions. Muntz said there was no reason to look at all six. On the other side of the cold room, he added, were more of the same—including Lex Hahn and his associates.

"One side full of known criminals like Lex Hahn nobody but their mothers will miss," the German fed said. He made no effort to keep Slayton from examining each body. "But this group," he continued, "makes life very difficult."

"Why?" Slayton asked.

"Tell me what you notice."

"Military-aged men, similar haircuts, similar builds."

"Do they look German to you?"

"Hugo, half of Germany doesn't look German any longer."

"If you had to guess—"

"A terrorist cell. Connected to al-Rashid. We didn't think he had the resources here for anything like this."

"Bingo. We've checked these men back to front. They're students at the University of Applied Sciences. They are the protégés of a professor named Mohammed Nassaar, who goes by the name John. They didn't only hit Hahn, by the way. Another group ambushed a smuggler named Alfie Neuman, and another named Helmut Nichol."

"Why target—"

"What do you think?"

"They want to take out anybody who moves people. Or *can* move people."

"Why?"

"Exactly." Slayton forgot the chill as his mind connected the dots. "They're taking out the usual suspects to throw us off. But who else will they use?"

"Let's get out of this cold place. I have an informant we should go see, but she won't be available till tonight when her nightclub opens."

"Who's your informant?"

"A woman named Elke Becker. She has a lot of friends in low places."

* * *

Slayton continued the thought process as Muntz drove.

"What do they gain with murdering smugglers?"

"Keep us preoccupied," Muntz said. "We'll be chasing false leads while they arrange with lesser players we aren't considering."

"But al-Rashid knows—"

"You're here, yes. He made a specific attempt to get rid of you. He may try a second time."

And I left Reema alone...

Slayton dialed Reema's cell and let out a breath when she answered. He told her he was on the way back.

"She's okay?" Muntz said.

"Yes," Slayton said. "Who might these lesser players be?"

"Anybody. But my informant may be able to narrow it down. She runs with an odd crowd. They smuggle drugs, stuff like that. Al-Rashid can coach them on how to get him out of the country, perhaps."

"I don't see al-Rashid using amateurs."

"If they are off our radar, then so is he."

"You have a point," Slayton said.

"We will get him, my friend. We only need to be patient."

Slayton hoped so.

"What about this professor you mentioned?" Slayton asked.

"We have people watching him. We will know if al-Rashid shows up again."

* * *

Elke Becker opened the center drawer of her desk.

Her gun sat among the clutter within. She hadn't fired the old Walther P-5 in some time. She hoped she didn't need it tonight. Because if Darius found out what she was doing, he'd go for her throat.

She shut the drawer.

Patrons packed her club as usual. Bass notes from the DJ booth vibrated through the floor. Some club managers found the constant shaking a source of irritation. For Elke, the longer the floor vibrated, the more money she made.

Dance Berlin had become one of the premiere party places in the city. It had almost bankrupted her in the beginning. But now her labor of love was a thriving business.

Elke Becker wasn't the type of woman a conservative Catholic would take home to Mom. Curvy and plump all around, her bright blond hair matched her pale white skin. A black corset narrowed her middle to accentuate her hips and breasts. A black bullet tattoo sat smack between them. More colorful tats covered her shoulders and upper arms. Others covered by the corset and leather pants hid symbols representing the kind of people Germany worked hard to forget. Despite her extra weight, she had plenty of muscle and looked ready for a cage match.

Working as an informant for the BfV saved her from bankruptcy in the club's early days. Her unsavory connections often met at the club. She videoed every meeting. Often, the videos found their way to Hugo Muntz. And then money found its way to her account.

She expected to send him another video by the end of the night.

Darius had a meeting scheduled and asked her to reserve his usual back booth.

Her office door crashed open. Elke let out a clipped shriek. Then she sighed. "Dammit, Darius—"

Darius Kreigel, a big man with a spiked blond crew cut, laughed. He kicked the door shut and stalked toward her.

"I didn't think to call ahead. Since you're expecting me and all that."

"I'm busy." The mess of order forms on the desk confirmed the statement. But she left her squeaky chair and came around the desk to meet him. She tiptoed to kiss his cheek.

"Whoa, that's it!"

He grabbed her, shoving her back into the desk. She grunted as the edge dug into her behind. "Hey!"

"Come on. I'm early. We got time—" He tugged at the waistband of her leather pants. "Let's get out of these."

She had to look up at him. He ignored the anger on her face. He leered at her.

"*Not* now," she said.

"Come on—" as he pulled down her zipper and slipped fingers inside to feel her crotch.

Elke smacked him open-handed. The slap sounded like the crack of a pistol. Darius Kreigel recoiled as if the shot had struck him in the chest. He pulled back from her. Elke pulled up her zipper.

His face flushed red. "You little—"

"*Later*, you ass! We *both* have things to do, and you need your mind on your meeting."

"You're gonna get it. *Later.*"

"You'll get it right back."

"I'm counting on it," he said.

Their volatile relationship wasn't without benefits. Sleeping with the boss of a wannabe neo-Nazi gang involved in drug trafficking brought her plenty of nuggets to pass along to Hugo Muntz.

"Is my booth ready?"

"Yes."

"Good. Bring out the beers yourself like a good girl. Oh, and put on a coat. I think our guy is one of those religious nuts."

He laughed. And exited. He left the door open this time. She had to cross the office to close it.

51

Darius Kreigel liked the back booth. A partial wall blocked off part of the dance floor. He heard the music but had enough of a shield so the conversations he often hosted weren't overpowered. The noise provided another advantage. If somebody was watching them, they wouldn't hear a thing. Unless they knew how to read lips. Kreigel had yet to come up with a way to cover his mouth in such meetings.

Aside from his height, his spiked crew cut stood out the most. He had the blue eyes of many Germans; nobody noticed those. They noticed his haircut, his plentiful tattoos. None of the tats covered his face or neck, unlike some people under his employ.

Kreigel wasn't a true neo-Nazi, though he ran with them. They were a convenience and provided manpower and structure for his activities. He didn't care one way or another for the philosophy. *Or* the re-emergence of the Fourth Reich of the Fifth or Sixth or whatever number the bozos were up to now. What he liked was freedom. What he enjoyed was sticking it to authority. In his quiet moments, he admitted his lifestyle was a way of getting back at his strict parents. They'd tried to shape his growth with rules and punishment. He rebelled. The unintended consequence was his lifestyle also made him rich. Via drug sales.

Germans hooked on chemicals were no different than any other culture on the planet. They liked drugs; they liked *good* drugs; they were willing to pay, and Kreigel was happy to supply. His drug business brought him in touch with many other like-minded people. Some of them smuggled things other than drugs. Careful investments with those parties netted profitable returns.

The music held his attention. The DJ spun up-tempo tracks and the floor thumped with the beat. He liked to dance, too. He liked watching the girls on the dance floor. Most of them were fit and wore party dresses to show off their curves—or lack thereof, with the skinny ones. He liked curves. He liked Elke's curves.

Then he saw Elke leading a man toward him. She wore a long leather coat—good, she'd listened to him. The man with her had dark skin, a businessman's short haircut, and was overdressed in a tan suit. As he got closer, Kreigel noticed the scar on his face. But he had a fighter's build, a solid frame, and his eyes missed nothing. When his eyes settled on Kreigel, he stepped around Elke and dropped into the booth. Kreigel extended a hand across the table. The two men shook. Kreigel asked Elke to bring two beers —but the new arrival declined. She promised him water instead. She departed. The two men began their conversation.

* * *

ELKE WATCHED the video from her desk. A row of security monitors sat to the right of her chair. The audio came through a Bluetooth speaker. Their voices sounded clear despite the small amount of interference from the DJ.

The camera captured enough of the visitor's face to identify him.

"Never mind my name for now," the guest said. "If you must have one, call me Michael Jones."

"Okay."

Her phone rang. The landline on her desk. But the double ring meant the inside line. She muted the Bluetooth speaker and answered.

"What? He is? For what? All right, send him up. And the other two, fine."

Presently the office door opened. Elke scoffed as she stood. The door meant nothing to anybody. Any jackass who wanted could waltz into her office at will. She needed to start greeting such arrivals with a whip to the face.

"This is an odd hour for a sales call, Hugo," she said.

"We have a deal too good to miss," Muntz said, and walked toward her.

The two people with him, a man and a woman, both younger than Muntz, stayed back. The man shut the door.

"I have some questions—" Muntz began, but the dark-haired woman who looked too thin for her own good cut him off.

Her eyes widened at the sight on Elke's monitors.

"That's him! That's Kameel!"

* * *

Slayton moved beside Reema to look at the monitors. He had to force himself not to look at the curvy blond oozing out of her corset as if her pale skin was being squeezed out of a tube of Colgate. Women still wore corsets? He hadn't realized they still existed.

"Is there sound?" Slayton asked. "We came looking for this guy."

The blond casually flicked a switch, and the table conversation filled the office. Nobody spoke while they eavesdropped.

* * *

"...WE can do that, but how much are you planning on spending?"

"You can do it for ten thousand US," Kameel al-Rashid said. "Yes?"

"No. Ten grand will barely get you out of Germany. Pal, my friend, you need to go through Austria to Hungary and from there to Romania. I have no idea how to get you to Syria after that. You better pull a rabbit out of your hat."

"My what?"

"Forget it. I need fifty thousand US. Minimum. You got that much, or are you hitching a ride with gypsies hoping they don't kill you?"

Al-Rashid sighed. "I will do sixty thousand US. Does this three-country journey come with a guide?"

"You'll have a guide, yes," Kreigel said. "There are people who need to be paid off at several stages along the way."

"Acceptable."

"I thought it would be. It will take me twenty-four hours to make the proper arrangements. Then when it's time, you need to be ready."

"I'm ready now."

"You have a place to hide in the meantime?"

"I do."

"How do I reach you?"

Slayton pulled Muntz aside and spoke urgently.

"If we can follow him—"

"He'll run to Mohammed Nassaar, I'm sure of it."

"Let's not waste time."

Slayton grabbed Reema and they hurried out. Muntz followed, saying goodbye to Elke. Slayton looked back as Muntz closed the door. The blond watched them with a mix of shock and surprise.

52

Kameel al-Rashid left the noisy club and the disgusting decadence within. Any other time, he'd have bombed the place. The Western lifestyle. Repugnant. They all needed to die.

But Kameel needed Darius Kreigel and his connections. He could come back another day and blow the place.

Kameel climbed back into Nassaar's Honda and merged into traffic. Twenty-four hours. An anxious period of time, but he accepted the necessity. He trusted the German to make the arrangements. All the man wanted was Kameel's money, and Nassaar vouched for him—claimed Kreigel was true to his word.

Kameel changed lanes. He wanted to make a few random turns in case the Americans or German authorities somehow picked up his trail.

* * *

Muntz worked the radio as he drove.

He followed the Honda at a discreet distance. Unlike

Kameel al-Rashid, he knew the streets back and forth. When the October Blood leader executed an obvious turn or even a U-turn to shake surveillance, Muntz knew the counter-maneuver to get behind him again. It only cemented his claim of Kameel returning to the professor's apartment.

He called other agents on the handheld radio unit, ordering his team to assemble near Nassaar's and prep for a raid. He wanted a special tactics team, too. Rallying GSG9 to the case would have been nice, but they didn't have time. The local special unit would more than suffice.

Slayton sat in the back with Reema. She clutched his hand. Her hand felt warm in his. They were close. Close to ending her three-year nightmare and bringing an end to October Blood.

"You all right?" he asked Reema.

"Never better. We're together. Nothing else matters."

She squeezed his hand. He squeezed back.

Muntz hooked his radio unit to the dash.

"We're almost there. My crew will be assembled by the time we arrive."

"Reema and I aren't sitting this out, Hugo."

"I figured. You two stick close to me. If there's shooting—"

"Oh, don't worry. There will be."

* * *

MUNTZ'S BFV team occupied an empty building at the rear of Mohammed Nassaar's apartment complex. The lower level was set up for retail space but had gone unleased for months. The agents parked along the street and assembled inside the gutted interior. Cold concrete floor, bare walls, miscellaneous debris scattered across the floor.

Some of the BfV agents wore full combat gear. Body armor, helmets, submachine guns. Muntz gave his briefing and held everyone's attention as he spoke. The tac team would lead the charge. They expected only two people inside. Muntz wanted both alive. But his side glance at Slayton and Reema as he said the words communicated the opposite. Slayton hoped the pair presented the needed requirement to open fire. In any other case, Slayton wouldn't have bothered with such legal necessities. But this wasn't a case where he could shoot first and forget about the questions. If Kameel and his friend surrendered, there were other ways of disposing of the trash later.

Instructions delivered, Muntz broke up the meeting.

Time for action.

Slayton and Reema stayed close to Muntz as they moved out to the street. Slayton was well aware neither he nor Reema had any body armor.

* * *

BfV agents on the roof of the building across the street watched the windows of Nassaar's place. They used a thermal imaging scope. The infrared image the scope produced confirmed two people inside. One paced the floor. The other sat and moved his arms as he spoke. The BfV team entering the building evacuated tenants from the floor. The thermal imaging remained constant. As the BfV worked, the occupants of the target apartment didn't notice any disturbance.

With the floor cleared of civilians, the special tactics team moved in. Helmet lights on, radios silent; bringing up the rear was Muntz and Slayton and Reema. There had, surprisingly, been little chatter among the BfV about the Americans. Which suited Slayton fine. The special tactics team reached Nassaar's door. Slayton, Reema, and Muntz stopped. The team used a steel battering ram to attack the locked door and hit hard. Slayton felt the wall and floor jump at the impact. The special tactics team launched into the apartment one after another, their bulks only filling the narrow doorway for a moment. Slayton fought the urge to follow. When he shifted, Muntz blocked his movement with a raised arm.

I should be in there!

But the BfV had their procedures and protocols and he had to abide by them.

The raiding party yelled a series of orders as they swarmed inside. Loud, aggressive commands; their jumble of voices flowed into the hallway. But no gunfire sounded. The overwhelming force of the raiders caught al-Rashid and Nassaar empty handed. Slayton tried to see the action in his mind's eye, but all he heard was noise. The heavy steps of combat boots shook the floor.

Muntz's radio crackled as the voice of the special tactics commander came over the speaker.

"Two in custody, no casualties."

"Bring 'em out as soon as you can," Muntz replied. He began to relax. So did Slayton, who turned to Reema. She seemed relieved as well.

"Let's get down to the street," Muntz said. "We aren't needed here."

* * *

LOOKING BACK LATER, Slayton decided he should have expected an attack. How the BfV didn't detect the shooters was never answered to anybody's satisfaction. In the end, they lost far too many people because somebody else missed a detail.

Three black armored SUVs and an armored transport van waited in the street. Flashing police lights created multiple strobe flashes to mess with everyone's vision. The special tactics team hustled a cuffed and silent Kameel al-Rashid and Mohammed Nassaar into the back of the armored van. Several of the heavily armed officers climbed in with them. Slayton and Reema stood with Muntz near the building, watching.

Muntz said, "I know you'd prefer them dead to alive—"

"We'll see. Accidents have a habit of...happening."

He was turning to Reema, on his left, when the rocket hit.

The flash of fire from the RPG came from up the street, out of the mouth of an alley. The high-pitched whine of the rocket motor filled the street. Slayton knew of only one reasonable response.

"Get down!"

53

He pulled Reema with him and covered her body with his. Muntz dropped beside him. Too many others didn't move fast enough.

The rocket-propelled grenade struck one of the armored SUVs. The plating was no match for the armor-piercing impact. Flame erupted, filling the street with a brilliant flash of light. Fire raged and consumed the vehicle. Glass and debris rained down in flaming chunks of lethality. But the danger wasn't over.

Gunfire from the other end of the street, where Slayton and Reema were, popped at a rapid rate. It wasn't aimed fire, but a sweeping pattern. The gunners avoided the armored van in which al-Rashid and Nassaar waited.

Slayton rolled off Reema, stopping beside her, like a shield. He drew his pistol. At least this time he had something to shoot at. He fired at the alley across the street where the shooting originated. Reema screamed his name and shifted beside him. She rested an arm across his back and fired her own gun. More shooters from down the sidewalk on their side of the street converged. Slayton stole a glance. The gunners ran hard, damn the torpedoes, into the street. The crew from the other alley joined the rush.

"Find cover!" Slayton shouted. "Now!"

Slayton and Reema fired at each group, flame spitting from their pistols. Muntz was on the radio calling for more help. Gunfire from the special tactics squad drowned out his words. The return fire did nothing to dissuade the onrushing fighters. A few fell, but the others didn't stop. They were going for al-Rashid and Nassaar in the van.

The only way to run was toward the flaming SUV, and it wasn't a good choice. The RPG had come from that direction. Luckily, no gunfire. The jihadists could have easily boxed them in on either side. He and Reema and Muntz scrambled back from the onrushing fighters. The scorching heat of the flaming SUV hit them within a few steps. They hunkered down near the building entrance. Thick smoke filled the street, choking hurried breaths, making eyes water as defenders tried to aim. Gunfire raged as the jihadists and German agents engaged. A group of jihad fighters clustered around the van, aiming at any target available. Their comrades rushed the van's interior. Slayton cherry-picked targets wishing for a more powerful weapon than a handgun. His 9mm hollow points brought down gunners when the shots connected.

One of the other armored SUVs partly blocked Slayton's view of the transport van. He had no chance of stopping the rescue. The rocking van suggested a violent fight within. He yelled the information to Muntz. At the same time, one of the jihadists ran along the street, blasting at the muzzles of the German agents. Others joined him. Slayton slapped a full mag into his CZ and triggered single shots. One jihadist fell, another dropped from a shot delivered by Muntz. Shadows under the SUV nearest them caught Slayton's attention. He shot the sneaking gunman in the neck when he cleared the front fender.

"Jack!"

Reema swung her gun to the back of the SUV; Slayton followed. They both fired. She tagged a second gunman as he appeared around the rear of the SUV. The gunner fired as he fell. Slayton felt one bullet pass under his nose. Then Reema jerked and fell against him, knocking Slayton off his feet. He clutched at her. Blood covered the front of her shirt. He couldn't see where the bullet hit.

"Reema!"

Her face looked pale in the light of the fire.

Slayton laid her on the cement and was about to yell for help when he saw the same thing Muntz saw. The jihadists were pulling back. Down the street, gunners loaded al-Rashid and Nassaar into a vehicle and screeched rubber driving away. Others ran back into the alley from which they arrived. The echo of gunfire faded. Yelling replaced shooting as agents still on their feet rushed to help the wounded. Muntz spoke into his portable radio and called for as many ambulances as were available.

Slayton held Reema close. She clutched at him, but her grasp weakened with the passing seconds. Her wide eyes stayed locked on his face.

"Don't...don't let me go," she said.

Slayton tried to answer, but no words escaped his lips.

* * *

Reema's blood spotted the front of Slayton's shirt.

He held her hand in the back of the ambulance. The siren wailed at high volume and distracted his thoughts. Her grip felt stronger, at least. An oxygen mask covered her nose and mouth. Slayton's face remained stoic but worry broke through. It showed in his eyes. The hollow feeling in his gut communicated even more to him, but resolve filled his mind. They hadn't come this far for her to die at random.

The ambulance shook over a rough patch of road. The driver made a slow left turn. Slayton hoped they were almost at the hospital...

He wondered how Muntz was doing. The German fed was already at the hospital where so many of his men had been taken.

* * *

HUGO MUNTZ PACED the hospital waiting area. Spots of black soot marked his face. His suit was torn and dirty—not even a good cleaning would save it. His shock of white hair remained in place.

He was surrounded by white walls and a white-tiled floor. Chairs sat on a carpeted patch, but his agents occupied the chairs, all of them speaking on phones. Like him.

"We need access to the traffic cameras. Nobody got the make or license plate of the car they used."

He spun toward the elevators as the bell sounded. The doors rumbled open. Slayton stepped out alone but looking worse for wear. Blood covered his shirt. His eyes held a faraway stare.

The BfV boss kept talking.

"At least twelve dead and more wounded. We had the evacuated tenants around the corner in an empty building. None of them are hurt."

Slayton reached him and waited.

"When the chief wakes up, tell him I'll be here for the

duration," Muntz continued. "Yes, let me know as soon as possible."

Muntz stowed his cell phone and took a deep breath. He coughed. Then he turned his attention to Slayton.

"You need a jacket." Muntz slipped off his own and handed it over. Slayton took the jacket. He'd shed his during the fight. It remained either on the street somewhere, or in an evidence bag.

"Is she all right?" Muntz asked.

"Where do I find Elke Becker?"

"Jack—"

"We'll see," Slayton snapped. "They're operating right now. Bullet didn't pass through."

"Jack, we're all—"

"Stop talking. I want to know where to find Elke Becker. I'll go back and knock down the walls of the club if I have to."

Muntz sighed.

Then answered the question.

54

Elke used her key on Kreigel's lock. The door opened inward.

"Who's there?" he called from another room.

"It's me," she said. She slammed the door and kicked off her heels. She found him sitting shirtless on the living room couch. He used a remote to turn off the television. Only a lamp beside the couch gave them any light. The digital clock under the TV read 3:22 a.m.

"Well?" he demanded. "You just going to stand there?"

She unbuttoned the front of the corset and pulled the strings in back loose. It dropped like a shell and let everything loose. Her breasts hung in a droopy inverted V. The bullet tattoo between stood out against her pale skin.

Kreigel raised an eyebrow.

She unzipped the leather pants, let them drop to her feet, and stepped out. She kicked the pants in his direction. He grinned.

Panties next. Down her legs to her feet in a smooth motion. She crumpled them into a wad and tossed. *Smack.* In the face. He laughed and shook them off. She put her hands on her hips and a pout on her face and thrust her chest out.

"It's *later*, you asshole," she proclaimed.

He grinned wider as he stood and approached. When he was close enough, she kicked him in the belly as hard as he could. With a startled grunt, he doubled over and fell to a knee. He raised his head. Kreigel's face was red, and his lips pressed tightly together.

"You bitch," he managed between gasps.

She laughed, turned, and marched to the bedroom.

Kreigel groaned as he stood but remained hunched over. He wandered after her.

* * *

ELKE ROLLED OFF HIM—*MUCH* later—and while he seemed satisfied, he continued to stifle groans from the residual pain of her kick.

Whatever, she thought. *He deserved it.* She grinned to herself. *So did I.*

The cell phone on the nightstand bleeped. Darius Kreigel rolled away from Elke to answer. She stared at his back tattoos as he spoke.

"Stop the panic attack and tell me what has happened," he said after listening a moment. He listened further. He interrupted fifteen seconds later. "Okay, okay, I get it. Direct them to the safe house and I will meet them there. They will be with us till we can get them out."

He ended the call and rose from the bed. As he pulled clothes from the closet and dresser, he told Elke to get dressed.

"What's going on?" she asked. She didn't leave the bed.

"Our Middle Eastern friends had a bad night," he said,

and explained the raid and escape. "Now we have two people to get out of Germany. Get dressed and scoot. I'll call you later."

Elke didn't argue.

She hoped she could reach Muntz with the update.

* * *

Slayton grabbed Elke around the neck and stuck his gun in her back.

Elke sucked in her scream.

"Unlock your door and let's go inside. We're only going to talk."

"I'll tell you—"

"Shut up. Open the door."

He maintained his grip as she inserted the key and turned the lock. Slayton moved with her into the house and kicked the door shut. He shoved her ahead and Elke fell. She landed on her hands and knees and stayed there. She looked ridiculous in her outfit. The way she landed only made her ooze out of the corset more than intended.

"Get up. Slowly."

She did and brushed off the front of her top.

"They called," Elke said. She stood with her back to him but tried to see Slayton over her right shoulder.

"Who called?"

"*Them*. The men you're looking for. They called Darius. I know where they're going."

"Turn around."

"None of this was necessary!"

"Turn. Around."

She did. She then explained the late call Kreigel received and told Slayton about the safe house. Slayton held the gun on her as she spoke. The muzzle didn't waver from her face, but she spoke as if the gun wasn't there.

"Where do I find this safe house?" Slayton asked once she finished.

She told him.

"If you put the gun away, and let me see your phone," she added, "I will also show you."

Slayton did.

She did.

* * *

SLAYTON DROVE Muntz's government car. The German fed had the option of tracking the car if he wanted, but Slayton didn't let the detail bother him. He also didn't report what he'd learned from Elke. He wanted to take Kameel al-Rashid himself.

He didn't check with Muntz for another reason.

He was afraid to ask about Reema.

Once al-Rashid was at his feet, he'd find out. Meanwhile, he let cold rage power him.

Slayton drove north into open country, turning off the autobahn and driving deeper into the middle of nowhere. Narrow roads, open fields, trees—he saw very little of the scenery through the beam of his headlamps. He didn't care. He was looking for an isolated house and it was the only thought on his mind.

He presently found the safe house where Elke promised it would be, drove past, and parked off the road. He popped the trunk. Time to see if Muntz had any lethal toys in the back.

The trunk revealed a zipped tote bag, heavy. Slayton pulled the zipper open. Inside, a Heckler & Koch UMP9 and spare magazines. A combat vest, too. He slipped on the vest and filled the front pockets with spare magazines. The UMP looked well-oiled. He chambered a round and slung it over one shoulder. Last, he grabbed a pair of road flares from the emergency kit, closed the trunk, and started toward the safe house.

Slayton stepped off pavement onto soft ground and tall grass. Dropping low, he kept the house in his peripheral vision while he advanced. The dry grass brushed at his exposed skin, tiny pin pricks he ignored. But he was well aware anybody watching for unusual movement in the grass might catch sight of him. With a naked eye? Maybe not. But if they had night vision...

He stopped, parted the blades before him, and examined the house. No exterior light—there was much about the structure he had trouble making out in the dark. But lights burned in the rear. Three cars sat in front. The dirt driveway looked smoothed out, a few weeds breaking through. The back end of one car looked familiar. Slayton had seen it before. During the fight outside the apartment.

Which car belonged to Darius Kreigel, and who belonged to the third? How many inside? What weapons did they carry? Slayton's mind raced with the questions but he had no answers. He'd find out. All he wanted was al-Rashid at the end of his gun. He resumed his forward movement as a plan began to take shape.

He cut left, moving parallel to the house. No sentries? What was going on in back? Maybe the guards—

Then he froze.

Because there *were* sentries.

Three gunmen in dark clothes loitered on the opposite side of the three cars, close to the corner of the house. They spoke in quiet tones, and left their weapons slung. Slayton picked up bits of German. These were not the same men who participated in the rescue raid. What had happened to them?

Slayton cursed under his breath.

He cut left again and followed the edge of the driveway to where it began at the paved road. He crawled across the dirt gap on his belly, then slipped into grass again. He grabbed one of the road flares, popped the cap, and let the tip blaze to life. The sentries shouted in alarm. Slayton tossed the flare at one of the cars, and watched it arc through the air to land close by. Shouldering the HK UMP, he fired at the car's gas tank. The full-auto blast sounded like a buzzsaw in the quiet night; the HK's flash hider prevented muzzle blast from marking him. The flammable gasoline landed on the burning flare and science followed its natural course.

A ball of fire engulfed the car. Slayton dropped flat and covered the back of his neck. The ground shook as the first car exploded.

Brightness lit the night. Chunks of car debris rained down, smacking the ground hard. The stench of melting rubber filled the air.

Slayton moved left, at speed, because now being seen didn't matter. The first explosion touched off the next car and this time the house caught fire, too. Flame splashed onto the roof, stayed there, and began eating at the roof tiles.

The three gunmen began firing at random. Slayton shoved a full mag into the HK and pivoted to face them. Less than twenty yards between him and them. The flames may have pinpointed Slayton's position, but he saw them too. The HK bucked against his shoulder. Two shots—one down. Another pair—*pop, pop*. Second man fell against the wall. The third tried to run, but Slayton's pair of 9mm slugs caught him in the back. He landed in the dirt face first.

Slayton bent below the top of the grass and ran to the back of the house.

He ran wide and cut right, taking a knee as the back door opened. Three men hustled out. One spoke rapid German into a cell phone. The flames on the roof spread rapidly. Orange embers flew into the sky. The air filled with smoke.

Slayton shot the man on the phone. Exit Darius Kreigel —he stopped talking mid-sentence and fell. Slayton shifted his aim as the last two men paused in the open. Al-Rashid and Nassaar and Slayton had no doubt. He started to squeeze the trigger. Then al-Rashid made a move Slayton didn't expect.

55

AL-RASHID DREW A PISTOL WITH ONE HAND AND GRABBED Nassaar with the other. He pulled his ally in front of him. Nassaar screamed as Slayton's bullets hammered into his chest and neck. The scream stopped, turned to a choked gurgle, and down went Nassaar. Al-Rashid shoved his pistol forward. Slayton rolled right as the October Blood leader returned fire.

Slayton poked his head up, dropped, rolled again. Al-Rashid dove into the grass. Slayton kept his head low. Listening for al-Rashid's movement was useless; but he *might* see the grass shift.

He started forward, HK at the ready. The pressure of his finger on the trigger held it half-back. Smoke stung his eyes. He changed direction every few steps, stomping down the blades before him, rustling those on either side, to try and get al-Rashid to reveal himself.

The jihadist did. Al-Rashid fired one shot. It came nowhere near Slayton. The CIA man held his fire. Let the enemy waste his ammo shooting at shadows.

Another pistol shot cracked. This one passed overhead.

Slayton lowered himself some more and caught movement ahead. He fired. No joy—al-Rashid didn't scream; no body struck the ground.

Then al-Rashid leaped at Slayton from the left. Slayton attempted to pivot, but the jihadi tackled him, and brought Slayton to the ground. Al-Rashid hammered at Slayton with the butt of his handgun. Slayton blocked with the HK but had no way to extend the bulky sub gun. He thrust the buttstock right to left, smacking al-Rashid in the face, but the blow didn't slow the assault. As al-Rashid brought his right arm back for another strike, Slayton rolled left, forcing al-Rashid off him. Slayton scrambled back. Al-Rashid pointed his gun at Slayton's face.

Slayton kicked, deflecting the muzzle away. Al-Rashid's shot went wide. Slayton held the HK close to his belly and pulled the trigger. The buzzsaw noise filled the night once more. The salvo slammed into al-Rashid with the force of a runaway train hitting a wall. Al-Rashid's face only registered a small amount of surprise before life left his body, and the now-empty shell flopped still amid the tall grass.

Slayton back away further, rose, and held up his left arm against the glare of the burning house. He didn't stop to examine the results. There was no time. He had to get out of there and back to the hospital. It was time to find out if Reema had survived her surgery.

He ran back to the car.

* * *

"You're a mess."

Slayton didn't argue with Hugo Muntz's statement. He'd splashed water on his face in the men's room but still had plenty of sweat and dirt on his clothes and skin. His clothing in particular looked filthy.

"Reema?" Slayton asked.

Muntz shook his head.

"Still in surgery. The bullet did a lot of damage."

"Not what I wanted to hear."

"She's in better shape than most of my guys."

"I suppose...I'll have to hold on to that."

"Let's sit down. Tell me what happened."

"Well, I started a fire..."

* * *

FBI AGENTS in four SUVs pulled up at the home of Max Hudson two days later. Agents in blue jackets with "FBI" across the back entered the house. Armed FBI SWAT officers accompanied them. Hudson, in the middle of breakfast, did not try to resist arrest or dispute the warrants. The search warrant alone was almost twenty pages.

The only thing he told the arresting agents was they needn't have brought so many guys.

Once seated in the back of a black Suburban, he stopped speaking entirely. He stared out the side window as the FBI began dismantling everything he'd worked so hard to build.

But he'd known the day would come. Once Wolf and Chapman had been arrested, it was only a matter of time. He still believed in his work. He believed he was keeping America safe. He'd plead his case. Ignore the detractors. Explain to those who needed to hear the reasons why.

He wasn't going down without a fight.

* * *

Slayton called Dylan from his hotel room. He stood in front of the window looking out at the window. Before he talked about al-Rashid, he told Dylan about Reema.

"Surgery went well. They put her back together, and she's resting in a private room."

"Good. I got the report from the fight you had with al-Rashid. You started the fire?"

"Yeah. How far did it spread?"

"Couple acres. Took out the house. *Almost* reached power lines, but you lucked out. And they confirmed the identities of all the bodies. October Blood is officially no more."

"Good," Slayton said.

"That professor, Nassaar, opened a can of worms, though. There will be a long investigation into his activities, and Muntz and his people are actively searching for the gunners who pulled off the street raid."

"He mentioned something about it, yeah," Slayton said. "I'm out of it. Job is done."

"I think Muntz will take down a sleeper cell or two."

"Or three or four."

"How long are you staying in Berlin?" Dylan asked.

"Till Reema can fly home. May be a few weeks."

"Stay close to the embassy. If I need you, I want you available."

"No problem. Um—"

"What, Jack?"

"How are *you* doing?"

Dylan didn't answer right away. Slayton didn't blame him. Then: "I'll be fine. Emily is being arraigned tomorrow. Wolf will be arraigned too. Max Hudson may take a little longer. They arrested him yesterday."

"That's it?"

"All I got, Jack."

"Okay." Slayton didn't press. When his pal wanted to talk, he'd open up all the way. "We'll be a while cleaning this up," Slayton added.

"But it's not our job any longer. When you get back, there's other matters we need to tend to."

"When I get back," Slayton emphasized. "Call if you need me, Dyl. I gotta get to the hospital."

"Take it easy."

Slayton ended the call and put the phone in a pocket. He had his rental keys in another pocket of his jacket—returned to him by the BfV. He grabbed the jacket from the back of a chair and left the room. Time to visit Reema.

* * *

She was awake and sitting up in bed when he arrived. He leaned down to kiss her. They held the kiss a few seconds. Grabbing a corner chair, he sat next to the bed to hold her hand. A German sitcom played on the mounted television, and they watched and chuckled.

Her hand warmed in his.

There was no need to talk.

She was okay. She'd recover. They'd go home. Together. And start again. They'd pick up where they left off as if the last three years had only been a bad dream. Anything that came up, they'd deal with together. They'd changed in three years, but what they went through cemented their bond.

All was well again.

A LOOK AT: IRON GHOST (JACK SLAYTON 2)

Once a SEAL. Always the Hunter.

Jack Slayton was once a battle-hardened SEAL commander—until the night a terrorist bomb ripped through the Shipwreck Bar and left his brothers-in-arms dead. The man responsible vanished into the shadows, leaving Jack with nothing but ghosts, guilt, and an unrelenting need for justice.

Now operating inside the CIA's shadowy Z Section, Slayton gets a whisper of hope from an informant embedded in a violent extremist network. Before the lead can turn solid, assassins strike. And the trail erupts into bloodshed. Andreas Ritter is still alive, still pulling strings, and still one step ahead.

What follows is a relentless pursuit across Europe's deadliest terrain. From Berlin's dark backstreets to the brutal heights of the Swiss Alps and the glittering deception of the French Riviera. Ritter's syndicate responds with savage precision: bombings, ambushes, and waves of chaos that leave civilians trapped in the crossfire.

As the body count rises and time runs out, Slayton faces an enemy who may finally be his equal. An invisible mastermind who knows how Jack thinks, how he fights, and how far he's willing to go. To stop Ritter, Slayton must confront the crimes of the past...and decide how much vengeance will cost the future.

AVAILABLE APRIL 2026

ABOUT THE AUTHOR

A twenty-five year veteran of radio and television broadcasting, Brian Drake has spent his career in San Francisco where he's filled writing, producing, and reporting duties with stations such as KPIX-TV, KCBS, KQED, among many others. Currently carrying out sports and traffic reporting duties for Bloomberg 960, Brian Drake spends time between reports and carefully guarded morning and evening hours cranking out action/adventure tales.

A love of reading when he was younger inspired him to create his own stories, and he sold his first short story, "The Desperate Minutes," to an obscure webzine when he was 25 (more years ago than he cares to remember, so don't ask).

Brian Drake lives in California with his wife and two cats, and when he's not writing he is usually blasting along the back roads in his Corvette with his wife telling him not to drive so fast, but the engine is so loud he usually can't hear her.

briandrakebooks.com

www.ingramcontent.com/pod-product-compliance
Lightning Source LLC
LaVergne TN
LVHW041111080826
845145LV00007B/1764

* 9 7 8 1 6 8 5 4 9 4 5 8 2 *